MURDER SEASON

MURDER SEASON

Robert Ellis

Minotaur Books
New York

MURDER SEASON. Copyright © 2011 by Robert Ellis. All rights reserved. Printed in the United States of America. For information, address St. Martin's Press, 175 Fifth Avenue, New York, N.Y. 10010.

www.minotaurbooks.com

Library of Congress Cataloging-in-Publication Data

Ellis, Robert, 1954–
    Murder season / Robert Ellis. — 1
        p. cm.
    ISBN 978-0-312-36617-9 (hardback)
    1. Policewomen—California—Los Angeles—Fiction.   2. Men—Crimes against—Fiction.   3. Murder—Investigation—Fiction.   4. Vigilantes—Fiction.   5. Los Angeles (Calif.)—Fiction.   6. Los Angeles (Calif.). Police Dept—Fiction.   I. Title.
    PS3605.L469M87 2011
    813'.6—dc22   2011026899

First Edition: December 2011

10 9 8 7 6 5 4 3 2 1

This book is dedicated to two friends.

Joe Drabyak and John Truby.

ACKNOWLEDGMENTS

I owe a great deal of gratitude to my editor, Kelley Ragland at Minotaur Books, for her brilliant effort in making this novel what it is.

I would also like to thank my agent, Scott Miller at Trident Media Group, for his support and enthusiasm for this book, and Eileen Hutton at Brilliance Audio, for the audio editions of my work featuring LAPD Detective Lena Gamble.

This novel wouldn't ring true without the help and guidance of LAPD Detectives Mitzi Roberts and Rick Jackson from the Robbery-Homicide Division, Cold Case Homicide Unit, and from Harry Klann, Jr., DNA Technical Leader from the LAPD Scientific Investigation Division. I can't thank you all enough.

I am also deeply grateful for the help I received from John Truby, H. Donald Widdoes, Pat Schrevelius, Peter B. Crabb, Peter & Terry Ellis, Robert & Ruth Ellis, Joe Drabyak & Reggie Painter, Michael Conway & Meghan Sadler Conway, and Debi Watson. Last, but even more, I'd like to thank Charlotte Conway for encouraging me and standing by me all this time.

ACKNOWLEDGMENTS

Somehow there's gotta be a thread that
stretches across the whole universe.
A motherfucking life jacket.
Something that will pull my sorry soul
out of this ditch and into the light.

—Jimmy the Dime, street poet
Santa Monica, California

MURDER SEASON

1

She could smell it in the pillow as she pulled it closer. On the sheets as she rolled over in the darkness and searched out cool spots that were not there.

Murder season.

She was floating, drifting. Cruising through an open seam between sleep and consciousness.

She glanced at the clock radio but didn't really see it, then fell back into the stream and let go. It was somewhere after midnight, sometime before dawn. Early spring, and the air inside the house was already deadened from the oppressive heat. A steep, lifeless desert wave had swelled over Los Angeles two days ago, pushing the marine layer and the cool breezes out over the ocean where they could be burned up and erased without a witness.

The city that was left behind felt dusty and canned in. Vacuum-packed. The air perfumed with spent diesel fuel and gasoline.

Murder season would come early this year. It would roll in with the heat like they were best friends. Lovers.

She reached across the bed, probing gently for a warm body but finding only emptiness. Only her dreams. A smile worked its way through her body. The one that came with her dreams. She could feel it in her chest and between her legs. She could feel it spreading across her face and blistering through her skin before it rose up and faded away.

She had spent the night on the terrace drinking ice-cold Irish reds with Stan Rhodes and Tito Sanchez. Sanchez had brought over a flank steak, marinating the meat, and working the grill with mesquite the way his grandmother had taught him. After dinner they sat on the stone wall and gazed down the hill, the lights of the city caught in the dust and glowing like cotton balls from downtown all the way across the basin to the Pacific. They laughed and told stories in the eerie light, opened fresh bottles, and talked shop. Rhodes and Sanchez were deep in on a new murder case and had worked the last forty-eight hours straight out. Both detectives needed to regroup and get some sleep. Lena had tomorrow off and could afford to relax, maybe even get buzzed. When they left around ten, she popped open the last bottle of ale, stripped off her clothes, and slipped into the pool.

Murder season. Trouble ahead. When the streets get hot, business burns.

She rolled onto her back, her mind cutting a jagged path to the surface. She could hear something going on in the house—something in the background behind her thoughts. A noise pulsing through the still air. She tried to ignore it, fight it. Tried to pretend that it wasn't real. After a while, she wondered if it wasn't part of her dream, a noise in the darkness breaking up her sleep.

Until she finally realized that it was her cell.

She opened her eyes and saw the light glowing from her phone. She grabbed it, recognized the caller, and slid open the lock on the touch screen. It was her supervisor, Lt. Frank Barrera, Robbery-Homicide Division. She didn't need to guess what he wanted. She checked the clock and read it this time: 2:54 a.m.

Murder season. The train was rolling in.

"You cool, Lena?" he said. "I know it's your day off, so I'm asking if everything's cool."

"I'm good. What's up? What's that noise in the background?"

She turned and looked out the window. Sirens. She could hear them in the distance, and she could hear them over the phone. She made the match—Barrera was close. He was in the neighborhood. She tried to look down the hill and thought she could see flashing lights. Something was going on just west of the Capitol Records Building.

"We're in deep shit, Lena. Real deep shit."

His voice broke. Barrera's usual demeanor—steady as she goes—had become tainted with fear.

"Tell me what you want me to do," she said.

"We've got two dead bodies in Hollywood. That's all I can say over the phone."

His voice cut off like he needed to catch his breath. Most homicides in Los Angeles were handled by investigators at the local level. For a murder to bounce up to RHD, the crime had to involve a high profile victim or be particularly horrific. For a Homicide Special detective to get the call with a crime scene still open, it had to be more than that. Some unlucky combination of the two.

Lena switched on the light, feeling the rush of adrenaline eat up whatever alcohol remained in her blood. She still didn't have a partner and wouldn't until the fall.

"Why me?" she asked.

"Orders from Deputy Chief Ramsey. You'll know why when you get here."

Ramsey was one of the few members of the old guard who had survived the department's reorganization. He reported directly to Chief Logan, and had become his trusted right hand. His fixer. She knew that Chief Logan had left the city on a ten-day recruiting tour for the Scientific Investigation Division. With the success of the CSI franchise on television, the line of students wanting to become the real thing was a long one. Logan was offering better than decent money and the chance to move to L.A. He knew that he would have his pick of the best and brightest. He also knew that SID had taken a big hit recently and the division needed the fire that came with new blood.

"Where?" she asked.

"You ever hear of a place in Hollywood called Club 3 AM?"

Lena glanced at her .45 on the night table as Barrera gave her the address. She didn't bother writing it down. Everyone in L.A. knew about Club 3 AM. It had become a celebrity hangout. A private nightclub catering to the A-list.

"Who's dead?" she asked.

"Can't do it, Lena. Not over the phone. Get here as soon as you can."

Barrera's cell punched out. Lena lowered her phone.

Murder season. It had come early this year.

2

Showered and dressed in fifteen minutes, she raced down the hill, hit the straight track on Gower, and floored it past the Monastery of the Angels, estimating her time of arrival at less than five minutes. She was driving a metallic-green Crown Victoria with tinted glass that had "cop" written all over it. The take-home car floated over the road, cutting a wide path through the air. But Lena wasn't thinking about the ride, or even the fact that her Honda had finally hit the skids and needed to be replaced at a time when money was tight. Instead, she was keyed in on the sound of Barrera's shaky voice.

The roads were empty. She blew through the light at Franklin, the V8 kicking like a shotgun. She was thinking about Club 3 AM. And she was thinking about the man behind the club. A man with a certain reputation who knew things.

Johnny Bosco.

She made a right on Yucca Street. As she crossed Ivar and sped around the bend, she could see the nightclub in the distance and slowed down some. Club 3 AM was tucked in between Yucca and Grace Avenue. The place looked more like a three-story European villa than a nightclub. Easing closer, Lena noticed the high wall around the property and guessed that the front of the building was only a facade. The main entrance would be around back so Hollywood's A-list could come and go without fear of being seen or photographed. Her view cleared as she passed a white van on the right. Ten black and white cruisers fenced in the street. Searching for a way through the blockade, she spotted a cop waving at her with a clipboard. But as she idled through the intersection, night became day—her car shelled with bursts of white-hot light.

She flinched, then turned to see the press crowding the other side of the street. One hundred cameras were blasting away on full automatic. The paparazzi could smell blood in the water: two dead bodies in Hollywood. They were pushing against the crime scene tape and shouting at each other—screaming at the patrol units holding them back.

She rolled down her window, squinting as the tinted glass gave way and the strobe lights penetrated the car bright as lightning. After signing in, the cop shielded his eyes and pointed at the gated drive.

"The place is set ass backward," he shouted. "The front's around back."

There was no smile on his face, and no verbal acknowledgment of the chaos. But there was something in his eyes that reminded her of the fear she had heard in Barrera's voice. He stepped away before she could ask him anything, then grabbed his radio mike and waved her through. Lena waved back, easing the Crown Vic down the drive and out of the paparazzi's bent view.

She found a place to park, got out, and hit the door locks. As she scanned the lot beneath the palm trees, she was struck by the number of city cars already at the crime scene. There were too many patrol cars here as well, too many detectives' cars. And that black Lincoln idling in the shadows could only mean that Deputy Chief Ramsey was here, too. She glanced over at the SID truck where a team of criminalists were preparing their evidence kits, then gave the lot another quick look.

What she didn't see was what she had expected to see and wanted to see.

There wasn't a single Ferrari here, or a single Lamborghini, or the possible witnesses that would have come with them. Club 3 AM never closed. It looked like the A-list had run for cover before anyone dialed 911. The Hollywood Station was just a few blocks south. The first responding units would have arrived in minutes and not let anyone walk away. Hollywood Homicide would have been right behind them.

"This way, Lena. Hurry."

She turned to find her supervisor on the elaborate set of steps encircling a fountain. Barrera was clutching the rail with his left hand and waving her up to the porch and main entrance. She took the steps quickly and met him at the door. When she got a look at his face in the light, the worry in his eyes frightened her.

"What's happened, Frank? Who's dead?"

He couldn't meet her gaze. "Not here," he said. "Follow me."

Barrera turned away, leading her through the foyer. As they passed the main bar, Lena saw a group of RHD detectives sitting at several tables. Some were working their cell phones. Others appeared to be on standby, watching her walk by with subdued faces and quiet nods, and drinking cups of takeout coffee. Behind them she recognized Johnny Bosco's partner, Dante Escabar, standing alone behind the bar and pouring a glass of bourbon as if he needed it.

She turned back to Barrera, following him down the hall, and thinking about what she had just seen. "How many guys got tonight's callout?"

"Everyone," he said.

Barrera picked up speed, leading her up the main staircase. They were moving so fast that Lena didn't have time to pick out many details. All she knew was that the nightclub exuded elegance and didn't have the feel of a public place. That the European villa had high ceilings, ornate moldings, and appeared to have been built around a large courtyard that included a pool. She could see the light shimmering from the water through the windows and painting the stairwell blue.

They reached the top floor. As they swept past a series of open doors, Lena noted the private lounges with stocked bars and full windows that opened to recessed balconies she couldn't see from the parking lot. Turning the corner, the private lounges gave way to a long line of equally private bedroom suites.

Things happened here, she thought. Johnny Bosco took care of people and learned their secrets. The A-list.

They made a final turn, passing through a set of French doors at the end of the hall and entering an office. The doors to the balcony were open. Barrera told her to wait and stepped outside into the darkness. There were people out there. Five or six shadows speaking in voices so low they didn't carry into the room. Lena was beginning to lose her patience. She was thinking about crime scenes and the fact that an investigator only gets one shot at it. That this crime scene had the touch and feel of being filtered down or even swept away. She wanted to know where the bodies were. Why the entire division had been called out, but no one was doing anything. Why, if this was her case, she hadn't been the first call, but obviously instead the last.

She shook it off, taking in the room as she waited. Shuttered windows of one-way mirrored glass gave way to views of the main bar and dining rooms on the floor below. What couldn't be seen with the naked eye was picked up by security cameras feeding into a paper-thin flat panel TV monitor hanging above the fireplace mantel. She glanced at the couch and sitting area, then stepped behind the desk for a better look at the walls. The wood paneling had been carved to mimic the ripples in cloth curtains. She had never seen anything like it before and couldn't imagine how it was done or what it might cost. This had to be Bosco's office, not Dante Escabar's. When she spotted the photographs on the far wall, that thought was confirmed. The wall was covered with pictures of Bosco arm in arm with his celebrity friends. Actors who had received Oscars, athletes who had won championships, and one of the few U.S. senators from California who served four terms without an indictment. When her eyes came to rest on a photo of Bosco with District Attorney Jimmy J. Higgins, she felt something hard pull at her chest.

She knew that Bosco and Higgins were friends. She even recognized the photograph. A copy had been published in *The Los Angeles Times* a few weeks ago.

Two dead bodies in Hollywood. Two heavyweights requiring a division callout. All hands on deck.

Lena checked her right palm, noticed the tremors creeping up her fingers, then turned as she heard someone enter the room from the balcony behind her.

3.

Deputy Chief Albert Ramsey stepped around Johnny Bosco's desk with his steel-blue eyes pinned on her. Ramsey was a tall, stiff man with a shaved head, a square jaw, and pale, blotchy skin that had been ruined by too much time in the sun chasing the great white whale. There was something frightening about his presence, something about the glint in those eyes of his and the fact that he was a man of few words. Ramsey had survived for more than thirty-five years in a police department often drowning in political turmoil, and he knew where the bones were buried. When he entered a room, like Ahab in the flesh, everyone noticed. But something about tonight was different. Tonight, the deputy chief appeared more like a prizefighter who had just walked into a straight right and taken it on the chin. He may have been standing, Lena thought. He may have even had two legs. But tonight he looked punch drunk and ready to fall.

"Thank you for getting here so quickly," he said in a low, raspy voice. "Detectives Sanchez and Rhodes are on their way. But we've made a decision, Gamble. This is your case now. What happens next is up to you. After tonight, you're on your own."

He didn't wait for a response, cutting a sharp path to the set of double doors on the other side of the fireplace. Barrera had followed Ramsey into the room, but was still avoiding her gaze. Lena expected the others to join them, but they remained on the terrace whispering in the night.

Ramsey gave the doors a hard push. As they entered another foyer, Lena could feel the finish line approaching. They were walking through a private bedroom suite, bigger than the rest because it belonged to Bosco. They were passing a changing room and entering a large bathing area that included a massage table, an open shower, and a spa.

Lena's eyes sprinted across the tiled floor until she hit pay dirt. The two dead bodies in Hollywood. She looked at the blood pooling on the floor—there was a lot of it—her hands instinctively digging into her pocket for a pair of vinyl gloves.

Two dead men. Two heavyweights. One faced down in a fetal position. The other, all bloodied up and leaning against the far wall.

Ramsey kept his eyes on her. "Everything remains the way we found it, Detective. As far as we know, nothing has been touched."

As far as we know . . .

Lena took in a deep breath, pushing the air out of her lungs as if it was smoke. She noted the open windows by the spa. The cocaine piled on a marble slab—at least 10K's worth—and the razor blade that went with it. The dead man in the silk suit had been shot in the back, a plume of blood oozing through his jacket just below his left shoulder. She checked the floor, stepping over the blood for a look at the man's face. He was about forty-five, with wide shoulders, short brown hair, and a strong chin. Until a few hours ago, he had been the kind of man people like to look at. But not now. One eye remained open—his capped teeth jutting out—and Lena could see a double load of white powder still lodged in his flared nostrils.

No doubt about it, Johnny Bosco had been killed before the thrill and never saw the grim reaper coming. The bullet in his back—his last hit of hits—had been a complete surprise.

Lena glanced at the second corpse, taking in the view quickly just to make sure. The district attorney would have been a barrel-chested man in his mid-fifties with silver, overgroomed hair. The dead man propped against the wall with the bloody face was wearing jeans and a T-shirt and obviously much leaner and younger than that. Late twenties, early thirties at best. District Attorney Jimmy J. Higgins may have lost one of his celebrity friends tonight in Johnny Bosco, but he himself was alive and well, and still loose somewhere in the city.

She turned back to Barrera and Ramsey, feeling a certain degree of relief. But both men remained by the door, studying her like just maybe there would be no relief. Not tonight. Not with this crime scene.

"Body number two is who?" she said. "An actor? A dealer? A VIP's son?"

Ramsey's sharp gaze faltered as it shifted to the corpse. When he didn't respond, her mind started churning. Why had she been the last call? Why the oppressive silence? It felt like they were playing her. Testing her. Bullshitting her when everyone in the room knew that a homicide investigation thrived on a quick start.

But there was something else going on. Something extra.

Johnny Bosco had been a player in this city. His murder would easily make the front page of *The Times*. His friendship with the district attorney, along with that pile of nose candy on the counter, would ensure that the story appeared above the fold and make things complicated for everyone. But Higgins was already damaged goods, particularly with the LAPD. According to *The Times*, his reelection next year was in trouble. Lena wondered if the politician really had enough clout with the department to insist on a division callout. Enough power to bring Deputy Chief Ramsey to a crime scene in the middle of the night. Even more unsettling, what about anything at this crime scene could create fear in two of the most seasoned police officers she knew?

She crossed the room and knelt before the second body, her heart pounding in her ears. The dead man was hard to look at. Although he had been shot in the stomach, it was the wounds to his face that made things difficult. His lights had been blown out. Even through all the blood, Lena could see the burned flesh and scorched eyebrows. The shooter had pressed the muzzle into the man's eyes and pulled the trigger.

Both rounds had punched through the back of his skull, drawing brain matter out like a vacuum and splashing it against the wall.

Worse still, he was a lot younger than she first thought. She could see it now. Low to mid twenties.

She leaned closer and checked his nostrils, but found no visible sign of white powder. As her eyes drifted off his face, she noticed a large bruise on his neck. Similar bruises tattooed both arms. When she spotted the scabs on his knuckles and his clean fingernails, she took a moment to think it over. The kid had been in a fight sometime within the past week or two, the cuts and bruises in various stages of healing. But nothing she saw indicated that he had a chance to defend himself tonight. The shot he took in the stomach knocked him to the floor. From the amount of blood puddling around him, the round struck an artery. The two shots in the eyes came after that. He would have been alive, maybe even conscious when the killer approached. But he would have been bleeding out. He would have been docile and unable to fight back.

The shot in the stomach was enough to ensure the kid's death. The shots to the eyes were about something more than the murder. Something psychotic. A killer overdosing on rage.

A memory surfaced—a movie she had seen more than ten years ago. A western. The Comanches believed that without eyes a victim couldn't enter the spirit world. Without eyes, the victim would be forced to wander between the winds forever. She thought the scene might be from John Ford's *The Searchers,* but wasn't sure. It was too far back in her history and too late at night. Still, as she forced herself to take a second look at the kid's broken face, she couldn't help but wonder if his soul was lost between the winds.

After a long moment, the wonder vanished and she finally lowered her gaze. She didn't recognize him. Not without his eyes and through all the blood masking his face. She doubted anyone could.

She climbed to her feet, checking the floor for shell casings but not finding any. When she looked up, she saw Sanchez and Rhodes standing beside Barrera. She hadn't heard them enter, and for reasons she couldn't explain, Barrera seemed to be holding them back. It didn't really matter. Both detectives looked spent, their eyes glassy from working two days without sleep and topping the night off at her place.

Lena turned to the deputy chief. "Tell me what's going on," she said.

Ramsey broke open a roll of Tums, choosing his words carefully. "Escabar found the bodies, but didn't call it in until after he cleared the place out. Hollywood detectives got here around one-thirty. They identified Bosco and passed the case up to Robbery-Homicide. When two of your colleagues arrived, they made an ID on the kid and called your supervisor. Frank called me, and then I briefed the chief at his hotel in Philadelphia. Once we got here and everything checked out, I called the chief back and we made a decision. Then Frank called you."

She wondered if Ramsey had any idea that the shortest distance between two points was a straight line. Nothing about who called who or even why was important anymore. Body number two was the main event, not Bosco. She was sure of it now.

"Who is he?" she asked.

"A motherfucker," Ramsey said. "A real asshole. As much trouble to us dead as he was alive. That's why you got the call on your day off. The department needs you now. The people you work with, Gamble."

Lena watched Ramsey dig an evidence bag out of his jacket. He held it up, displaying a pair of wallets, then passed it over.

"They found them over there in the trash," he said. "The shooter took the cash, but left their credit cards. Johnny Bosco was known to carry a lot of cash, and there's a fire escape right outside those open windows. His partner, Dante Escabar, believes that this was a robbery. That the mess we're looking at was done by a pro. What's your take?"

Lena glanced at the corpse, then turned back to the deputy chief. She lowered her voice because it seemed obvious that Ramsey already knew what she was about to say. She didn't understand the play. Why was he running this out in slow motion?

"Number two was the target, not Bosco," she said.

"You sure about that?"

She nodded. "The killer knew him. And whatever happened here to-night was payback. You don't blow somebody's eyes out if he's a friend. And you don't waste time shooting a dead man if he's a stranger. You run."

Ramsey stared at her for a moment. His eyes felt like needles.

"How long have you worked homicide, Gamble?"

"Long enough to know that this wasn't a robbery, and that the killer wasn't a pro. This was about something more personal than that. Something between the two."

"I'm with you on that," he said. "But I know the identity of the victim and you don't. Tell me why you think it's personal, Detective. I need to hear you say it."

"If tonight was about a robbery, the coke wouldn't be here. And if this was done by a pro, these wallets would have been left in their pockets. No pro would've taken the cash. Just a single credit card from Bosco's wallet because everybody knows he's loaded. One card with a decent credit line that wouldn't be noticed for a day or two. That's all it would take to bleed the account dry."

Another moment passed as Ramsey considered what she had said. Lena traded looks with Rhodes, then moved to the counter and un-zipped the evidence bag. She was tired of waiting. Tired of being tested at a crime scene that was stuck on hold. She pushed the leather wallet aside and pulled out the one made of nylon and Velcro. Ripping it open, she found the driver's license and held it up to the light.

The victim was twenty-five years old. As her eyes slid over the name, those tremors began working through her fingers again. Lena finally understood why the deputy chief appeared so stunned. Why Barrera had been unable to look her in the eye all night. Why it didn't matter that Escabar had shut down the club before calling 911 and all the Fer-raris were gone. And why it didn't even matter if the victim's soul was lost forever between the winds.

The deputy chief had called it right. The kid with his lights punched out was more than an asshole. More than a motherfucker. And, in the end, he would be more trouble dead than alive.

She felt someone move in behind her and realized that it was Ramsey looking over her shoulder at the license. He was staring at it, but not seeing it—everything turned inward and lost in the black.

"Jacob Gant," he whispered in a voice taut with emotion. "Now you know why we need you, Gamble. Now you know why we're fucked."

4

Payback.

A killer overdosing on rage.

Lena didn't need to do the math as she exited Bosco's office and headed for the stairs.

Jacob Gant raped and murdered his sixteen-year-old neighbor Lily Hight. Six weeks ago he'd walked out of an L.A. courtroom a free man. Tonight the big wheel turned—yin finally met yang—and he was dead.

Gant's crimes were executed with extreme brutality. After assaulting the girl in her home, he drove a foot-long screwdriver into her back and watched her bleed to death.

The NOT GUILTY verdict had stunned everyone in the courtroom, producing utter silence for almost ten minutes with only the faint sound of Lily's father, Tim Hight, weeping in the background. Lena could still remember the moment—still hear the sound of Hight sobbing. Like everyone else, she had watched the trial on television from her desk. The shock of the verdict worked like an infection. In a single instant, the entire city knew what had happened in that courtroom and felt sickened by the result.

But the tent was bigger than Los Angeles. Jacob Gant's trial for the murder of Lily Hight had juice and flowed like a river rising over its banks wherever satellites and computer servers and smartphones could take it. Particularly after Gant's initial arrest when Lily's father had given the district attorney's office snapshots and home videos of his beloved daughter, his only child, to be distributed to the media outlets.

The images fed a fire that could no longer be contained. In the world of senseless murders, Lily Hight was what came next: a gorgeous blonde with striking blue-gray eyes and a gentle but outgoing spirit. An innocent teenager who faced the ultimate violation just as she had begun to flower. A grieving father who tried to protect his grieving wife and maintain their privacy, but seemed to look years older every time he was photographed.

And then there were the rumors that began soon after Gant's arrest, salacious stories appearing in the rag sheets that the twenty-five-year-old killer and his teenage victim were lovers.

The public's outrage to the crime, their compassion for Lily and her father, seemed to burn without end and evolve into near myth. Lily Hight's image began showing up on coffee mugs and T-shirts months before the trial. Street artists blanketed the city with her face on posters and wall paintings that read IS JUSTICE REALLY BLIND? Local TV news stations from coast to coast could point to interviews with teens who claimed to have known Lily, or met Lily, or seen Lily and wanted to be just like *their friend.*

It was another circus. Another media trial set in L.A. Another slam-dunk murder case in which every piece of evidence collected at the crime scene pointed to one person and only one person.

Jacob Gant raped and murdered his next-door neighbor Lily Hight. And the LAPD blew it. The district attorney's office blew it.

Again.

Blood samples were mishandled by SID techs at the crime scene and misplaced in the lab.

Again.

DNA analysis of semen collected from the victim pointed beyond all doubt to Jacob Gant, but like the blood evidence, it went missing and couldn't be found in the lab.

Again.

Two deputy district attorneys, outmatched by Buddy Paladino, sat back and watched the defense attorney rip their rock solid case apart while making them look like bunglers and fools in a way that only Buddy Paladino could do.

Again.

A killer was released, free to enjoy the pleasures of life here in the City of Angels or anywhere else he wanted to go.

Again and again and again.

Lena hit the stairs, feeling the words ripple through her body until she reached the club's foyer on the main floor. She was looking for Dante Escabar, but didn't see him behind the bar. Someone had turned down the lights, and the place was empty now. Just the spent coffee cups left behind by a division callout, the detectives finally released and sent home. She pulled a stool away from the bar and sat down. When she noticed the pack of cigarettes left beside an open bottle of bourbon, she fought the urge and pushed them away. Her mind was still skipping through the details. Still reeling. But there was anger, too. Anger at the situation and for what she was being asked to do.

Payback.

A killer overdosing on rage.

A father who could claim both reason and cause. In some circles, even the moral high ground.

Other than Jacob Gant's family, no one in the city would have a problem with his death tonight. Far from it. Lena imagined that when the news broke, the bars would be packed with people celebrating. But the party wouldn't last very long. Once Tim Hight was arrested for killing the man who murdered his daughter, once Lena put the case together and slapped the cuffs on the grieving father's wrists—a father in ruin doing what any father might do . . .

"Are you okay?"

She turned and saw Rhodes walking into the bar. She tried to find her voice, and it came out deep and scratched.

"I was going to ask you the same thing," she said.

He shrugged without an answer, crossing the darkened room for a peek out the window. Lena could hear the press corps still shouting at the patrol units holding them back. After a while, Rhodes joined her at the bar.

"The coroner," he said. "Barrera asked me to show him the way up when he gets here."

"Who got the call? Who got lucky?"

Rhodes gave her a look. "Besides you?"

She nodded. "Besides me."

"Ed Gainer," he said.

"Well, he's not gonna like the stairs."

"You're right. Eddie won't like the stairs."

Rhodes reached for the pack of cigarettes, found a lighter beside a tray of spent candles, and lit up. When he passed it over, Lena shook him off. Neither one of them really smoked. Although tonight more than qualified as a crisis, she was no longer in the mood. Instead, she looked at the scar on Rhodes's left earlobe. It was in the shape of an X, and she liked looking at it. His brown hair was cropped short again, his body lean and trim from daily jogs around Hollywood Reservoir. He looked good. The gunshot he'd taken to his left shoulder a few years back—a distant memory that only surfaced when it rained.

Rhodes stepped behind the bar and found a plate to use as an ash-tray. "I guess Hight held it together for as long as he could," he said. "I've never met him, but during the trial he looked okay. Wearing down maybe, but okay."

Lena nodded again without answering. No one in the division had met Tim Hight because his daughter's murder investigation had been handled by local detectives on the Westside. The case didn't ignite until prosecutors released those family snapshots to the press. By the time the public met Lily Hight, Jacob Gant had already been arrested and moved from his parents' home in Venice to an isolated cell at Men's Central Jail.

Rhodes leaned on the bar directly across from her. "After tonight people will think that Tim Hight's a hero. They're gonna say that he did what we couldn't. That he did what he had to do. That he finally got justice for his daughter."

"He's not a hero," she whispered.

"It doesn't make any difference, Lena. They'll call him one."

The words settled in for a while.

"He's not a hero," she repeated. "He didn't shoot Gant, lay down the gun, and wait to face the music. He walked into the room and shot Johnny Bosco first. And he shot him in the back, Stan. Then he tried to make it look like a robbery and ran away. He hit the wall and blew."

"I agree, but it won't play that way. It's still poison for us. Sugar-coated poison. Leave it to the LAPD to set the bad guys free and send the good guys to jail."

Lena remained quiet because she knew that what Rhodes had just said was true. Barrera and Deputy Chief Ramsey knew how it would play as well.

She started to reach for that pack of cigarettes after all, but stopped when she heard movement in the foyer behind her. It was a group of about ten people walking toward the front entrance as if on autopilot. She recognized the mayor's chief of staff, a city councilwoman from Hollywood, and the LAPD chief's new adjutant, Abraham Hernandez. It seemed like a good guess that this was the group who had been whispering in the darkness from the balcony outside Bosco's office. When she saw Steven Bennett and Debi Watson, she reached out for Rhodes and gave him a nudge.

Bennett and Watson were the deputy district attorneys who had brought the case against Jacob Gant to trial. Until Buddy Paladino humiliated them in front of a courtroom wired for TV and the electronic universe beyond, they were considered to be two of the best and brightest deputy DAs in Los Angeles. Particularly Steven Bennett, whom the district attorney had taken to and was grooming to replace him if he won reelection for his third term in office. Tonight, it looked like Bennett and Watson were anything but the best and brightest. Tonight, they were shuffling their feet and keeping their heads down. Tonight, they were passing the investigator from the coroner's office at the door—mere shadows of their former selves—and leaving another crime scene in shame.

5

She found Dante Escabar in the courtyard at a table by the pool. Although it seemed clear that he wanted to be alone, she pulled a chair out and sat down. Several moments passed before he even acknowledged her presence. He was deep within himself, sipping bourbon and brooding on automatic, with sheets of sharp blue light from the water ricocheting off his dark eyes.

"I've already told you people everything I know," he said finally.

He hadn't looked up, but was still staring at his drink. The ice was melting away.

"Sometimes in the heat of the moment details get left behind," she said.

"Heat of the moment? Is that what the LAPD calls it?"

She could hear the fury in his voice. The venom. Escabar was younger than his partner by at least ten years. He was a handsome man with clear brown skin, a strong frame, and black hair as fine as silk cut just above the shoulders. Lena knew very little about him because Bosco had been the front man for Club 3 AM. She thought that she could remember reading somewhere that Escabar had spent his childhood on the street. That it had been a long climb that began at a taco stand on San

Fernando Boulevard. That he met Bosco, who gave him a job and eventually took him under his wing. A few months back *The Times* photographed Escabar's home on Mulholland Drive and the actress he was living with. The climb was part of his history, but Lena wondered about his temperament. She watched him take a long pull on the glass, his eyes settling somewhere over by the pool.

"How much will you benefit from Johnny Bosco's death?" she said.

"What's that supposed to mean?"

"How much will you make?"

Escabar finally turned to her. "You're right, Officer. After tonight I'll be rich. I've been sitting here, counting it in my head. All that fucking money. While you assholes have spent the last three hours trying to cover for the fact that every one of you fucked up, I've been out here celebrating the murder of my best friend."

A long moment passed. A long stretch of jagged silence.

"I know it's not easy," she said. "The timing's worse than bad. But I need to clear a few things up and I need to do it quickly."

Escabar took another swig of bourbon. "Sounds like you need to clear up more than that. You're way off base."

"I hope so," Lena said. "But I still need an answer."

"This isn't about my partner. This is about that asshole kid."

"How much are you gonna make from your partner's death?"

Escabar glanced back at her, shaking his head at the inevitable. "Nada," he said. "Nothing. Not a single cent. I'm lucky to be one of seven partners. More than lucky."

"Who are the other five? Studio execs?"

"Three of them are. The other two are actors. If you want their names you'll have to call our lawyer. But no one profits from Johnny's death. The club grew out of his business with the studios. This was his place. His idea. Nothing changes, not even the split. He's got family on the East Coast. South Jersey. A mother and father. If you really want to waste time, talk to them. Maybe they killed their own son tonight. It's either that or you've gotta face the fact that Johnny Bosco's dead because the LAPD couldn't cut it. Someone else had to put Jacob Gant down, and he fucked it up. He killed Johnny. He's even more lame than you are."

Escabar turned away. As she thought it over, she studied his posture. His face and hands. Although she didn't trust him, she believed that his reaction to her questions was genuine. That her gut instincts about the case were more right than wrong. Gant was the target. Bosco got in the way.

"Why did you tell the deputy chief that you thought this was a robbery?" she said.

Escabar didn't move, didn't blink—his eyes fixed on the memory.

"I heard the shots," he said in a quieter voice. "I ran upstairs and found them. I saw Johnny lying on the floor, but the kid's face was all fucked up. I didn't recognize him. When I found out who he was, I knew I'd been wrong. It wasn't a robbery."

"Who told you his name?"

"I don't know. I overheard some cops talking about it in the bar after you showed up."

"What time did you hear the shots?"

"About twelve-thirty," he said.

"What was Gant doing here? Why was he upstairs with Bosco?"

Escabar tossed his drink on the ground and set the glass down. "I've been asking myself the same thing. I have no fucking idea."

"You ever see him here before, Dante?"

He shook his head again. "No."

"Did Bosco ever talk about him or mention his name?"

"Never."

"What about the girl's father? What about Tim Hight?"

In spite of the blue light masking Escabar's eyes, something changed. Lena could see him thinking it over. The fire inside the man was flaring up again.

"He knows the club," Escabar said. "Way back before his kid got killed, he used to come here. Not often, but enough to know how the place works and where things are."

"How could Tim Hight get into Club 3 AM?"

"He used to direct a TV show on cable. People liked it. The show did well."

"Did you see him here tonight?"

"No, and I've already checked. He didn't walk through the front door and sign in. But like I said, he knows the place."

Escabar's voice died off. After a long moment, he climbed to his feet and reached for the table to steady himself. Lena glanced to her right and saw Barrera wave at her through the windows as he circled the foyer inside and searched for the door.

"One more thing, Dante."

"Just one, Detective Gamble?"

"You know my name."

He nodded, but remained silent.

"The cocaine," she said. "You knew it was there. Why didn't you get rid of it?"

He paused to consider her question, but only briefly. "What cocaine? I never saw any cocaine. It must have been planted by the killer."

"Nice try. Why didn't you get rid of it?"

He looked down at his empty glass and wouldn't answer.

"What?" Lena said. "You think that I'm gonna bust your partner? After tonight, I don't think it would play in court. Tell me why you left it there."

The door opened and Barrera stepped out. As he approached from the other side of the courtyard, Escabar lowered his voice.

"I was trying to take care of things," he said. "I needed to call my partners and tell them what happened to Johnny. There was confusion. People were frightened. I gave myself an hour to shut the place down."

"Did you call the DA?"

He appeared surprised by the question and didn't know how to answer it.

"They were friends," Lena said. "It's seems only natural that Higgins would be your first call."

He shook his head, but kept quiet.

"Is that an answer?" she said.

"I didn't call the DA."

He walked off just as Barrera reached them. Lena turned to her supervisor. From the look on his face, Barrera had news.

"We've got him," he said under his breath. "It's Tim Hight. Street cameras picked him up driving away from the club. His car. His plates. His face behind the wheel."

"When?"

"About a half hour ago. He probably hung around to watch the chaos. Most of them do."

Lena checked her watch. The night was slipping away. Too many people were involved.

"I want to notify Gant's parents," she said. "I don't want them to find out what happened to him on their own."

"He had a father and one brother. His mother's dead."

It had come up during the trial. Gant's mother had been murdered when he was fourteen, her body found on a ball field a block from Santa Monica High School. Lena had forgotten. As Barrera handed her a three-by-five card with Gant's contact information, she realized that she needed to pace herself better. Think things through more carefully and keep focused.

"Take Rhodes with you," Barrera said. "Tito can help me get started on the warrants. But these guys need rest. I want to release them as soon as you've talked to Gant's father. We'll meet back at Parker by seven. The deputy chief is setting something up with the DA's office. We can work things out then. You okay?"

She nodded, slipping the three-by-five card into her notepad. Then Barrera met her eyes and offered a shrug.

"I'm sorry, Lena," he said gently. "I'm sorry that it turned out to be Hight. I'm sorry that you got stuck with this one. I kept hoping we were wrong."

"I'm okay, Frank. I'm okay."

"Maybe so. But that doesn't change the fact that they're using you. The way your last two cases played out. You've got capital to burn, and they're gonna burn it."

"I'll do whatever it takes to put this behind us," she said.

Barrera flashed a warm smile beneath his mustache. "That's what I told them you'd say. Now grab Rhodes and hit the road. And remember, Hight lives next door. Keep your eyes open. Be careful and be safe."

6

The wall of heat hit them as they exited Club 3 AM and started down the steps. Lena glanced at Rhodes, caught his weary smile and pointed at the Crown Vic parked in the back of the lot.

"Hope the air works in that thing," he said. "How'd you get a take-home car with all the cutbacks? You pay somebody off?"

She knew what he was up to. Next-of-kin notifications were never easy. Under the circumstances, letting Jacob Gant's father know that his son had been murdered tonight was almost beyond the pale.

"I stole it," she said. "Two days ago when my car died. No one's noticed."

Rhodes laughed. "But they will. And then a little man with a clipboard's gonna show up and ask you for a credit card. I'm not kidding. They're gonna charge you for the ride. The money goes to—"

Lena grabbed Rhodes's arm and pulled him to a stop, her eyes on the Crown Vic. There was movement in the car. It was difficult to see, yet it was there in the darkness. A set of bad shocks moving ever so slightly on a still night. A rear window cracked open to let in air.

"I locked the car," she whispered.

"You sure?"

"I locked it."

They traded looks and separated. Rhodes drew his gun, moving slowly around the passenger side. As Lena approached the left rear door, she slid in behind the slope of the roof and hit the clicker. Then the alarm chirped, the locks popped, and the interior lights switched on.

She peered through the darkened glass and saw a man in the back-seat hiding below the window line. He was staring up at her through a pair of glasses and trying to conceal his face beneath the bill of his baseball cap.

"Out of the car," she called through the window.

The man shook his head at her.

"Step out of the car right now, mister."

The man shook her off again without saying anything.

Lena's eyes flicked up to his hands gripping the front seat. When she didn't see a weapon, she nodded at Rhodes and they ripped open the doors. Unaware that Lena wasn't alone, the man panicked and started squirming. As Rhodes dragged him backward, Lena pushed his legs through the car and they wrestled him onto the ground. The guy was still kicking, still pushing and pulling, but they had him. Rhodes rolled him over onto his stomach, driving a knee into his shoulder and pushing his face into the pavement. Once Lena got him cuffed, she turned him onto his back and looked him over.

The odd-looking man appeared soft and round. His suit and tie, rumpled and sweat stained and permeated with body odor. For some reason he couldn't stop bouncing up and down off the asphalt. She had seen it before when she worked narcotics, particularly with people overdosing on ecstasy. Once their core temperature overheated, they became the equivalent of a live fish hitting a hot frying pan. As Lena watched, she couldn't decide if he was using or just writhing in anger. Either way, the ground was hard and it looked painful.

She reached out to check his forehead. When he tried to bite her, she pulled her hand away, leaned over him, and shouted.

"You got a name, mister?"

He shook his head back and forth and started grunting. It sounded a lot like he was telling her to fuck off.

She glanced at Rhodes. "We don't have time for this, Stan."

Rhodes agreed and they started going through the man's pockets and tossing his possessions aside as quickly as they could. When Lena found his wallet, it seemed larger than most and she flipped it open. Inside were a set of press credentials. She read the ID, then checked the man's face against the photo. She hadn't recognized him with the baseball cap and glasses, but she could see it now.

"Who is he?" Rhodes said.

She held up the ID and noted the fear and uncertainty washing over their captive's face. Rhodes scanned the document and started laughing.

The man squirming on the pavement was Dick Harvey, a lowlife gossip reporter from *Blanket Hollywood*. Seven nights a week, *Blanket Hollywood* played in the mud, promising its viewers another thirty minutes beneath the sheets with their favorite stars. Lena suspected that the TV show and the Web site that went with it killed brain cells.

"Dick Harvey," Rhodes said, his voice peppered with a joyous sarcasm. "Crossing a police line and breaking into an LAPD car at a homicide investigation. Man, you're good."

Harvey finally settled down and found his voice. But it all seemed a little too smooth, and Lena wondered if the convulsions hadn't been some weak attempt to fake them out.

"Come on, guys," he said, pleading. "You've gotta understand the spot I'm in."

Rhodes laughed again. "We get it, Harvey. You're on a secret mission. You're working undercover. But what I really want is your autograph. I can't wait to see it right below your fingerprints when you get booked tonight. Remember to smile when they take your picture. I guarantee it'll make the rounds."

"But I've got a deadline to make. Give me a break. I'm just covering a story."

Lena had reached her limit. "Not anymore," she said. "What were you doing in the car? What were you up to?"

Harvey's voice rose an octave and he began whining. "It was just a mistake. It's late and I didn't know where the fuck I was going. Come on. I'm working a story, guys. Jacob Gant's dead, right? Lily Hight's old man blew his brains out. You're in charge, right, Lena?"

Something inside her clicked as she measured him. The hat and glasses, the sudden barrage of questions, his use of her first name. The dirtbag reporter was cuffed but still busting—still running out line.

"You stink, Harvey," she said. "You need a shower and clean clothes. And what's with the hat and glasses? What are you up to?"

She reached out for his glasses, but he jerked his head away.

"Fuck you both. I want a lawyer."

He flashed a big smile at them like he'd just said the magic words. Like he thought he was in charge.

I want a lawyer.

Rhodes slapped the smile off his face and yanked him back. "You're gonna need one, Harvey. And if you bite me, you're gonna need a new set of teeth. Now shut up and don't move."

Lena ripped away the glasses, tossing the baseball cap over to Rhodes. Within a few moments, she knew that they were on the right track. Both items were wired for video and sound. Harvey had probably hoped that he wouldn't be seen in the car. At least not until he'd recorded a sound bite with enough juice for tomorrow's broadcast of *Blanket Holly-wood*.

"I want a lawyer," he repeated. "I want one now."

Lena didn't respond to the magic words. She'd found the camera lens, but the frames were split. On the left was a battery pack. On the right, a small thumb drive. She switched off the power and turned to watch Rhodes. The camera hidden in the hat was about the size of a dime with a high-capacity media card attached. Rhodes was holding them in front of Harvey's face as if he'd won them at the racetrack.

"You're a wild man, Harvey," he said.

"I'm a reporter, and I have rights. That's my stuff and I want an attorney."

Rhodes shook his head. "Sounds like a mantra, but it won't work until we've processed the crime scene. You're the crime scene, Harvey, so answer the question. Did you plant something in our car?"

"I don't have to say anything. I'm a reporter. This is a free country. You guys are assholes."

"And I think I saw you running out of the building," Rhodes said. "Where did you hide the gun, Harvey? Is that what you were doing in our car? Getting rid of the murder weapon?"

Harvey stopped and cocked his head as he tried to read Rhodes's face. "What are you saying?"

Rhodes traded a hard look with Lena, then turned back to the reporter. "You were found hiding in a detective's car on the wrong side of a police line. Maybe you don't get it. Maybe you think homicide investigations are a game. You're a suspect, Harvey. A person of interest."

"You can't pull that shit. Jesus Christ! You know it's not me."

"I don't know jack," Rhodes said. "All I know is where we found you."

Lena could see fear crystalizing all over Harvey's face, dirty little wheels turning inside his dirty little head. As Rhodes continued to pat him down, she glanced at his possessions piling up on the asphalt. She noted the pad and pen, his cell phone, and a small leather case that looked like it held his business cards. After a second glance, the case seemed too big for cards. She picked it up and felt the weight in her hand. As she unzipped it, she noticed Harvey staring at her with those beady eyes of his. He was more than nervous now. Unusually quiet. Utterly still.

Once she opened the case, she understood why. It was a complete set of lock picks and auto jigglers.

Most of the auto jigglers Lena had seen on the job were handmade from hacksaw blades. After a few minutes with a Dremel grinder, the flat pieces of scrap metal could be shaped to look a lot like skeleton keys and were capable of opening a car door in less than a minute or two. But Dick Harvey's set was better than that. These jigglers were made of stainless steel, crafted with precision, and could unlock a car door as well as the owner's key. Lena knew how well they worked because she owned a set herself. She'd found the manufacturer over the Internet and made the purchase for about twenty dollars, plus shipping and handling.

She held up the case and noticed a label on the back that read THE ESSENTIAL BURGLAR. Rhodes's eyes sparkled as he gazed at the tools.

"You're better than a dream, Harvey," he said with delight. "You're the gift that just keeps on giving."

7

Lena cruised off the Santa Monica Freeway and made a left on Lincoln. She was driving Rhodes's Audi, the Crown Vic left behind until SID could sweep the car and dust it for Dick Harvey's greasy fingerprints. Harvey had been left chained to a streetlight in the parking lot under the supervision of two patrol officers. By now, detectives would have arrived and Harvey was probably on his way downtown.

The thought brought on a smile and she glanced over at Rhodes. His head was back, his eyelids shut but fluttering. Obviously, Harvey wasn't really a person of interest in the murders tonight. But for ten minutes, Rhodes's play against the man had provided a short break from the pressure. Depending on the charges, Harvey would spend anywhere from a few hours to a night or two in jail. He would be confined to a cell for however long they could stretch things out. Lena had to admit that the image of the gossip reporter being hosed down with disinfectant and issued a jumpsuit before he got that jail cell felt pretty good, too.

She blew through the red light and started up the hill on Ocean Park. The streets were dead, the trip from Hollywood to the beach made in record time. As she turned onto Sixteenth Street, she tried to think

through what she would say to the father of a young man who murdered his sixteen-year-old neighbor, got away with it, then got himself
killed. She had mixed feelings about it because what Jacob Gant did to
Lily Hight was essentially irrelevant for the next half hour or so. Gant's
father would feel the same pain any parent would feel upon hearing
that they had lost a child. No matter what the circumstances of his
son's life, Lena would be delivering bad news.

She made the final turn, following the road around the rim of the hill.
To the right, she could see Main Street and the blackness of the ocean
cutting into Venice Beach. To the left, the hill flattened out and homes
with sidewalks and oak trees began to appear one after the next. She
checked the address Barrera had given her. When she spotted the house,
she killed the headlights and pulled over.

Gant's father was already awake. Every window in the entire house
glowed with bright incandescent light. Two windows on the first floor
of the house next door were lit up as well. When she turned to wake up
Rhodes, she found him staring through the windshield completely alert.

"Who lives where?" he said.

"Tim Hight's is the one here on the left with the picket fence. Gant's
father lives on the other side of the drive."

"The one that's all lit up."

"Yeah," she said. "He lives there with his son."

She saw Rhodes check the clock on the dash and look back at Gant's
house.

"Their lights wouldn't be on unless they knew, Lena. Someone
called."

"The way things happened—the number of people involved—it
would've been a hard secret to keep."

"If it's already filtered down to trash like Harvey, it's no secret. He
probably knew before we did. But now it's gonna be even harder to
knock on that door."

Lena shut off the engine and they climbed out. She listened to the
silence, the rest of the neighborhood still in a deep, seemingly untrou-
bled sleep. Just the hum of air conditioners getting an early start on the

year. In spite of the heat, she could feel a chill between her shoulder blades as she gazed at the two houses standing side by side. It seemed so odd that these people still lived next door to each other. After all that had happened, it didn't make sense that one or the other hadn't sold their house and moved on. Although the ocean views were better ten houses back, both homes were built on prime real estate. Eclectic versions of California bungalows that had been stretched into two stories with front porches and sunrooms. Both lots were big enough to include driveways and garages. From what Lena could see from the curb, each home even had a small backyard. She couldn't believe that either place would have been hard to sell.

"We should have brought Tito," Rhodes said.

"Why?"

"Look."

She followed his eyes across Gant's driveway to Tim Hight's house on the left. She could see someone through the living room window. Stepping up to the picket fence, she realized that it was Hight—still dressed and pouring a drink at the kitchen counter. Even from this distance she recognized the bottle by its blue color. Hight was pouring vodka into a very tall glass.

"It's five," she said. "Nothing like a cocktail after a hard day's work."

Rhodes took a step closer. "Kill'n and chill'n, Lena. The man likes a big glass."

"You have those cigarettes?"

"No. I left them on the bar, but it looks like he's got one."

She watched as Hight lit a cigarette and grabbed his drink. Exiting the kitchen, he hit the wall switch and the house went dark. After a few seconds, they picked up the bead of light from the head of his cigarette. The light was passing through the living room and moving into the sunroom on the side of the house. Lena could see his silhouette in the window and guessed that the LEDs from a radio or cable box were filling the room with a muted light. When he sat down before the windows overlooking his neighbor's house, the glow from his cigarette brightened, then faded some. The man was smoking and drinking and probably playing back the last three hours in his head. More than likely, he was replaying everything that went down over the past year, all those images that he would be forced to carry with him for the rest of his days.

His love for his daughter cut against finding her dead body lying on her bedroom floor. Passing the blindfolded statue of Lady Justice on his way to the courtroom two or three times a day, cut against a trial that fell apart and washed away. Holding on for as long as he could, then buckling under the strain and blowing out Jacob Gant's eyes.

Blind justice.

Lena heard a ticking sound and spotted Hight's car in the drive beneath an oak tree. A black Mercedes still cooling down after a hard drive on a hot night. She turned back to Rhodes and kept her voice down.

"I think I should go talk to the Gants on my own," she said. "You should stay out here and keep an eye on this guy."

"You sure?"

She nodded, her eyes returning to Hight's eerie silhouette in the window. "Maybe he's done for the night," she said. "Or maybe he's just getting tuned up for more. Either way, I've got a feeling about the guy."

"Me, too," Rhodes said.

The front door opened tentatively. On the other side of the threshold stood an eighteen-year-old boy Lena recognized from the trial as Jacob Gant's brother, Harry. He didn't look at the badge she was holding in her hand. Instead, he kept his eyes on her face and called out to his father.

"They're here, Dad."

His father didn't respond. The kid pointed to the left and she followed him through the dining room into the kitchen. William Gant was sitting at the table in his bathrobe with a cup of coffee. As she crossed the room, the man held up his hand as if to say, *Stop, you're close enough.*

"Mr. Gant?" she said. "I'm—"

He cut her off with another raised hand. "You know what, Detective? I really don't care who you are. If you're here to tell us that Jake's dead, you're more than an hour and a half late. If you're here to say you're sorry, save yourself the trouble. I don't want to hear it. And I don't think Jake's brother wants to hear it, either. Nothing you say or do could make a difference now."

Harry had moved around the table to stand behind his father. The weight of their eyes on her felt corrosive and heavy. She knew that she could handle their anger. She expected it and understood it. But what charged the moment with electricity had nothing to do with them or even why she was here. It was the view out the slider behind their backs. It was that bead of light from Tim Hight's cigarette. She could see it in the sunroom window. The man was watching them, and he was close. Just on the other side of the driveway.

Lena tried to ignore it. Tried to keep in mind that Rhodes was somewhere outside, watching the watcher.

"I'm sorry for your loss," she said. "I know that you don't want to hear it from me, but I mean it."

William Gant didn't say anything. His eyes drifted away from her to something he was holding in his hand. A small photograph. When he set it down on the table, Lena was close enough to get a decent look. It was a family snapshot of William Gant with his two sons. They were aboard a ship and dressed for cold weather. A whale was swimming just off the bow. All three were caught up in the moment and flashing wide smiles.

Gant saw her looking at the photograph and covered it with his hand. "I think we're done here," he said. "I think that you should get back in your car and drive away."

"We need to arrange a time when you can come down to the coroner's office and identify your son."

"It's already been arranged," he said.

"By whom?"

"My son's attorney, Buddy Paladino."

It hung there. Paladino had told Gant that his son was dead an hour and a half ago. Rhodes had been right. The leak had become a flood before she even got the case.

"What about the circumstances of your son's death?" she asked.

Gant shook his head, chewing through the words as if they were toxic. "The circumstances of my son's death," he said. "That's a good one."

"Do you know why he was at Club 3 AM?"

Neither one of them responded. Lena looked at them staring back at her just the way Escabar had—despair spiked with poison. She checked the slider and saw Hight's silhouette in the window, that bead of light from his cigarette still piercing the darkness.

"What about Johnny Bosco?" she said. "Why was Jacob with him?"

The father pushed his coffee aside. "I have no idea."

She sensed something in Harry's face and turned to him. "Did you know Johnny Bosco?" she asked. "Do you know why your brother was with him, Harry? Did he use cocaine?"

The kid remained quiet and appeared nervous at being singled out. When she repeated the question, his face hardened.

"My brother didn't do drugs," he said finally. "And you're just another stupid cop. Why don't you leave us the fuck alone?"

He pushed past his father and rushed out of the room. After a few moments, a door slammed on the second floor. Then Gant pocketed the snapshot and got up from the table. Curiously, he turned his back on her and looked out through the slider. The man seemed to know that Hight had been watching them all along.

"You need to leave," he said, still gazing across the driveway. "You've fulfilled our every expectation, Detective, and I don't want my asshole neighbor to see me get angry. That's what he wants. That's why he's watching. Why don't you knock on his door tonight and ask him if he feels any better now. I can already see the stories on the news. The man who murdered my boy will get a parade. A street named after his sorry soul. I'll bet you cops are actually happy about the way things worked out. Not short-term happy because you look like the stupid jerks that you truly are. But long-term happy because you're finally off the hook."

"No one's off the hook, Mr. Gant."

He turned from the window and stared at her for a long time. His weary body was trembling slightly and it looked as if he'd aged ten years in the past few minutes. Like something deep inside him had given way. As he pushed the chair into the table, he seemed a lot like his neighbor. He seemed like a man being forced to carry a monkey on his back for the rest of time—a bag overflowing with memories and nightmares he couldn't shake out or get rid of.

He stepped around the table and pointed at the door, his voice hoarse and barely audible. "This is over," he said. "Get out."

8

The ride back to Parker Center was quiet—the eastern sky just beginning to catch some light from the sun still waking up below the
horizon. With "rush hour" underway—an event that ran continuously
from 5:30 a.m. until 2:00 a.m. every day of the week in Los Angeles—
Lena assumed that she would be late for the strategy meeting at seven
and had called ahead to let Barrera know.

It couldn't be helped. Tim Hight and William Gant were way too
wound up to be left alone. The air was too hot, the tinder too dry, and
too many nerves were exposed.

Murder season was in full bloom, and Lena couldn't walk away.

Her first thought was to request a surveillance team from the Special Investigation Section. SIS was their primary surveillance unit and
could easily handle the job. But this was a unique situation. After talking it over with Rhodes, they decided that everyone would be better off
if the surveillance units were out in the open for all to see. Two or three
black and white cruisers parked right at the curb to underline their
presence, and with any luck, cool things down.

Lena swung around the block and pulled up to the building. As she
climbed out and Rhodes moved in behind the wheel, she could see

what three nights without sleep had done to him. She watched him wave and pull away from the curb, trying not to worry about his drive home. Losing sight of her friend in traffic, she headed for the lobby on her own.

The meeting was being held in Captain Dillworth's office on the third floor directly behind the Homicide Special Section. Her captain was in New Orleans, so the room was available and always left unlocked. Her desk stood just on the other side of the wall at one of four homicide tables. Her early morning arrival, more than routine. But Lena could sense something was different about today from the moment she passed through the lobby doors. The lunch stand across from the front desk. The guys working the turnstiles and X-ray machine. The three or four groups of people she passed in the hall.

The usual morning banter had been replaced with muffled voices and dull eyes pinned to the ground. The read she picked up was disappointment. But she thought that she could see fear and uncertainty, too.

The mood followed her into the captain's office, only it was more pervasive here. As she slipped into an open seat and listened, Deputy Chief Ramsey was standing at the head of the table, laying it out for anyone who might have missed it. His audience was a select group that included the two prosecutors from the district attorney's office who had failed, Steven Bennett and Debi Watson, another deputy DA Lena recognized but had never worked with, Greg Vaughan, along with their boss, District Attorney Jimmy J. Higgins. Aside from Ramsey, the only other LAPD official was her supervisor, Lieutenant Frank Barrera. That could only mean that Lena really was on her own.

She pushed the thought away and tried to concentrate on what the deputy chief was saying. Most of it was a repeat of her conversations with Rhodes and Escabar. But Ramsey had found his voice—gravel rinsed in an ashtray—and spiced things up with new details.

"We're making news again," he said. "Department of Justice attorneys will be meeting with the judge in two hours. Every reform we've made under Chief Logan—the progress we've achieved, the performance records we've broken—everything we've stood for over the past few years burned up with this case. This trial. And now, two men murdered in Hollywood. Termination of the consent decree has been tossed to the side of the road. Another monitor will be selected to look over our shoulders and report to the judge. The department is under the microscope again. You are, too, Higgins. We're in this mess together. And right now, we're roadkill. We're fucked."

The deputy chief's words settled into the room sharp as broken glass. When Higgins didn't react, Lena looked around the table and wondered what she'd missed over the past forty-five minutes. Bennett and Watson were sitting with the district attorney directly across from her. Barrera was on her left, but seemed to be focused on Greg Vaughan who was in a chair by himself at the far end of the table.

Something was going on. The more she thought it over, the more convinced she became that Vaughan's presence was out of place. And from the grim expression on his face, it seemed obvious enough that he didn't want to be here, either. Of all the prosecutors in the DA's office, Greg Vaughan was the total package and could have worked for any law firm in the city. Lena had only met him in passing, but was well aware of his reputation. He was an exceedingly bright and gentle man, and looked to be about forty. His hair was more brown than blond. His frame, lean and athletic. When she had seen him in the past, he walked with an easy confidence. But it had been his eyes that set him apart. The glint and energy in those light brown eyes.

Today it looked like the lights had been shut down.

Lena glanced at Higgins, then back at Vaughan jotting something down on his legal pad. Vaughan had been shut out of the Jacob Gant trial early on when it looked like the kind of high-profile case that could make a deputy DA instead of breaking one. Higgins had kept Vaughan away because it was well known that he had become the district attorney's chief rival. To Vaughan's credit, he didn't seem to have an interest in the rivalry and had made no attempt to compete with Higgins for his job. Roy Wemer, a deputy DA Lena had worked with over the past few years, once told her that Vaughan would never give up being a prosecutor. In spite of the years he'd put in, in spite of the over-whelming support he would have received from his colleagues, Vaughan still enjoyed presenting a case at trial and working in front of a judge and jury.

The deputy chief opened a file folder, tossing a photograph on the conference table. Everyone leaned in for a closer look. It was a single frame from the street camera that had picked up Tim Hight driving away from Club 3 AM. Although the image had been taken at night, the clarity was good enough to make an ID. Tim Hight's face showed clearly through the windshield, looking triumphant and completely mad, along with a dark shape on the passenger seat that could easily have been the murder weapon.

Ramsey rolled a chair over, turning to Lena as he sat down. "SID has already made a preliminary review of the security tapes from the club," he said. "Unfortunately, the fire escape is a blind spot. Hight could have been waiting out there all night and never been picked up on camera."

Lena thought about the way the building was configured—what the cop with the clipboard had called *ass backward*. "The fire escape is on the far side of the building," she said. "Out of the way and facing north."

"Exactly. No one can see it from either the street or the parking lot."

She looked back at the photograph of Hight in his car. "What about this shape on the passenger seat?"

"They're working on it," Ramsey said. "But don't get your hopes up. At this point, they think it's a flashlight."

Lena settled back in her chair. Something about the way Bennett and Watson and even Higgins were looking at the photograph both-ered her. She wasn't a mind reader, but she began to get the feeling that they were trying to *appear* interested. That it required an effort and that they couldn't quite get there. Bennett's eyes were emerald green, his body short and stocky. He was old enough have grown up at a time when "supersize me" sounded like free food instead of garbage, but young enough to have two kids in daycare and worries about what he and his wife might do with his career sinking to the bottom of the pool. Watson looked as if she shared the same unnatural lack of concern. She was about Lena's age, with blond hair and a sleek body hidden beneath her business suit. Every time Lena had ever seen Watson, she was dressed conservatively. Only rumors stood in her wake: rumors of a boob job last year while on vacation, and rumors that she and Bennett were having an affair—one reason among many why they'd lost the Jacob Gant trial and a murderer had walked free.

As Lena's eyes moved to Higgins all puffed up in his pinstripe suit—his weak, pudgy face and a haircut that looked over processed and more like a do—it suddenly occurred to her what was going on.

All three of them were running away. Greg Vaughan would be left behind to sit on the hot seat. Higgins had picked his rival in the office to handle the case because he knew that it would destroy whoever sat in the chair.

No one prosecuting the father of a murdered girl would ever have a political future in Los Angeles.

Higgins had picked Vaughan, not to save the office, but to save himself and possibly even his protégés: Steven Bennett and Debi Watson. Vaughan's face would be attached to the prosecution of Tim Hight, a father who sought justice for his only child, rather than the prosecutors who had blown the trial, or the district attorney who claimed to have overseen them.

The move was ice-cold and vicious. As Lena looked Higgins over, she wondered if he hadn't worked out the details with his political consultants last night. It had seemed more than odd to her that he hadn't shown up at the crime scene. Especially when one of the victims was someone he called a friend.

She turned away and caught the deputy chief scrutinizing her. His face remained completely expressionless, yet it felt as if he knew what she had been thinking. He pushed a second copy of the photograph her way and cleared his throat.

"Here's what we need to make happen, Detective. You and Mr. Vaughan are now partners. You need to work together to build a case against Tim Hight. You need to do it quickly and with as little noise as possible. Hight's arrest must occur without incident. I'm sure that the district attorney hasn't had a chance to think about what a deal might look like. There's Bosco's murder to consider, which complicates everything for everyone. Your case must be strong enough that Hight and his attorney are willing to listen—the deal from the DA good enough that they just might be willing to avoid a trial. Admittedly, we're talking about a best-case scenario. Hight will have public opinion on his side. More than likely, he'll choose to roll the dice in front of a jury. People will say that if we had done our jobs, if we hadn't been asleep at the wheel, if we hadn't fucked everything up, none of this would have ever happened. So the odds would be in his favor. Chances are, he'd win. That being said, the key words here are speed and building the case against him quickly. That's really the only option we have left. The longer this goes on—the longer Hight's in the news—the deeper the wounds will be for all concerned. Is that clear? Does everyone here understand exactly what's at stake?"

Vaughan didn't move or say anything.

The district attorney ignored his silence and turned to Ramsey. "I've been talking to some people," he said. "They think that if we work quickly, everyone will forget about what happened in six months."

A moment passed. Then another, as Ramsey measured the DA with complete dissatisfaction showing on his face.

"Six months?" Ramsey said finally. "We're talking about restoring the public's trust, Higgins. The people you spoke with should have told you the truth. Nobody's gonna forget this one. By the time they do, you'll be dead."

His words hung there. The room darkened as the sun slipped behind a cloud.

Higgins took the hit and blinked. "I need to speak with the chief," he said.

Ramsey shook his head. "He's out of town on business."

"But I have a problem. I need to talk to him."

"It's not gonna happen."

"Then I need to speak with you privately."

"That's not gonna happen either, Jimmy. What's your problem?"

Higgins remained quiet, checking the door, then glancing from face to face until he came to Lena and Barrera. He was tossing something over in his head and rubbing his polished fingernails across his chin. His eyes appeared dull and watery. Several moments passed before he seemed to come to a decision. Then he reached down for his briefcase and pulled out a copy of *The Los Angeles Times*. As the paper splashed onto the conference table in front of the deputy chief, Lena read the headline:

Double Murder At Club 3 AM:
Jacob Gant and Johnny Bosco Dead

Head shots of the victims were included above the fold, along with shots of Lily Hight and her father. But Higgins was pointing at another photograph in a box to the right of the lead story. It was the same picture Lena had seen hanging on the wall beside Johnny Bosco's desk. A shot of Higgins and Bosco together.

Higgins met the deputy chief's eyes, his voice low and shaky. "Bosco's life needs to be cleaned up. The drugs that were found at his place. They need to go away."

Ramsey actually smiled as he took it in. Lena had never seen him like this before. The smile matched his hardened face and shaved head. There was a vicious underside to it—a slow, dark curl—like he was holding a knife to Higgins's throat and ready to make the cut.

"This is a no-win situation for all of us," he said. "Everybody's gonna lose something this time around."

Higgins grimaced and looked frightened. "The drugs are a real problem. They're a negative we can't beat."

Ramsey leaned over the table, still working that tainted smile. "You mean, a negative *you* can't beat, Jimmy. When are you gonna stop talking to your asshole consultants? When are you gonna realize that what we're facing isn't about you?"

9

The meeting ended quickly with Higgins chasing the deputy chief down the hall and pressing the man for a private moment that Lena knew he'd never get. Bennett and Watson had stayed behind to talk to Vaughan. Lena could see them through the plate-glass window as she hung up the phone from an empty desk in the staff room. She wanted to verify that everyone was ready while Barrera checked on the progress of the warrants. She had also placed a call to SID and received preliminary confirmation that a 9-mm weapon had been used to murder Jacob Gant. Because the slugs had fragmented as they broke through his skull and entered the wall, no exact determination could be made until the medical examiner removed the additional slugs from each victim's body. With any luck, they were lodged in soft tissue and remained in decent shape. The autopsies would occur simultaneously and were scheduled for early this evening.

Lena wrote the time down in her notebook and glanced back at Vaughan through the glass. His conversation with Bennett and Watson appeared heated. Returning to her notebook, she went through her checklist.

The group heading out to Hight's place included Barrera and six additional detectives from the division. Of the six, Joe Carson and John Street had the most experience working high-profile cases. Both were RHD bulls known for being extremely thorough. A team of seasoned criminalists from SID would roll out as well. Three patrol units were already there keeping watch from the street. According to the patrol supervisor, both Tim Hight and William Gant had refrained from killing each other last night. Hight had passed out in his chair by the window, while Gant fell asleep on the kitchen floor.

The situation was more than tragic. But Lena pushed it aside, listening to Barrera finish his call with the chief's new adjutant, Abe Hernandez, and hang up.

"The judge gave us a break," he said. "The warrants are signed. I guess it didn't hurt that they were shepherded through by the chief's office. You ready, Lena?"

"As soon as Hernandez gets here with the paper, we'll head out."

"Good," he said.

Barrera exited the staff room, heading for his desk at the other end of the section floor. Lena glanced at her watch, guessing that she had ten or twenty minutes and weighing her options as she examined the beat-up coffeemaker on the counter. She was starting to feel the sleep she'd missed last night, but a run to the Blackbird Café wasn't an option because she needed to speak with Vaughan. She gave the glass pot another look, then poured a cup and took a short first sip. The thick syrupy brew tasted like it had been sitting on the burner for a week or two. It may have even qualified as the worst cup of hot java ever poured. But none of that really mattered right now. All she wanted was the fix. She took another sip—longer this time—letting the burned caffeine wash through her system. Then she crossed the room to the captain's office and pushed open the door without knocking.

Bennett and Watson turned toward her so quickly that she caught the foul sneers on their faces a split second before they switched to glowing smiles. Lena had pegged them right but ignored it, glancing at Vaughan, who seemed grateful for the interruption, then back at Bennett as he spoke.

"We were just talking to Greg," he said in a smooth voice. "If there's anything we can do to help, we're here for you. That probably means keeping our mouths shut and staying out of your way. But whatever you need, both Debi and I are willing to do it."

Bennett was good, she thought. Just not good enough to win.

Watson stepped forward, extending her hand. "Think of us as silent partners, Detective. If you ever need background on the trial, I'd be more than happy to walk you through our case."

There wasn't time for their particular brand of bullshit, but Lena thanked them anyway, making a conscious effort to avoid looking at Watson's breasts. She couldn't tell if they were real or not, and she didn't care.

And then the two of them gave Vaughan one last nod and took off. They moved through the doorway quickly—a series of short, choppy steps. As they vanished around the corner, it seemed to Lena that their backs shivered and they broke into a run.

Lena closed the door. "Nice people," she said.

Vaughan gave her a look. They didn't know each other. When he figured out what she meant, he tried to smile but only made it halfway.

"Two of the very best," he said. "Especially now that they think they've found a way to squirm out of their own mess."

"The way out of their mess is you," she said.

"We're in the same boat, aren't we?"

"Yes and no."

He thought it over as he moved to the window and looked out at the city.

"I guess you're right," he said. "They just told me that they won't be attending the press conference. Higgins can't make it, either."

"At least they're predictable."

Vaughan shrugged. "When I heard that Gant had been murdered, I pretty much knew the way things would go."

He was dressed in a light brown suit, a crisp white shirt, and a red tie with thin gold stripes. He wore the clothing better than most, but still appeared wiped out by the bind he was in. Lena joined him at the window and followed his eyes up the block to the new building that would serve as LAPD headquarters. Although construction had been completed and the move would occur next month, the building didn't have a name because members of the city council were still arguing about it.

"I heard a story," he said in an easier voice. "Not about your new building, but the one that went up in the Valley last year. The contractors blew the installation, reversing the one-way glass in the interrogation rooms. If we'd put some guy in the box, he could see us, but we couldn't see him. Is that true or what?"

Lena caught Vaughan's grin and smiled. "They fixed it before they opened."

"How 'bout in your new place?" he asked.

"The builder got it right this time. I checked."

She watched him turn away from the window and lean against the sill. He was gazing at the conference table as if he might be replaying the meeting in his head—as if he'd finally realized his fate and knew that it was time to start putting things back together again. His anger was dissipating. A certain spark was returning to his eyes.

"How do you want to work this?" she said.

"I don't know yet."

"Let's see what happens at Hight's place."

Vaughan nodded. "He's had some time to think things over. Maybe he'll feel the need to get it off his chest."

"Or maybe we'll find the gun."

Vaughan popped open his briefcase. "I'll be in my office," he said. "It'll take me a day to go through my cases and clear my schedule. We should talk when you get back."

They traded business cards. Then the door opened and Barrera entered, waving a sheaf of papers in the air.

"We've got the warrants," he said. "Let's roll."

10

The front door opened. Tim Hight's eyes hit the bright daylight but remained dilated. They were hollow, almost colorless—a faint, even decayed blue. They swept across the group of detectives and criminalists assembling on the porch, moved to the tow truck inching toward his Mercedes in the drive, then slid back to Lena.

"Tim Hight?" she said.

"You already know who I am."

"We have warrants. We're coming in."

"I didn't do it," he said.

Barrera held out the warrants. "We're still coming in."

Hight moved away from the door. As the team pushed past his slight figure and split up, Lena remained with Hight and Barrera in the foyer. She noted Hight's rumpled clothing, didn't see any signs of blood, and wondered if he had changed. It didn't look like he'd showered or shaved, and he seemed groggy and burned out. She checked the kitchen and saw the bottle of vodka still on the counter, then took a quick look at the living room. The fine carpets. The art on the walls. The shutters blocking out the light. The house had a definite feel about it. Dark and empty.

"Where's your wife?" she said.

"Visiting her sister in Bakersfield."

"When did she leave?"

"About three a.m. this morning."

"Seems like an odd time to go on a trip."

Hight gave her a look that mirrored the feel of the house. "I knew you'd come," he said. "I didn't want her to see this."

Barrera cleared his throat. "How did you know we'd come? How could you at three a.m.?"

"I heard what happened on my scanner."

Hight pointed to the sunroom on the other side of the French doors. Gazing through the glass, Lena cataloged the items she saw and cut them against what she remembered from last night. An armchair was pointed toward the windows facing the Gants' house. Hight's drink sat on the sill more than half empty. On a shelf within reach of the chair, she spotted the scanner and an ashtray overflowing with spent butts. The LEDs on the scanner were blinking, the unit still on.

"It's the only room I'm allowed to smoke in," Hight said.

Lena knew that victims' identities weren't broadcast over the air, but let it go for now.

"We'll need the keys to your car," she said.

"I didn't do it."

"Everybody says that, Mr. Hight. We'll need your keys."

Hight grimaced, digging his hand into his front pocket and fishing them out. As he fumbled with the key ring—his fingers trembling— Lena tried to keep her mind focused on the job.

It wasn't easy.

No matter what she thought of him, no matter what he'd done, the fact that he had lost his daughter was impossible to ignore. Barrera was standing just off the foyer in the living room. She could see him struggling with it, too. It didn't help that an array of framed photographs of the man's daughter were arranged on the baby grand. Lily Hight's gentle face and bright eyes were more than striking, her intoxication with life set against her horrific fate more than palpable. It almost seemed as if the girl was watching them build the case against her father—keeping an eye on them from somewhere on the other side.

Lena turned away. Tosh Mifune, a criminalist from SID, was standing in the kitchen doorway.

"We'll do it in here," he said. "The light's good."

She ushered Hight into the room, Mifune pulling a chair away from the breakfast table. Hight started to protest, but finally sat down, perhaps due to Mifune's patient and well-seasoned manner. As the middle-aged criminalist unpacked his evidence kit and laid the items on the table with great care, Lena could see the concern growing on Tim Hight's face. Mifune's tools appeared better suited for a doctor's office than a crime lab.

Hight began fidgeting in his seat. He glanced at Barrera leaning against the stove, then turned back to Lena. "Aren't you gonna read me my rights?"

"You're not under arrest," she said. "But yes, I'd be happy to."

She hoped that she didn't sound too confrontational. Hoped that she could light a fire beneath the man and the flame wouldn't burn out. But when she finished, Hight started to get out of the chair.

"So I'm allowed to call my attorney," he said.

"You can do anything you want, as long as you do it from that chair."

"You mean you're holding me here? I can't leave?"

"We've got a body warrant, Mr. Hight. We're gonna take a sample of your hair, swab your mouth, and get a set of your fingerprints."

"You already have my fingerprints. You took them when Lily died."

"We're doing it again. Were you wearing these clothes last night?"

He nodded.

"Then we'll need to take them as well," she said. "There's nothing your attorney can do to stop it."

Hight fell back into the chair, shaking his head as he reached into his pocket for his cigarettes. Unfortunately for him, the pack was empty. Lena watched him crumple it up in disappointment, then traded a quiet nod with Barrera on the other side of the room. They had talked it over before their arrival. Barrera had more experience than any detective he supervised. He had a way of seeing things, and wanted to keep his distance.

She turned back to Hight, acknowledging the man's distress. "You could make things a lot easier on yourself," she said. "A lot easier on everyone."

"How?"

"Tell us what you did with the gun."

"What gun? I didn't shoot Jacob Gant."

"Would you be willing to take a polygraph?"

He ran his hands over his head, ignoring the question. His hair was a mix of blond and gray, cropped short enough to stand on end.

"If you didn't shoot him," she said, "then why are you afraid to take a polygraph?"

He crossed his arms over his chest and shrugged.

Lena took a step closer. "When was the last time you saw Jacob Gant?"

"Not since the trial," he said. "Not since he walked out of that courtroom a free man."

"Do you expect anyone to believe that?"

"People believe what they want to. I'm guessing you're no different. I haven't seen him."

"But he lived next door, Mr. Hight."

"He hasn't been around. Maybe he got a job. Or maybe I wasn't looking for him. Maybe I didn't want to see him."

She glanced at the nicotine stains on the first and second fingers of his right hand. Hight noticed and buried them underneath the fold of his arm.

"How many cigarettes do you smoke a day?" she asked. "How much time do you spend in the sunroom? How often do you sit in that chair by the window with the lights out?"

Hight didn't respond, and silence overtook the room. Lena circled the table. As she passed the pantry she noticed pencil marks on the inside of the door. Beside each line was a date. The months and days remained the same—only the year changed—and she realized that the marks on the door were Lily Hight's measurements, recorded on her birthday each year.

Lena felt the gloom creeping in. A sudden hard pull. Hight's daughter had been five feet nine inches tall on her sixteenth birthday. Her last birthday.

She turned back to Hight. He had been watching her. Studying her. As Lena measured him in the chair, he appeared broken, but not frightening—like a man who stared into the abyss, lost his footing, and fell in.

"Why are you afraid to take a polygraph?" she said in a softer voice. "Why go through all this? Why not clear your name and move on?"

Hight had turned away, his eyes fixated on the bright sunlight spilling into the room from the window over the sink. The polished brass faucet and white porcelain tub sparkled and glowed, giving his ultra-pale skin the illusion of life.

"Move on?" he whispered, more to himself than anyone in the room.

"That's right," Lena said. "Clear your name and move on. Or take responsibility for what you've done. Own up to it."

A moment passed, the man staring at the rays of sunlight dancing on the counter. "You don't know what it's like," he said. "If you did, you wouldn't be here. You wouldn't be doing this to me. You are the people I trusted. The people I counted on. The people who were supposed to bring me just—" The words stopped coming with Hight thinking things over as if in a trance. "I won't do it," he said finally. "I won't take a polygraph because nothing in this world is guaranteed. I won't do it because I'm glad that Jacob Gant was murdered last night. I wished for it. I dreamed about it over and over again. Lily's gone. She's gone and I wanted him dead. I'm glad he's dead. I only wish there was something past dead. Something worse than dead."

His voice shook, then faded into silence. Lena traded looks with Barrera and Mifune, but she was thinking about the way Jacob Gant had been murdered. The two bullets in his eyes. The anger that the killer had been harboring. The bitterness and hatred that had rushed out the barrel of a gun.

Payback.

Hight gazed up at her, his dilated eyes wild with emotion. As he lowered his hands to his lap and tried to pull himself together, Lena noticed a bandage on his left palm. The blood leaking out. Hight had been cut—wounded—and he was trying to hide it.

Someone tapped on the door from the foyer, breaking the moment. When she turned, John Street motioned her into the living room. She could see his partner behind him. Exiting the kitchen, she joined them by the far window beside the baby grand. Carson was holding something: a plastic evidence bag containing a single sheet of yellow paper. Both detectives were big men. Both were experienced and not in the habit of showing much emotion. But everything about today was different.

Carson glanced at Hight through the doorway, then passed the bag over. "It's a receipt for a gun," he said quietly. "A nine millimeter Smith, Lena. Check out the gun dealer's address."

Carson opened the window shutter. Lena lowered the receipt into the light and started reading. The 9-mm pistol had been purchased in Arizona. The address was nothing more than a Web site, and nothing less. She didn't see a phone number, but the date of purchase caught her eye.

"He bought the gun six weeks ago," she said.

Carson nodded, his wide face flushed with color. "The day after the verdict," he said. "No wait time and no background check. Hight types in his credit card number, and some asshole ships him the piece, no questions asked."

"Where was the receipt?"

Street answered for his partner. "He's got an office upstairs. We found it in his desk with a stack of other receipts. Looks like he was trying to write it off as a business expense."

Lena felt someone move in behind her. It was Barrera. He reached for the evidence bag and examined the receipt.

"Business is business," he said. "Find the gun. Tear the place apart."

She had asked Mifune to remove his instruments from the table and wait outside. Barrera was seated on the couch in the living room, out of sight but within earshot. Hight remained in the kitchen, alone for the last thirty minutes with whatever was going on inside his head. She didn't think that time would soften him. The man had been running on fumes for more than a year. When she finally entered the room, he was staring at that empty pack of cigarettes.

"What's happened?" he said. "Why is this taking so long?"

Lena opened a file she'd pulled from her briefcase. "Do you keep a flashlight in your car, Mr. Hight?"

"I don't think so. Why?"

She found the surveillance photo and set it down on the table. Hight looked at himself behind the wheel and seemed amazed that his ride home had been documented. Lena pushed the photo closer, pointing at the dark object on the passenger seat.

"What do you think this is?" she asked.

"What do you mean?"

"On the seat beside you. What do you think it is? What's your best guess?"

Hight didn't answer and seemed confused. Leaning over the table, he tried to study the image.

"We're not talking about six days ago," she said. "It's more like six hours. You've just left Club 3 AM. You said that you don't keep a flashlight in your car. So what is it, Mr. Hight? What's on the passenger seat of your car?"

His eyes returned to the photograph. "I don't know. It could be a shadow. It's nothing."

Lena tossed the receipt for the gun on the table.

"A shadow?" she said.

Hight's body stiffened as he realized what was in the evidence bag. Beads of sweat began to percolate on his forehead. His mouth quivered. Lena pulled a chair away from the table and sat down. Nothing about her voice or manner was confrontational.

"Where's the gun, Mr. Hight?"

He took a deep breath and shuddered as he exhaled. He tried to look at her, but couldn't. He seemed embarrassed. The room went quiet again.

"Make it easy on yourself," she said. "You're so close. Just tell me where it is."

Another long moment passed. "I can't remember," he whispered finally. "I don't know what I did with it."

"You mean you got rid of it. After you left the club, you tossed it."

He shook his head. "No. I mean I can't remember where I put it. It came in the mail and I put it somewhere. I didn't know what I was doing. I was confused."

Lena sat back in the chair, unable to hide her disappointment. "That's your story? You bought a gun, but you can't remember what you did with it. You were at Club 3 AM last night, two men were shot, but all you took with you was your shadow."

The cynicism in her voice registered on his face, though only for a brief moment.

"I think I should call my lawyers now."

Lawyers. He didn't have one attorney. He had more than one.

"I do, too," she said. "And here's what you'll need to tell them. It won't work, Mr. Hight. What you're doing. What you're trying to get away with. It won't work."

"I'm not trying to get away with anything."

"Sure you are. You're trying to get away with murder. But all that depends on it looking like a crime of passion. And you'll need public opinion on your side to pull it off."

"If I had killed Jacob Gant, it would have been a crime of passion."

"But what happened last night wasn't a crime of passion," she said. "And that's your problem. It doesn't look like it. It doesn't feel like it. So how do you expect your lawyers to sell it?"

"If I'd murdered Jake, it would have been," he repeated with less conviction.

"I can only speak for myself and the people I work with, Mr. Hight. The whole thing looks planned. Everything you did looks scripted, like you spent a lot of time in that chair in the sunroom thinking it over from every angle. Watching the Gants from your window and letting it eat you up from the inside. You dreamed about murdering Jacob Gant. Like you said, you wished for his death over and over again."

A beat went by. Then another, and Hight started weeping like a man overcome by his memories. His ghosts.

"But Jake murdered Lily," he whispered into his hands. "My girl. That's how a crime of passion works."

Lena spotted a box of tissues on the counter and brought them over to the table.

"You planned it, Mr. Hight. You bought the gun six weeks ago. We checked. It's not registered. You followed Gant to the club last night. You knew the layout and waited on the fire escape."

"I haven't seen him since the trial. I told you that."

"You shot an innocent man. You shot Johnny Bosco."

"I didn't. I couldn't. I liked Johnny. He was nice to me."

Lena lowered her voice. "You shot him in the back. You'll need to tell your lawyers about it because that's what it really comes down to. The gristle on the bone. You shot an innocent man in the back."

His body shivered—a tremor from deep within that came and went.

"Why do you keep repeating it?" he said.

"Because you're playing us. Because you're trying to take the city down with you. No matter what I might feel for your loss, you're hurting other people now. You shot Bosco and then you killed Gant just the way you dreamed about it. You took care of business. You wasted him. You disfigured him beyond recognition. Just the way you wanted to. Just the way you planned it."

"No."

"When you talk to your attorneys about selling what you did as a crime of passion, remember the details and don't leave anything out. You took the time to pick up your shell casings, Mr. Hight. You took the time to go through their wallets and make it look like a robbery. You knew Bosco. Everybody knew he carried a lot of cash. So you took his money and tried to make the murders look like something else. You tried to cover your tracks. And then what?"

"I didn't do any of these things."

"And then what?" she repeated. "You stayed behind to watch. You got lost in the crowd outside the club because you wanted to see the fallout. You called ahead and sent your wife to Bakersfield. You came home and mended the wound on your hand that you've been trying to hide from us. You made a drink and sat down in your chair by the window. And then you waited. You waited for the news to arrive next door. Your dream came true. You made sure it came true. Jacob Gant is dead."

Lena paused a moment, her words settling into the room.

"That's not a crime of passion," she said finally. "That's the death penalty, Mr. Hight. That's a trip to the dead room. That's a ride on a gurney and a needle in the arm."

He looked up from the floor. His eyes had hollowed out, and the tears were gone. He hadn't weakened or given anything up. But he was looking through her now. All the way through her—his jaw tight, his gaze bitter and ice-cold.

12

People are capable of anything.

Given the right circumstances, the most gentle and meek can lash out in a single instant to become the most vicious and unforgiving.

It was the great lesson she had learned from her first partner in the division. Her last partner. Humanity can be shed as easily as clothing. Everything you know about someone can change in the blink of an eye. For anyone who works in law enforcement, this was the premise, the foundation, the key to survival.

She was standing in the foyer. Barrera had stepped out onto the back porch, smoking a cigar, and talking to the deputy chief on his cell. As she watched Mifune work with Hight in the kitchen, it occurred to her that Hight wasn't necessarily as disappointed with the way things had turned out as he showed himself to be. He had dreamed about killing Jacob Gant, and the botched trial had given him the opportunity to realize that dream. A shrink would probably call it the quickest way through the grieving process. A shortcut to closure. Gant would never appear in an interview, never be seen in public, never be an issue again. He was nothing more than a memory now.

The thought faded as she climbed the stairs to the second-floor landing. Carson and Street were searching through the master bed-room at the end of the hall. Toward the front of the house she could see a small guest room, well furnished with large double-hung windows and a decent view of Venice and the ocean at the bottom of the hill. A door was open to her left. She noted the unfinished stairs leading to the attic and could hear a pair of detectives moving things around. Across the hall she found Hight's office and walked in.

It was a large room with the same footprint as the living room. And like the room below, window shutters kept the space in a perpetual state of near darkness. She understood why when she noticed the large TV mounted on the far wall. She looked at the glass coffee table, the leather couch and chairs. The room served as both an office and a screening room. As she walked over to the desk, she realized that Fred Wireman, a senior detective due to retire next year, was searching the closet. Like Carson and Street, Lena knew Wireman to be extremely thorough.

"Lots of movies, huh," he said.

Lena nodded, eyeing the bookshelves. Hight's library of films looked to be as extensive as the music collection she had inherited from her brother. Several thousand titles filled the shelves from floor to ceiling. Skimming through the collection in the dim light, it took a moment to grasp that they were sorted by the director's name, not the title of the film. Because this information wasn't printed on the spine, Hight had to possess a certain knowledge of each film's history. All the same, some of Lena's favorites were here. Films by Truffaut and Bresson, Buñuel and Bertolucci. Works by Hitchcock, and Huston, Kubrick, Kurosawa, and Herzog.

It all registered even though she was thinking more about Jacob Gant's murder and the memories that had surfaced while she examined the gunshot wounds to his head. She was looking for John Ford. When she found Hight's copy of *The Searchers*, she pulled it from the shelf.

The cover was a reproduction of the original poster: John Wayne and Jeffrey Hunter on horseback with their rifles set on their saddles. Across the image the words, *He had to find her . . .* were repeated twice. Still, nothing registered.

"Hey, Fred," she said. "Are you into movies?"

"Since I was a kid."

"You ever see this one?"

She turned and held out the cover. When he read the title, he smiled.

"One of my favorites," he said. "Along with *Stagecoach, The Man Who Shot Liberty Valance,* and *My Darling Clementine.*"

"Someone shoots someone in the eyes. This is the movie, right? Without eyes, you can't enter the spirit world."

Wireman thought about it for a moment, started to nod, then stopped as he put it together. "That's the one," he said. "Of course, it doesn't prove anything."

"I'm not saying it does. All it means is that he owns the film and probably watched it once or twice."

"More than once or twice would be my guess, Lena. Before Hight's career tanked and he moved to reality TV, he directed *Prairie Winds.* The poster's over here on the wall."

Wireman swung the closet door shut, revealing the framed poster. Lena crossed the room. She had seen the film more than once and liked it. Once with her brother, and once with Rhodes.

"You look surprised," he said.

"I didn't realize it was him. What went wrong? Why'd he stop making movies?"

Wireman shrugged and got back to work. "Shit happens, I guess. Seems like he got more than his share."

13

ena noticed a second door in the hallway. Because it was slightly more narrow than the door leading to the attic, she assumed that it opened to a closet. But when she gave the handle a push, bright sunlight flooded the entire landing and swirled around her feet.

It turned out to be another bedroom. Lily Hight's bedroom.

And there was a feeling inside—something undefined and difficult to absorb.

The girl's room was almost the size of her father's office across the hall. On the left, Lena could see a walk-in closet—a chest of drawers and a bathroom. On the right, a small desk stood beside a pair of bookcases and two sets of windows facing the Gants' house on the other side of the drive. Curiously, a window was cracked open, a slight breeze filtering warm air into the air-conditioned room.

Lena walked in, letting the door drift shut behind her. As she stepped into the middle of the room, she looked at the double bed pushed against the far wall, noted an armchair, the computer, and various keepsakes the sixteen-year-old had collected before her death. But what struck her most was the condition of the room itself. That feeling she got when she first opened the door.

One year ago this bedroom had been a crime scene. After the investigation, the space would have been released and the Hights given the names of several companies specializing in bio waste and crime scene cleanup. It seemed as if their work had been thorough. Even the white carpet looked spotless. But it was more than that. What struck Lena about the room was that the Hights didn't appear to have sealed it off. Unlike most families who have suffered a devastating loss, the room had the odd feeling of openness that comes from continued use.

She moved over to the bed. Pillows were propped up against the headboard with several books stacked by the lamp on the night table. An impression left by a body was visible on the mattress. On the carpet by the window Lena noticed marks from the chair and was surprised that the carpet fibers hadn't filled in after the cleanup. The chair must have been placed in front of the window for a long time before someone moved it closer to the bed.

She turned back to the chest, found it filled with the girl's clothing, and started searching through the drawers. She tried not to think too much about what she was seeing, the sadness and heartbreak that came with such a loss. Still, Lily Hight's clothing was clean and neatly folded. And Lena couldn't help but smell the girl's body lingering here and there throughout the room. The fragrance of her hair and skin. She knew from experience that no matter how well you cleaned a room, no matter how much you scrubbed everything down, the scent of a human being lasted until the walls were repainted and the furniture was removed.

She tried to push her thoughts away. Tried to work at a steady pace and quiet her mind. When she finished with the last drawer, she heard something outside and checked the window.

Through the tree branches she could see a crowd beginning to form in front of the Gants' house. Members of the press corps were unpacking cases and setting up their cameras. When she spotted the Acura RL parked at the curb, she knew who it belonged to and understood what was about to happen.

Buddy Paladino was inside conferring with Jacob Gant's father. There was a buzz in the air—anticipation—the media's nervous chatter easily reaching the open window. The defense attorney with the million-dollar smile was preparing to make his statement.

Lena's pulse quickened slightly as she played through the possibilities in her head. Paladino wasn't going to be talking to the press from his office or even the courthouse. He was here because he knew that they were here—the truck from SID, the marked patrol units and detective cars parked in front of Tim Hight's house. Paladino was a genius at seeing the single flaw in a prosecutor's case and working a jury until they saw it, too. But he was even better at playing the press. He had won freedom for Jacob Gant, and now Jacob Gant was dead. He needed someone to blame for his client's death, someone with deep pockets, and his finger would be pointed directly at the police. He'd stick the blade in as deep as he could and twist it. He'd deliver his message, smear the department, and use their marked vehicles as a visual backdrop only an art director from one of the studios could match.

It was the reason Buddy Paladino was Buddy Paladino, she thought. The reason she found him so fascinating, even dangerous at times.

She stepped away from the window and moved back to the bed. When she noticed the memory box on the night table, she picked it up and sat down. The box appeared to be handmade from cherry wood, the lid inlaid with silver leaves around a glass picture frame. Behind the glass was a snapshot of a wet dog, an English cocker spaniel, sitting on the beach, panting and looking up as if he were waiting to continue a game of fetch. Lena recognized the Santa Monica pier in the background but couldn't tell when the photograph had been taken.

She opened the lid and removed the pad of notepaper on top. Underneath she found pieces of jewelry and sorted through them with her finger. Mixed in with the jewelry was an old silver dollar, a stamp commemorating Babe Ruth, and finally, an ID tag Lena guessed had been worn by the spaniel in the snapshot. Lily Hight's dog had been named Mr. Wilson.

She looked away.

There was a sustained sadness here, a presence even the sunlight couldn't bleach out. The feeling dissipated when Barrera called out her name from the landing and she called back to him. As the door opened and he popped his head inside, she set down the box.

"We need to talk," he said.

Barrera closed the door and crossed the room for a look out the window.

"We're fucked, Lena. And the DA's full of shit. This isn't going away. Not with Paladino reminding everybody that we fucked up. It doesn't matter what people thought of Jacob Gant. It doesn't matter that they're glad he's dead. Paladino's smart enough to know that. Watch him rip us apart and milk the cash cow dry."

His words came out in a jittery spin that ran out of gas and died. Sitting on the arm of the reading chair, he took in the room and seemed as uncomfortable by the setting as she was.

"You find anything?" he said.

"Not yet."

"Same with everybody else. Let's face it, the gun's not here. It's not anywhere. When you finish in here we're done."

He gave her a look. Something flared up in his eyes.

"You've got something," she said. "What is it?"

"Cash and coke. Street found it in Hight's dresser drawer."

"How much?"

"Two grand in hundred-dollar bills. That's what Bosco carried. Hundred-dollar bills."

It wasn't the gun, Lena thought, but it remained a small piece of luck because most people counted their money. Especially when they carried hundred-dollar bills. If the cash found in Hight's drawer belonged to Bosco, there was a chance that both had left their fingerprints.

"What about the coke?" she said. "How was it packaged?"

Barrera raised his eyes. "A number ten envelope, like Hight found it in Bosco's desk and scooped the shit in. About fifteen grams worth. Maybe twenty. Enough for a lot of good rides."

"His eyes," she said. "He looked strung out."

"I thought so, too."

Lena got up and walked over to the window. Paladino was still inside, the number of reporters gathering in the street, too big to count.

"The cameras, Frank. How do you want to handle this? We can't walk Hight out the front door."

Barrera had been holding what was left of his cigar between his fingers. As he thought things over, he jammed the cigar into his mouth and started chewing and puffing. It didn't seem to matter that it had burned out.

"Hight's not going anywhere," he said finally. "Even if the cameras weren't here, we'd have to give him a pass. Charging the guy with possession . . . it can't look like we're badgering him. It would only make things worse."

"Where's that coming from?"

Barrera gave her a look and shrugged. "It's got to be solid, Lena. Rock solid like the case was made by God. Every piece has to fit. Every road drawn on the map. Then everything changes. Then we walk the guy out the door no matter who's outside." He got to his feet and gave the room another look. "It's weird in here. I've gotta get out. I need more air."

"What's Hight's status?"

"Mifune's got what he needs. Everybody's packing up. Until Paladino's finished and the cameras go away, we're here."

"You mean we're trapped."

Barrera opened the door, flashing a slight smile. "I just got off the phone with the coroner's office. Paladino's taking Gant's father down to ID his son. It's scheduled to take place in about an hour and can't be changed because of the autopsy."

"I thought the autopsy was set for tonight."

"It is, but they're backed up. If he wants to see his son, it has to happen now and Paladino will have to keep his press conference short."

"As long as we've got time, I want to dust this room for prints."

"Why?"

"You said it yourself—it's weird in here. As long as we've got time, why not?"

He shrugged. "I'll send somebody up."

She watched him close the door and listened to his footsteps move down the hall. When she noticed the press corps raising their voices, she looked back through the window.

Paladino had just exited the house next door with William Gant. As they reached the attorney's car, they stepped around the hood and stopped as if cued by that art director from the studios. Lena didn't need to look through a lens to verify her guess about the background. And even if a reporter somehow missed the marked truck and patrol cars, no one did after Buddy Paladino turned and pointed them out.

The scene was difficult to watch. The fact that she had a history with Paladino didn't make it any easier right now.

Her eyes moved up the drive and found the Gants' house through the tree branches. She could see Jacob Gant's brother Harry watching his father from a window facing the street on the second floor. And Paladino's voice was clearer now—the attorney all warmed up in the hot sun and working the crowd as if selling snake oil.

This is what revenge looks like. This is what's left when people take matters into their own hands and commit acts of violence. This is what's left when the L - A - P - D falls asleep at the wheel.

Lena stopped listening. Paladino had delivered his sound bite like the master that he was. There would be no need for a second take.

She turned away from the window and noticed that she'd left the memory box on the bed. Returning it to the night table, that photo of the dog caught her eye again. It was an old black-and-white shot—dark and grainy with rain clouds in the sky. She was still curious about the date and wondered if it had been printed on the back. Lifting the wooden lid, she pulled off the back cover and removed the cardboard filler. When the snapshot fell away from the glass, she turned it over.

The paper hadn't been date stamped, but she realized that a second picture had become stuck to the first. She lowered the box to the table and pried the two pictures apart. Then she flipped over the second shot and gazed at it. She sat down on the bed and stared at it for a long time. The photo Lily Hight had kept hidden. The one in her memory box by her bed.

It was a snapshot of her killer. It was a picture of Jacob Gant.

14

Harry Gant wasn't answering the door. Lena walked down the drive between the two houses and found him in the kitchen eating a bowl of cereal. The slider was cracked open, and she didn't wait to be invited in. As she slid the screen shut behind her, shock waves rippled across the kid's face.

"What do you think you're doing?"

"It looked like you had something on your mind," she said. "Before you ran upstairs last night, you had something to say."

He stared back at her, open mouthed. "You want to talk, save it for when my dad gets back."

He dug his spoon into the bowl, trying to look bored and probably hoping that if he ignored what just happened, the homicide detective standing in his kitchen might go away. He was dressed in a pair of jeans and an old T-shirt, and hiding behind his long hair. But Lena knew that he was faking it. She could see his legs beneath the table, his bare feet tapping the floor like all his batteries were charged up. The kid was in a situation and didn't know what to do.

"I realize that you haven't had much time to think things over," she said. "But has it occurred to you that we're on the same side?"

He took another spoonful of cereal, still feigning boredom. "Which side is that?"

"I'm trying to find out who killed your brother, Harry."

He laughed. She could hear the pain in it. The loss.

"You just spent three hours in the killer's house," he said. "Lily's dad murdered Jake. It's like you're blind."

"He says he hasn't seen your brother since the trial."

Harry finally pushed the bowl away. "Then he's blind, too. He saw Jake every day. He sits in that chair spying on us like a lunatic. The two of them got into an argument yesterday."

"Over what?"

"I wasn't here. All Jake told me was that they had another shouting match."

"Did he say when?"

"Sometime in the morning. Jake was out by the garage shooting hoops."

Lena remembered Hight telling her that he hadn't seen Jacob Gant since the trial. She had read it as a lie the moment it came out of his mouth. One among many. But what seemed important right now was Harry. He had stopped hiding. He'd made some sort of turn.

"Any chance you could show me your brother's room?" she asked.

He looked at her for a while, then nodded without saying anything. Walking through the foyer, she followed him upstairs and started down the hall. The layout mirrored the Hights' house next door. She checked the room on the right and saw an electric guitar laid out on an unmade bed. When she turned back, she found Harry standing before the door directly across the hall.

A moment passed, like he didn't want to enter the room. Lena sensed his hesitation. Giving the door a push, she led the way in, then paused a moment herself.

Jacob Gant's bedroom faced Lily's. And they were close, just a driveway apart. She wondered why she hadn't seen it before, then noticed the large oak tree standing beside the Hights' house. The tree branches had given Lily's room a false sense of privacy, obscuring the real view.

Harry joined her by the window, his voice so soft she could barely hear it. "My dad told me that David Gamble was your brother." He hesitated again but pushed through it. "And Mr. Paladino says you helped him with a problem last year. He says you're okay, too."

It laid there for a while. Lena turned to him and knew that they understood one another. Her brother had played guitar and was murdered shortly after his band performed at a nightclub on the Strip. Although the murder occurred eight years ago, it worked like a shadow, changing sizes from day to day but never going away.

"I'm on your side, Harry. I really am."

He sat down on the bed. Tears began to well up in his eyes and he covered his face with his hands.

Lena rolled the desk chair over and sat down. "Tell me why Jake was at Club 3 AM last night. Why was your brother with Johnny Bosco?"

This time Harry didn't run out of the room when she asked the question. He wiped his cheeks. She could see him putting the words together in his head.

"Bosco was helping him," he said.

"Helping him do what?"

"Find the guy who really murdered Lily. Jake told me that something had happened and he needed to see Johnny. He said he thought they knew who did it and hoped they could prove it last night."

A beat streaked by like a stray bullet.

Lena looked around the room, the violent sketches and artwork that Jacob Gant had created barely registering. All she could see was the road ahead. What had seemed like a clear but difficult path a few minutes ago was vanishing like a mirage. She leaned forward, searching for an even voice.

"Your brother was investigating Lily Hight's murder?"

Harry nodded.

"Why Bosco?"

He shrugged. "I don't know."

"What did your brother tell you?"

"He wouldn't tell me anything. He said it wasn't safe."

"What about Paladino?"

"Jake didn't tell anyone about it. Just Johnny Bosco. He knew what it would look like."

"What it would look like?"

Harry dropped back on the bed, raising his arms over his head and closing his eyes. "He said that no one would believe him because of the DNA. He said that if anyone found out what he was doing, it would only make him look even more guilty because that's what they all do. The freaks you see on TV. They kill their wife, then act like they're looking for the guy who really did it. It's fake, but the people on TV are so stupid, they buy it. They're fakes, too."

A moment passed. There was no stillness in it. No peace.

"Your brother had bruises on his neck and arms," she said. "His knuckles were scraped like he'd been in a fight."

Harry opened his eyes and looked at her. "He was in lots of fights."

"With who?"

The teenager shrugged. "Mr. Paladino may have gotten him out of jail, but he didn't change anybody's mind who wasn't on the jury. Jake couldn't go anywhere without people shouting at him or trying to beat him up. He wanted to find out who murdered Lily, but it was way more than that. Jake *needed* to find him. He said that if things worked out last night, he was going to Mr. Paladino's office and show him everything. That if they got the real guy, all the crap would stop and we'd be safe."

"What about Lily's father? You said they argued. Did it ever get physical?"

Harry rolled over on his side to face her. "I don't think so. But I always thought he was the one who murdered Lily. He's a head case. He's got issues. I always thought it was him."

Lena took it in, but her eyes were on the carpet by the window— the impressions left by a reading chair that had been moved just as Lily Hight's reading chair had been moved. Jacob Gant's chair was placed beside his desk.

Lena got up and pushed it across the carpet. Now the chair faced the bed with a soft, perfect light from the windows spilling in from behind. But when she checked the carpet, the footprint of the chair didn't match the impressions.

"Jake moved it," Harry said. "After Lily died. It goes the other way."

Lena turned the chair around. When she felt the legs slip into place, she sat down and gazed out the window. The view into Lily's bedroom was remarkable—so close and so crisp and clear that she could see the memory box sitting on the night table beside the girl's bed.

Harry got up and joined her by the window. Kneeling down, he folded his arms on the sill and stared across the drive.

"They used to sit in front of their windows," he said. "Every night they'd sit and talk to each other on their cell phones. They dug each other. I never understood why no one got that."

15

Trouble ahead. She could sense it, taste it, feel the dread reaching out for the back of her neck.

As she left Harry behind and walked out of the house, Lena understood that she had been thrust into an exceedingly dark and lonely place. That the number of loose ends, the number of questions rising out of the muck, only matched the speed at which the case was already unraveling.

She started down the cavernous drive between the two houses. Tim Hight's windows remained shuttered, and she wondered if they were meant to block out the sunlight, or to keep his secrets locked away in a perpetual state of darkness. She kept walking. She adjusted her grip on the evidence bag she was carrying and kept moving. Harry had helped her search his brother's room and seemed to know where the hiding places were. Among the items Lena had taken was a weekly planner that Jake had been keeping since the trial. They had found the graphic novel he had been working on as well. The same one that the prosecution team had used against him during the trial, but returned following the NOT GUILTY verdict.

She picked up her pace. She needed to see Vaughan. And she needed to see him fast.

As she turned the corner and started up the sidewalk, she realized that she needed to lose the Crown Vic as well.

The press had followed Paladino down to the coroner's office while William Gant identified his son's body. But a handful of reporters had already returned and were setting up shop in front of Tim Hight's house. She didn't recognize any of the faces. And the overweight man with the three-day beard and gelled hair appeared to be using the hood of her car as his desk. His laptop was open and he was munching on a double cheeseburger and an extra large bag of fries. As she approached the car, she could see open packets of ketchup strewn across the hood and fender.

She hit the clicker. When the car beeped, the big man nearly jumped out of his loose skin.

"Shit, lady. I'm eating lunch here."

His mouth had been filled with food as he spoke. Ketchup mixed with grease leaked out and dripped off his chin onto his gut. Lena didn't think she'd order a cheeseburger anytime soon. She tossed the evidence bag onto the front seat, the rest of the group approaching the car. From the way they were dressed, she guessed that they were from out of town.

"Is it a nice lunch?" she said.

The big man gave her a look as he wiped his shirt. "Yeah, sure. It's like eating at the Ritz with paper napkins. When's the hero coming out? We want an interview."

"Which hero is that?"

"Tim Hight. The dad who took care of business for his kid."

So there it was. The theme laid out in the open for all to see and hear. Tim Hight had been crowned a hero.

Lena gave the big man another look. "I don't see your press credentials."

"They're in my bag. So what? Are you a cop or a lawyer?"

She shrugged. "Neither one. I'm with the tax collector."

"Yeah, right," he said, still working on that stain. "You're a cop."

Lena climbed into the car and started the engine. As she shifted into reverse, the big man finally understood that he was about to lose his desk. He went for his computer first, then made the mistake of reaching out for his food. Grabbing the burger, he took a swipe at his fries and the supersized drink. But he didn't make it. He wasn't fast enough or smart enough. As she hit the gearshift and drove off, she saw the drink splash all over his keyboard. By the time she reached the freeway, the ketchup packets glued to the hood were finally starting to blow off.

She switched on her phone and toggled through her recent calls. When she found Samy Beck's number, she tapped it with her thumb and heard him pick up.

"I'm out of time," she said. "I need a new car."

He laughed at her. It was a wicked laugh—the only way he knew how to do it. Beck owned a shop just east of the airport in Hawthorne. When her Prelude died, Beck had been her first call. He owed her a favor, but hadn't come up with anything yet.

"Where are you?" he said.

"Heading downtown."

"When are you back on the Westside?"

"Later this afternoon."

"Then stop by."

"You got something?"

"I got it."

"Is it real?"

"It's better than real. And for the money we talked about."

"What is it?"

"What you've been looking for, Lena. Today's your lucky day. I'll be here all afternoon."

She could hear him laugh again as he switched off his phone. She dropped her cell onto the seat, watching the last open packet of ketchup slide up the windshield, lose its grip in the wind, and fly away. She needed to get rid of the official car. Anything that Beck came up with would work. Anything that restored her anonymity would do.

The district attorney's main offices were housed with the county courthouse and the public defender on West Temple Street in downtown Los Angeles. The building had been named after Clara S. Foltz, the first female attorney on the West Coast. But no one would have ever known that by looking at the sign out front. For whatever reason, most of the letters to Foltz's name had been ripped away from the concrete.

Even though most people referred to the building as the Criminal Justice Center these days, it always bothered Lena that no one seemed to take an interest in repairing the sign. Not so much because of Foltz's place in history, but more because of what went on here. Matters of life and death were discussed, judgments were rendered, and lives were changed. The fact that the sign had been vandalized a long time ago and no one seemed to care said something about the county and the people who lived here.

Lena found Greg Vaughan waiting for her by the information desk as the elevator opened. When she had called ahead, Vaughan expressed concern that what she wanted to tell him couldn't be said over a phone. Seeing her here in his office this early in the afternoon didn't change that.

"Are you okay?" he asked.

She nodded and they started down the hall.

"You look like you could use something to eat," he said. "A meeting was canceled. They brought in food."

"I'm good," she said.

"Well, I need something. Maybe you'll change your mind after you see what's there."

She looked him over as they walked. His jacket was off, his sleeves rolled up to his elbows, and he appeared less weary and more able than he had this morning. As they entered the meeting room, she saw a group of prosecutors standing before a long serving table with plates in their hands. The room was quiet, the tables and chairs set with pads and pens, not place settings. It looked like people were taking advantage of a free lunch, but returning to their offices and eating at their desks.

Vaughan poured a large cup of coffee. In spite of the caterer's obvious talent, Lena had too much on her mind to eat and too much caffeine already streaming through her body to add another dose to the mix. She turned away. When she looked up, she found Debi Watson staring at her through the crowd. Watson stood by the water glasses with a modest plate of food and tried to smile but was late with it. After an awkward moment, the woman stepped out of the room with her lunch.

Lena found the encounter unsettling. No matter how brief, she had just caught a glimpse of what Watson looked like stripped of her confidence. She had seen it in her eyes—a combination of weariness and pain. A certain recognition that the prosecutor had lost her standing in the office, and things would never return to what they were.

Lena turned back, following Vaughan over to a table by the windows.

"Let me guess," he said. "You searched Hight's place and didn't find the gun."

"He got rid of it. We found the receipt, but not the gun."

Vaughan tested his coffee with a short first sip. "And he has no intention of working with us. He's not gonna make it easy."

"It sounds like he's got more than one attorney," she said.

"He thinks he can win, Lena. And you know what? He's probably right."

Lena started to say something, but stopped when she saw Steven Bennett enter the room. He nodded at them, then turned away and picked up a plate. Although his purpose appeared innocent enough, the way he walked into the room carried the same lack of authenticity as Watson's delayed smile. It didn't feel true. He didn't enter the room looking for the serving table. Instead, his emerald green eyes had swept through the space searching out faces. It seemed obvious that Watson had told him that they were here. For some reason, he needed to see it for himself.

Vaughan took another sip of coffee, then spoke in a lower voice. "Why couldn't you say any of this over the phone? What else did you find?"

"Cash that may have come from Bosco," she said. "Fifteen to twenty grams of cocaine that may have been taken from that pile at the club."

"How long will it take SID to process everything?"

"We're at the top of the list."

Lena was still eyeing Bennett. The deputy DA was spending too much time staring at the catering trays with his back to them. He was close enough to hear them. Lena had no doubt that he was listening.

Vaughan tapped her wrist. "Is something wrong?"

"We need to go to your office," she said. "We can't talk here."

Her eyes were still on Bennett. Vaughan followed her gaze.

"I see what you mean," he said.

Bennett didn't turn or move as they walked out. When they reached Vaughan's office on the other side of the building one floor below, he closed the door and apologized for his housekeeping. Stacks of file folders two and three feet high lined nearly every square foot of the room. They were piled on his credenza, on the couch and chair, and formed a semicircle to the right of his desk chair. As he cleared off a seat for Lena, she looked out the window and saw an abandoned building just this side of the Hollywood Freeway.

"At least the DA gave you an office with a window," she said.

"Yeah. Higgins gave me a window."

She saw a picture on the sill of Vaughan playing with a young boy and girl, about three and four years old.

"I didn't know you had kids," she said. "I didn't even know you were married. You're not wearing a ring."

"Divorced," he said. "Irreconcilable differences, meaning that I work too much. We've stayed friends, and she's met someone who works nine to five and seems like a good guy. The kids love him. I told her I could change, but her attorney came by one day and got a look at my office."

He grinned at her, then settled into his desk chair and watched her sit down. A moment passed with Vaughan gently probing her face with his eyes.

"You didn't come here to tell me you couldn't find Hight's gun," he said finally. "I don't know you very well, Lena. But you don't strike me as someone who would waste that kind of time."

She leaned forward, thinking it through as she spoke. "What if Bennett and Watson screwed up?" she said.

Vaughan shrugged. "They lost a slam-dunk case. Of course they screwed up."

"But what if it wasn't a slam-dunk case? What if it only looked like one? What if Bennett and Watson *really* fucked up?"

"They're corporate types," he said. "All they see is the finish line and what they're gonna get out of it."

Lena nodded. "Exactly. So what if it started from the beginning? What if they got lost in the details and the headlines? What if Jacob Gant didn't murder Lily Hight and they tried the wrong man?"

It hung there. And for several moments, it looked like Vaughan had taken a punch. He pushed aside his coffee and leaned back in his chair, rubbing a finger across his forehead as he considered her question.

"If you're asking me if Bennett and Watson are capable of running the worst investigation and trial in the city's long history of blown investigations and even worse trials—if that's what you're really asking— it's possible, I guess. It's more than possible. But you'd have to get past the DNA, Lena. Lily Hight was raped before she was killed. Gant's semen was found at the crime scene and by the coroner during the girl's autopsy. That locks Gant in."

"You mean the samples that went missing at the crime lab?"

Vaughan nodded.

"SID doesn't lose things, Greg. It's not in their nature to lose things."

Vaughan got out of his chair and moved to the window. "What's this got to do with Tim Hight, Lena? All that matters is what he believed. He thought Gant killed his daughter and got away with it. He shot the kid. He put two bullets in his head. And he murdered Johnny Bosco along the way."

Lena glanced at the door, then back at Vaughan. "Bosco was helping Gant investigate Lily Hight's murder. They thought they knew who did it. Last night they were hoping to prove it."

"What are you talking about?"

"Gant's brother told me that about an hour ago."

"You don't believe him, I hope."

She thought it over. She thought about that feeling in her gut.

"I believe that he believes it, and that his brother wouldn't lie to him. That's all I'll say right now. Bosco and Gant—you've got to admit that it's an odd pairing because of who Bosco was. No one's been able to explain why they were together last night. Not even Bosco's partner, Dante Escabar."

Vaughan sat down on the sill. "Bosco catered to Hollywood. He gave them privacy. A place to go where no one had to worry about controversy or some asshole taking a picture that might embarrass them. Being seen with Jacob Gant after the trial would have been a risk to Bosco. So I guess the question becomes, what was worth the risk?"

Lena joined Vaughan by the window. "Exactly. There's something wrong. Something missing. What we're seeing isn't necessarily what's really there."

A moment passed—utter silence—while both of them gazed through the glass at an endless ribbon of cars breezing down the Hollywood Freeway.

"I know what you're saying," Vaughan whispered. "And now I know why you didn't want to say it over the phone. You want to take another look at Lily Hight's murder. You want me to go through the trial and figure out how Bennett and Watson built their case."

"And there's no way to keep it a secret from anyone we work with."

"I've got that press conference this afternoon. At least I can keep it from them."

She nodded, but remained quiet.

"We sure caught a good one, didn't we?"

"Yeah," she whispered. "We're fucked."

16

It was more than the number of loose ends. It was their size and scope and potential to ignite.

Lena sensed that she had found a new one the moment Dan Cobb walked out the door and greeted her in the lobby with his hands in his pockets. He settled back on his heels, staring at her with open suspicion.

Cobb had been the lead detective investigating Lily Hight's murder. Lena had made the drive across town to the Pacific Station and walked in unannounced. He had asked to see her badge, which seemed unnecessary and ridiculous. He already knew who she was.

"What's this about?" he asked.

The watch commander was on the phone behind the front desk. People were milling about within earshot. Lena glanced at the door leading to the homicide section.

"Any chance we could talk back there?"

He needed a moment to think it over. More time to stir the change in his pocket.

Cobb was a big, barrel-chested man in his mid-fifties. His hair was cropped short, a wild mix of gray on gray. His goatee was even shorter and could have just as easily passed as stubble lost within the creases of his leathery skin. Although he was staring at her, even measuring her at close range, she couldn't tell what color his eyes were because he wore a pair of glasses that grew darker in sunlight. The lenses were set in clear plastic frames, the shape as outdated as his clothing. He must have been looking out the window about the time she arrived.

"I guess we can talk," he said finally. "As long as it doesn't take too long."

He pulled open the door and walked off, letting her follow in his wake. His attitude was unmistakable. His contempt for her, his rudeness, was over the top.

Lena ignored his behavior because she knew that she had to. Her concerns for the case outweighed everything else and provided some degree of immunity. But even more, she wanted Cobb's cooperation.

They crossed the section floor. Lena didn't see a familiar face; the place was nearly empty. When they reached Cobb's desk, he waved her off.

"Not here," he said. "We'll talk in one of the rooms."

He grabbed a pad and started searching for a pen. There was nothing personal on his desk except for an old snapshot taped to the surface. Curiously, it wasn't a picture of a person, but of a place. A discolored photo of the sun setting into an ocean behind a grove of palm trees.

"Where was this taken?" she asked.

Cobb didn't look up, still rummaging through his drawer for a pen. "Hualalai," he said without interest. "Fifteen years ago. I was working a case. I've been trying to get back ever since." He finally spotted a pen and grabbed it. "Now let's get this over with."

He led her over to an interrogation room, flipped on the overhead lights, and pointed to a seat bolted to the floor. But as he started to sit down, he tested the pen on his legal pad and realized that it was out of ink.

"I'll be right back," he said.

It seemed clear enough that Cobb was dogging it. That his act was intentional. Unless he'd been dead for the past twelve hours, he had to have some idea as to why she was here. She turned and looked through the doorway. The detective wasn't at his desk. Just as she was about to get up, he reappeared from around the corner, breezed into the room, and kicked the door shut. She watched him take a seat on the other side of the table and test his new pen. Apparently, this one worked.

"Why are you here, Gamble?" he said.

"I'd like to see the murder book you kept on the Lily Hight case."

"Why? It's over. The man who killed her was shot last night. Case closed. He's dead."

"I met the girl's father. I want to know how you cleared him."

It had been a righteous request—one that any detective would have made no matter what questions they might have harbored about the case. Yet Cobb leaned back in his seat, chewing it over and giving her another hard look through those glasses. The lenses were beginning to fade, and she could see his eyeballs floating in the vanishing darkness.

"You're it, aren't you?" he said. "The new face of the LAPD's PR machine. The new deal. I know who you are, Gamble. They're using you to dig themselves out of the hole they're in."

"You're in it just as deep as anyone else, Cobb. We're in it together. Now, how did you clear Tim Hight?"

He shrugged, his eyes still pinned on her. "I already had the kid. Why would I have needed to clear Hight?"

Another warning beacon broke the surface. Lena took it in, but remained silent. Lily Hight had been murdered in the bedroom of her home. The investigation should have begun with her family—her parents—and continued until they were cleared one by one.

Cobb had been watching her put it together like a mind reader. When he laughed, it sounded raw and vicious and even crazy.

"I got it," he said. "I see where you're going now. You think Daddy diddled his little girl. That ought to go over well since he's a hero now."

He slammed his hand against the table in anger, then bounced to his feet and started pacing back and forth along the rear wall like an animal.

"If you're gonna muddy things up," he said, "if you're looking for someone to blame because the jokers who fucked this up don't want to admit they fucked it up—if that's where it's at, Gamble—then my memory's just hit the skids. I can't even remember what I ate for dinner last night. Was it steak, or was it lobster? Or maybe it was just a bowl of plain old bullshit."

Lena shook her head. "Sit down, Cobb. You're making me nervous."

"Making you nervous. I love it. I dig it. I'm making you nervous. What do you think you're doing to me? The kid killed her. There's no *but* to it. There's no doubt about it. I've been working homicide for twenty-five years and I knew that little shit did her the minute I set eyes on him. When I heard he got wasted, I poured a fucking Cutty Sark."

"Okay, Cobb. Take it easy and sit down. What happened when you put Gant through a polygraph?"

Cobb finally returned to the table. He seemed to need to inspect his seat. When he was satisfied, he sat down.

"Who said anything about a polygraph?"

"You didn't put him in the box?" she said.

"I didn't need to. The blood work came in. The DNA results. We got a hit and I made the arrest. Why risk a polygraph after that? The kid was a natural-born liar. I could see it. I know the type. What if the piece of shit beat it? What would Paladino have done after that? How fast would that asshole lawyer have blanketed the results all over the fucking city and poisoned the jury pool?"

Lena didn't respond.

Cobb smiled at her in triumph. "Got you, didn't I?" he said. "You wouldn't have risked it, either. No one would."

She was thinking about the year she decided that she wanted to become a police officer. She had written it down on a piece of paper. On one side, she listed what she hoped to accomplish, along with the reasons why. On the other, she wrote down what she didn't want to become and the reasons for that as well. As she looked at Cobb's weather-beaten face, his crude, even violent manner, his inability to control himself, she realized that he embodied everything she'd listed on the other side of that sheet of paper. Although there was some truth to what he'd been saying, the gist reeked of bitterness, incompetence, and self-posturing.

Lena gave him another look, hoping that he would succeed at reading her mind again. She wanted him to know what she thought of him but was too much a professional to say. She tried to adjust her seat but remembered that it was bolted to the floor. Glancing about the small room, she noticed a wave of perspiration in the stale air.

"Why are we meeting in here, Cobb? Why did you pick an interrogation room instead of a conference room?"

He shrugged like he didn't give a shit.

"It's all about power, isn't it?" she said. "Power and intimidation. It's your blowback pitch. You think it gives you the upper hand. Is this how you treated Jacob Gant? Did you hit him? Did you hurt him?"

His eyeballs flicked at her from behind those glasses. She could see them still swimming around behind the tinted lenses. She could see a glint breaking through—a stray spark hitting the water and fizzing out.

But he didn't say anything. And when a quarter fell out of his pocket and rolled across the floor, he didn't move.

Lena got up and yanked open the door. "Get me the murder book, Cobb. It's late and I want to get out of here."

Several moments passed before he finally pried his stiff body out of the chair and rose to his feet. He was dogging it again, moving toward her at a tortured pace. But he was brimming with anger, too. When he finally reached the door, he grimaced at her and showed her his clenched teeth as he passed by.

17

Dan Cobb, aka Mad Dog Dan, aka. "Hey You"—born and raised in Wichita, Kansas—ejected the tape that he had secretly recorded, jammed it into his pocket, and rushed out of the tech room. He would listen to it when he had more time and more privacy. Like tonight, when he went home. He'd listen to the tape he'd made and take notes.

His knees were shot. He sped across the section floor as best he could, tossing those horrible glasses on his desk. By the time he reached the windows, the world came back into focus and he could see Gamble crossing the lot toward a metallic green Crown Vic. She was carrying the murder book under her arm. The one he'd edited, rather than the one he kept at home. The one he'd put together for the day he knew someone would come.

Cobb understood with perfect clarity that everything was in jeopardy now. Everything was on the line. And he could see his life flashing before him.

It worked like a movie in his head—as clear and realistic as any of the new theaters in Hollywood. He tried to shut down the images as he exited the building through the rear doors and climbed into his Lincoln. He tried to switch channels but it was always the same scenes playing over and over again. Scenes that had begun haunting him about a year ago as he sat with Lily's dead body in her bedroom. Scenes that picked up speed during the trial, then died off over the past six weeks. But the peace was gone now. After last night, the movie wormed its way back into his head so ultra vivid, he would have sworn before a judge and jury that the stupid thing was shot in 3-fucking-D.

He could see the dead bodies piling up. He could see their faces in the muted light. He could see them staring at him and taunting him.

One, two, three.

Cobb tried to get a grip on himself, idling through the lot until he caught a glimpse of the ass end of Gamble's Crown Vic. The way the windows matched up at the corner of the building, he could look through the glass and see her standing beside the car. She was on her cell phone, jotting something down on a pad.

He hated the stupid bitch. The new fucking deal.

But he needed some sort of plan. A map that would show him the way through. Now more than ever—he'd already lost too much.

His house, his money, his retirement—everything he owned except for the car went through the greed machine on Wall Street. When it came out the other side, the big shots had moved to Easy City on the money they'd stolen while Cobb was sent back to the world of zeroes. He could see himself in his later years, his body hunched over, his knees locked up with bone chips, the arthritis already in his shoulders taking siege all over him. He could see himself working the door at Walmart with a smiley face pinned to his apron, nodding and waving at every shithead who grabbed a cart.

The stupid bitch started moving.

He must have blanked out. He hadn't seen her get into the car.

She pulled out of the lot and made a right, heading east on Culver toward the 405 Freeway. Cobb swung his Lincoln around the building, counted to five, then eased onto the street. Traffic was lighter than usual—the Crown Vic visible one block up. He changed lanes, anticipating that she would drive north to catch the Santa Monica Freeway for the return trip downtown. But as he settled into his seat, Gamble hit the entrance ramp heading south toward the 105 and picked up speed.

He spotted her one lane over as he hit the ramp and slid onto the freeway. Weaving through a long line of trucks and SUVs, she was hard to keep up with. He pushed the accelerator into the floor, launching the Lincoln forward and slipping in behind a F-150 pickup that provided good cover. When she exited onto the 105 heading east, he slowed down some and followed her onto the ramp.

The ride on the 105 didn't last long enough for Cobb to think about what he was doing. Within minutes they were back on surface streets, breezing past the airport in Hawthorne. Cobb glanced at the warehouses and small factories, but kept his eyes on Gamble hidden behind the darkened glass in her Crown Vic.

It seemed obvious that she was in a hurry to get somewhere. And *somewhere* wasn't anywhere near Parker Center or downtown.

She made a right turn at the corner, then another at the end of the block. Cobb began to wonder if she hadn't spotted him. A series of three right turns was standard operating procedure for anyone who suspected that they were being followed. Cobb could remember his instructor at the Academy grilling him on it as if it were yesterday.

Three right turns with three mirror checks. If you still see the son of a bitch back there, then it's decision time. You need to get your ass in gear.

Instant Karma.

But Gamble's third right turn never happened. Instead, she pulled down an alley and stopped in the rear lot of a nondescript building surrounded by razor wire and a twenty-foot security fence.

Cobb cruised past the alley to the end of the block, turned back, and found a decent place to stop. Through the buildings, he could see her getting out of the car and shaking someone's hand. The guy seemed happy to see her. And he was an odd-looking guy, way too young to have white hair—probably a dye job from one of those places on Melrose.

Cobb flipped open his glove box and reached for the Tylenol. After dry-swallowing two caplets, he grabbed his binoculars and adjusted the focus. Behind Gamble he could see a double set of extra-wide bay doors. A small sign on the wall read SAMY, INC., but gave no indication of what kind of business it was.

At first glance, it looked like some sort of garage or auto repair shop. But as Cobb considered its location, the place was hard to find, didn't offer a street entrance, and was surrounded by warehouses.

He took another look through the binoculars, steadying the image with his elbows pressed against the door. Gamble and the man with white hair were walking toward an Acura TSX parked in front of the loading dock. The car looked mint, a metallic version of gun-metal gray, but Cobb knew from the body style that the vehicle was two years old. He didn't see any plates. When he spotted them on a black 911 Carrera parked by the entryway—the only other car he saw in the lot—he wrote down the number and pulled out his phone.

He'd seen enough to make a guess. But everything was on the table now and he needed more than a guess. He called central dispatch, identified himself to the woman who answered, and gave her the plate number. While he waited, he looked through the buildings at Lena Gamble and used the time to think things over.

He hadn't been prepared for her. He hadn't thought anyone would show up so soon after Jacob Gant's death. He'd hoped to have more time to practice what he wanted to say, at least a couple more days to work on his performance. While he may have punched out one or two points, he knew in his gut that he'd blown it. That the way he'd acted meant more than what he'd actually said. That the dominoes were falling and could easily bring down his world and put him in the ground.

The dispatcher came back on the line. Cobb's eyes stayed on Gamble.

"Samuel Trevor Beck," the dispatcher said. "White male. Thirty-three years old. Lives in Manhattan Beach."

"What's it look like?"

"Clean for the last ten years," the dispatcher said.

"And before that?"

"Grand theft auto. Two counts."

"That's what I figured. Thanks."

Cobb slipped his phone into his pocket, giving Gamble a last look before driving off. He'd blown the interview with her. He couldn't change that. Still, he hoped this wasn't a new scene in the movie that kept playing in his head. A scene toward the end where he felt cornered and would be forced to rip her heart out of her chest.

18

Lena entered the Blackbird Café, ordering a large cup of the house blend and a toasted bagel with lox and cream cheese. Stepping around the bookcases, she passed a newly acquired photograph by Minor White and found a table on the far side of the room. It was late afternoon and the café was particularly quiet right now. If it had been an ordinary day, she would have called it soothing and spent a few minutes looking at the art on the walls and absorbing the atmosphere. Only a handful of people were here—two sat alone reading while the others sipped their drinks and gazed out the rear windows at the city. The view was magnificent: the sun passing through bands of carbon monoxide to the west, the tall buildings throbbing in a brilliant red light. If it had been any other day, she would have seen it and probably noticed the music in the background as well—soft and subdued and something she hadn't listened to in a long time—Keith Jarrett playing part one from *The Köln Concert*.

The Blackbird had always been her oasis, the place she came to when she needed safe harbor.

But nothing about today was ordinary. And nothing of what the café usually provided could prevent her from thinking about Dan Cobb or how he might have blown the Lily Hight murder case. Ever since leaving the Pacific Station, she had been plagued by the possibility that she and Vaughan were caught up in a catastrophe.

The sense of doom was so pervasive that her memory of buying the TSX from Beck seemed like a blur. She remembered him saying something about picking up another car tonight from someone who worked at NBC. That he would drop off the TSX on his way to the studio in Burbank.

But that was about all that cut through her growing feelings of dread.

Worse still, on the drive into town she had switched on the radio and listened to Vaughan's press conference. According to a reporter from KNX, Bennett and Watson were no-shows, along with their fearless leader, Jimmy J. Higgins. True to their word, Vaughan stood at the podium alone. And just as predicted, the fall guy with the stellar reputation got knocked down with the first two questions.

Are you going to arrest Tim Hight for shooting Jacob Gant? And how could you prosecute a hero—a father who sought justice for his daughter's murder because your office completely failed?

Vaughan did the best he could. He tried to remind everyone that two murders were committed at Club 3 AM last night, not one. That Gant was dead, but so was Johnny Bosco. That any decisions would be made after they completed their investigation. That he didn't want to jump to conclusions, and his office was trying to keep an open mind.

But nothing he said seemed to make any difference, and Lena thought that she could hear several reporters snickering in the background as he paused to take another question.

Their voices had become shrill, even moblike, the moment stained with cynicism and open contempt. Before Vaughan could recover, someone shouted a follow-up, *If Fred Goldman had put a bullet in O. J. Simpson's head after the killer stabbed his son to death, would you have prosecuted him? Would you have put Fred Goldman in jail?*

Lena didn't wait for Vaughan's response, switching off the radio and trying to clear her mind by concentrating on the road ahead. It was a safe bet that Higgins, Bennett, and Watson were more than pleased with the way things were going as they listened to the press conference from wherever they were hiding. While nothing could change the fact that their reputations had been tainted to the core, within a single day the press had found a new face and a new target. And for everyone following the story, a new memory had been born.

Lena reached for her briefcase. As she set it on the chair beside her, the fear that Dan Cobb botched the case and arrested the wrong man blew back through her like an ice-cold wind. She noticed her fingers quivering again, and struggled to steady them and to push away the thought. The panic.

How much worse would it be if the press found out what she and Vaughan were actually thinking?

She took a sip of coffee, then another as she pulled out Cobb's murder book and laid it on the table. The three-ring binder Cobb should have been working with for more than a year appeared almost new. Although she had checked before leaving the Westside, she took a second look at the table of contents just to make sure he'd given her the right one. Lily Hight's name had been written in blue ink at the top, with Cobb and his partner listed below the date of the murder. Lena didn't recognize the name of Cobb's partner, nor did she remember seeing any detective but Cobb testify when she watched the trial on TV.

The murder book was divided into twenty-six sections. Often an investigation required two or more binders—the first containing the chronological record, various forensic reports and photographs, while the additional books were filled entirely with field interview cards and witness statements. The book Cobb had compiled only required one binder. Lena paged through the reports, picking out his initials: DC. It seemed clear that Cobb didn't delegate much of the workload to his partner, and that he had put the book together himself.

She paused a moment to see who was seated around her in the café. Satisfied that no one could view the binder's contents, she flipped forward until she reached the crime scene photographs. The way Lily had been left by her killer. She didn't spend too much time on any one image. Just enough to get a feel for what Cobb and his partner had walked into.

None of the crime scene photographs had been made public. Only the jury would have had the opportunity to view them as they were presented as evidence at trial.

But as Lena skimmed through the series, she began to feel the weight of the crime pulling her in. The rape and murder of Lily Hight had been far more brutal than she imagined, the details recorded by the camera far more violent.

She could see the girl sprawled out on the carpet by her bed, her left hand clutching the head and shaft of the screwdriver that had been drilled through her chest from behind. But it was her right arm that made the photo all the more difficult to look at. Lily had died trying to reach the handle pressing against her left shoulder blade. From the amount of blood that had wicked through her T-shirt and blouse and pooled on the carpet, the girl had spent a lot of time trying to reach that handle.

Lena took a moment to collect herself, then turned back to the photo. The girl's boots and jeans had been tossed in a pile in front of the night table. Her panties had been pushed aside and hiked up to her hips. When Lena noticed the unnatural position of her right foot, she flipped ahead to the coroner's report.

Lily Hight's right ankle had been broken during the struggle. And it was a severe break, a complete break. Lena read the entire report, surprised, if not concerned, by how much detail she had missed watching the trial on television from her desk at work. It was almost as if the TV provided some sort of safe distance, some way of filtering out or smoothing over facts that she would have considered essential to the case.

This was particularly true of the evidence supporting the charge that Gant had raped the teenager. The rips and tears and bleeding from her genitals. Gant's semen collected from her thighs and stomach, her panties and vagina. The bruising on her cheeks and jaw and around her neck. The pinpoint hemorrhages in the whites of her eyes.

There could be no doubt that what Cobb and his partner had walked into was a vision of absolute darkness—a crime brutal enough to stun any detective, even a man like Cobb. As Lena thought it over, it seemed more than plausible that Cobb's judgment could have been compromised by the horror. That any hope of working a mistake-free investigation could have been in jeopardy the moment he entered Lily's bedroom and saw her body skewered to the floor.

The thought lingered as Lena noticed that it was dark outside and checked her watch. The autopsies of Bosco and Gant were due to begin in an hour. Paging to the front of the murder book, she found the chronological record and started reading as quickly as she could.

According to the official record as compiled by Cobb, Lily Hight's body had been found at 10:00 p.m. by her parents after returning home from dinner on a Friday night. By eleven, a pair of first responders had confirmed the death as a homicide, and Cobb and his partner were on their way. Even though more than an hour had passed, both parents remained hysterical when the detectives arrived. Cobb suspected that both had been drinking heavily that night and made the immediate decision to call for help.

Lena turned to the Death Investigation Report and read Cobb's notes, then paged back to the record. From the egregious nature of the crime and with no signs of forced entry, Cobb became convinced that Lily had known her killer. When he asked Tim Hight if he knew anyone who would want to harm his daughter, Hight named Jacob Gant and told him that the twenty-five-year-old had been stalking her. When asked if he knew where Jacob Gant lived, Hight pointed across their driveway directly at Gant, who happened to be watching them from the chair set before his bedroom window.

Cobb stated in his notes that his primary concern in that first hour was securing the crime scene and helping the Hights deal with their loss until assistance arrived. But during the course of the evening he made initial contact with Gant under the pretense that he might be helpful as a witness. Gant claimed that he had been alone that evening, that he'd gone to a bar by himself and had a couple of beers. By the time he returned home the police were already there. When asked about his relationship with the sixteen-year-old victim, he said only that they were friends and neighbors. But what struck Cobb about the interview was Gant's demeanor. While Cobb described the Hights as being in extreme emotional distress, he found Gant visibly nervous and afraid, even evasive.

Lena thought back to the conversation she'd had with the detective just a few hours ago in that interrogation room.

I knew that little shit did it the minute I set eyes on him.

After that meeting, that moment, that gaze, the case seemed to gain traction toward a single target.

Lily's cell phone couldn't be found and was never recovered. Cobb assumed from the beginning that the killer had had a reason to take the phone and get rid of it. Within twenty-four hours, the service provider came through and the detective thought he knew that reason.

Gant had left more than a hundred and twenty-five voice and text messages with Lily over the last two weeks of her life. And from Cobb's point of view, Gant had made a huge mistake, the kind of mistake most criminals make when they're in a hurry. The phone had been discarded without deleting the messages from the phone company's server.

Lena saw a note indicating that transcripts from a selection of messages, what Cobb called *Highlights,* had been added to the back of the murder book. She counted just over twenty and read through them carefully. Although the sampling wasn't complete, each message mirrored Tim Hight's claim that Gant was infatuated with his daughter. Even more, each message portrayed Gant as a young man driven by rage and overwhelmed with jealousy and paranoia.

Lena sensed movement in the café and looked up. A man was sitting down at the next table but seemed preoccupied with his food. Glancing at her watch, she realized that she only had another ten minutes before she needed to head over to the coroner's office, and turned back to the murder book.

With Gant's voice and text messages in hand, Cobb had no difficulty securing multiple warrants from a judge. And the detective made a decent effort to describe his thoughts as a team of criminalists and detectives took samples from Gant's body and searched the house. Lena was surprised by the quality of the detective's writing. Somehow it didn't match up with the man she had met this afternoon. All the same, it made the reading easier. When she finished, she set the binder down, sipped her coffee, and thought it over.

The search of Gant's room had convinced Cobb that he was on the right track. He saw the violent artwork Gant had created for his graphic novel, the close-up view into Lily's bedroom from the chair. He found a camera with a long lens in a desk drawer. Within hours of seizing Gant's computer, an SID tech called with news that several nude photographs of the sixteen-year-old victim had been found on the hard drive. While Cobb waited on the DNA analysis and SID reports, he focused on Gant's alibi and history. Gant claimed to have gone to a bar the night of Lily's murder, but his story fell apart when no one remembered seeing him there. When Cobb learned of Gant's troubled youth and the murder of his mother, the detective must have thought that he could see the finish line. And on the following day, he crossed it.

The results from the crime lab showed Gant's fingerprints in Lily's bedroom. But even more, the DNA analysis revealed a hit. A perfect match. The semen samples taken from the girl's body locked Gant in beyond all doubt.

Lena wasn't surprised that Gant hired Paladino after that, or even that his story changed. Most stories change once an attorney becomes involved and knows that his client has just hit the wall. Diffusing the circumstances of a murder—fitting the pieces together so that they make sense in another way—could almost be considered an art. And Lena knew of no one better at it than Buddy Paladino.

Now Gant was more than Lily's friend. More than just her neighbor. Now Gant was claiming to have had a secret relationship with the sixteen-year-old—a relationship they had kept quiet because of her age. Now he claimed that his semen was found because he had made love with her that night. That although they had been fighting over the last two weeks and he had left those angry messages on her cell phone, they had made up that night and all had been forgiven. That no one saw him at the bar because it was standing-room-only on a Friday during a Lakers game. That even though he owned a camera, he didn't need to take the nude snapshots of Lily because she had taken them herself and given them to him as a gift.

Gant tried to explain away all the details through his attorney. Every piece of the puzzle fit or almost fit or was forced to fit—except one.

There were still no signs of forced entry. No indication that anyone had been with Lily in the house other than Jacob Gant. All physical evidence collected at the crime scene still pointed to Gant and only Gant.

And then there was the harsh condition of Lily Hight's body that neither attorney nor client could explain away. The bruising on her neck. Her broken right ankle. The trauma to her genitals. The fact that she was dead. To Cobb, and now to Steven Bennett and Debi Watson who had just been assigned the case, the way Lily had been left didn't look or feel much like love.

19

Lena gave her protective clothing a final check. She was standing before a locker in the changing room at the coroner's office, trying to ignore the conclusions she'd reached while reading Cobb's murder book. Trying to pretend that the flaws in the case weren't really there.

But she knew she was fooling herself.

There was Cobb's take on the case—and then there was everything else. The lies and loose ends were beginning to pile up. If Cobb's investigation hinged on the father's claim that Gant was stalking his daughter, why did Lily keep a picture of Gant hidden by her bed? If Gant's brother knew that there was something more to the relationship, why didn't Tim Hight?

And that was the problem. Hight would have had to have known.

He sat in that chair in the sunroom every night. He sat in the dark smoking and drinking and snorting cocaine. He was probably watching them the same way he'd watched Lena when she notified the Gants that Jacob had been murdered. He probably tuned in every night.

But even more telling, if Cobb's case was as rock solid as it appeared in the murder book, why wasn't he willing to help? If Cobb had connected all the dots, why the psycho drama? Why all the insanity? Why didn't he just brief her on the case and wish her luck?

Lena slipped on a pair of gloves and grabbed her face shield. But just as she reached for the door, her cell phone started vibrating in her pocket. The phone shook five times before she was able to dig it out from beneath her scrubs and see Barrera's name blinking on the display.

"I just got a call from Jack Peltre," he said. "You know him, Lena?"

From the sound of Barrera's voice—the low rattle—it didn't take much to put it together. Jack Peltre was a lieutenant working out of the Pacific Station. More to the point, Peltre was Cobb's supervisor.

"I've heard of him," she said.

"Then I'm sure you'll be happy to know that it was a friendly call. It was friendly because we've known each other for twenty years and that's what friends do. They take care of each other. And from time to time, they make friendly calls. You know what I'm saying?"

Barrera was seething. The shit was hitting the fan.

"I think so," she said.

"You think so? Well, they do, Lena. Friendly people like to stay in touch, otherwise they don't consider themselves friendly. By the way, Peltre mentioned that you stopped by this afternoon. He told me that when you left the building, you took something with you."

She glanced across the changing room at the murder book stuffed in her briefcase. There was no point in denying it.

"I did," she said. "I took something."

Several moments passed. She could hear Barrera grinding his teeth and working a cigar.

"Bring it to me," he said finally. "I want to see you in my office. And that's an order, Detective. I want to see you right now."

The line went dead. He'd hung up on her.

Lena stared at the phone, weighing her options. She was already suited up and figured that she had five, maybe ten minutes—plus the short drive over to Parker Center before Barrera would start looking for her. Lowering her face shield, she gritted her teeth and entered the operating room. There were seven autopsies in progress tonight. Even better, the jar of Vicks VapoRub wasn't in its usual place in the changing room. She had nothing to block out the abhorrent smell of decomposing flesh and human waste. Nothing to filter away the dense, oppressive odor that permeated every inch of the room.

The experience was more than overwhelming—something her former partner once told her didn't get any easier after twenty years.

But tonight she welcomed it like a wake-up call.

Without looking too closely, she scanned the room and spotted Sid Kosinski working in the far corner. The two corpses were laid out side by side on stainless steel operating trays. Even from a distance neither Bosco nor Gant looked as if they were resting or had found much peace.

Mindful of the wet floor, Lena worked her way deeper into the room. Kosinski glanced up at her as she approached. He had begun with Bosco, and appeared to be more than halfway through. As he jotted something down on a clipboard, she turned to Gant and eyed his dead body. She took the shock with her game face on, thinking about how difficult it must have been for his father to stand here and identify his son.

Without clothing, she could see that the bruises Gant had received were significantly more extensive than what she'd seen on his neck and arms at the crime scene. The wounds from the beatings he had endured stretched across his shoulders, his chest and stomach, then circled around his lower back. His upper thighs were marred as well— almost as if he'd blocked a series of kicks to the groin.

She had no reason to doubt Gant's brother on this. No reason to doubt that the number of people standing in line to throw a punch Gant's way after the NOT GUILTY verdict would have extended across the entire city.

An image surfaced. She could see Cobb sitting before her with his eyes concealed by those strange glasses. She could remember how still the room became when she asked the detective if he'd hit Gant, if he had hurt him. She wondered what their interviews had been like before Gant signed up with Paladino. She hadn't seen any transcripts in the murder book. If they were there, she hadn't found them.

She pushed the thought away and looked back at what was left of Gant's face. The two rounds that had blown out his eyes carried more meaning now. The killer's personal rage for his victim remained all too clear. Yet the possibility that Gant had been murdered for what he'd seen—what he'd discovered—seemed just as clear.

Kosinski moved in beside her. "Some of these bruises have to be more than ten days old, Lena. Look at the change in color."

She nodded. "I can't stay, Sid. How come you started with Bosco?"

Kosinski met her eyes, then tipped his head toward the double doors that opened from the hallway behind them. Lena peeked over his shoulder. District Attorney Jimmy J. Higgins was watching them from the other side of the glass and seemed more than a little edgy. But at least she knew what had happened to that jar of Vicks VapoRub. She could see Higgins smearing the gel all over his handkerchief and pressing the cloth against his mouth and nose. He had a wild look in his eyes like a man huffing glue.

Kosinski lowered his voice. "He said he's got a meeting tonight. He wants whatever I can give him before he goes."

"Why doesn't he come in?"

"Because he's a chicken shit. I don't even know why he's here. I could have given him a call."

"It's Bosco," she said. "They were friends."

"What kind of friends?"

She shrugged.

"Well, Higgins asked me to do something I could never do, Lena."

"Clean the report," she said. "Don't mention what you found in Bosco's nose."

Kosinski gave her a long look and then nodded. "What kind of a DA would ask for something like that?"

She wished that Higgins's request would have surprised her, but it didn't. If the DA could press the deputy chief of police, he would have had no problem trying to corrupt a medical examiner. She turned and took another peek at him. He had stepped away from the window and was shouting at someone on his cell phone. She wondered if it was

Vaughan taking the verbal beating on the other end of that phone. She wondered if Cobb's supervisor had made another call on the "friends network"—this time to the DA because that's what friends do.

But Lena had her own reasons to be troubled by the cocaine found at Club 3 AM.

She still didn't understand why Dante Escabar had left it at the crime scene. And his explanation that somehow he had overlooked it— that he'd rushed to inform the owners about the murders and protect their clients by shutting the place down—didn't ring true. The quantity alone raised serious doubt. In the end, finding that much coke would jeopardize the club's place as an oasis for the A-list just as much as Bosco being seen with Jacob Gant after the trial. Escabar had both the time and opportunity to clean things up, but hadn't. Lena felt certain that he'd had a reason. Something she couldn't see yet.

Kosinski pointed to the worktable. Bosco's stomach had been removed and set on a plastic tray.

"I was just about to pull the slug," he said. "That's what you came to see, right?"

She nodded and followed the medical examiner over to the worktable, then watched as he selected a clean scalpel.

20

Unable to reach Vaughan on her cell, Lena hustled through the basement to the elevator at the end of the hall. She had taken the shortcut from the garage and entered Parker Center using the rear doors. It was after-hours—dark and still with just the sound of two guys talking in the distance. As she passed the men's locker room, she could hear them through the door. They were laughing about something, and she envied them for their apparent lack of worry and concern, for what sounded like a carefree moment between friends.

The single bullet that had ended Johnny Bosco's life entered his body from the back, missing his spine and ripping through his aorta. When the slug entered his stomach, a cheese burrito was waiting for it like a block of foam. Kosinski estimated that Bosco had eaten the burrito within twenty minutes of his death. The result was a perfect nine-millimeter slug. Once the slug from Jacob Gant's abdomen had been removed and the second autopsy completed, both would be hand-delivered to the crime lab. Still, it didn't seem like much of a priority. Not without Tim Hight's gun.

The elevator opened on the third floor. Lena hurried down the hall and entered the section floor. The overhead lights were dimmed and no one was around. As she passed Barrera's desk and started down the aisle, she looked through the glass off the staff room and saw him waiting for her in the captain's office. He was sitting at the conference table, smoking what was left of that cigar and tapping the ash into an empty can of diet Pepsi. Several cartons of Chinese food were set on the table as well, along with his cell phone and a charger that he'd plugged into the wall. She pushed open the door. Barrera nodded at her and pointed to a chair. He looked thin and weary—the circles beneath his eyes three or four shades darker than she remembered seeing this morning.

"Give it to me," he said.

She lifted the murder book out of her briefcase and slid it across the table. Barrera pulled it closer without taking his eyes off her.

"Cobb called Bennett," he said in a low, raspy voice. "Bennett called the DA. The DA tried to get hold of the chief, but couldn't reach him. When he tried the deputy chief, Ramsey refused to take his call, so he tried Peltre. Then Peltre found me. That's what friends are for."

He let it sit there, working his cigar and thinking it over before he continued.

"You're scaring the shit out of everybody, Lena. Cobb, Bennett, Higgins—they want you fired. They want worse than that—more than that. They'd like to do the same thing to Vaughan, but they can't. If they did, Bennett or Watson or Higgins would have to take over the case, and none of them want this one. Vaughan's safe. He's ruined, but he's safe. But you're not safe. The deputy chief might be using you because of the way your last two cases turned out, but you're too green to be safe. You understand what I'm saying? There's only so much give before your value runs out. No one on the sixth floor gives a shit."

Lena nodded and kept quiet, her mind locked on Cobb. He'd made a move—not to his supervisor, but to Bennett. She didn't like the feel of it.

Barrera leaned forward in his chair. "What I said to you this morning, what the deputy chief told you at the briefing—everything still stands. Your job is to build a case against Hight for the murders of Johnny Bosco and Jacob Gant, and to do it in a hurry. Taking another look at Lily Hight's murder isn't part of this investigation, nor will it ever be included. Why do I even have to say it, Detective? We need to put this behind us so that we can move forward, not back. Hight's a third rail. Touch him the wrong way and you're dead. We're all dead. And you're thinking that maybe we tried the wrong asshole? No wonder everybody's in a shit fit. I'm in a shit fit, too. The guy who murdered Lily Hight got shot last night. His name's Jacob Gant, and he's dead."

Lena glanced at the binder, then back at Barrera. "All I asked Cobb was how he cleared Hight for his daughter's murder, Frank. It was a righteous question. Anyone would have asked it. And I need that murder book for background. What Cobb thinks I said or thinks I think is his business, not mine."

"If that's all it is, then why is Vaughan reviewing tapes from Gant's trial?"

She shrugged, wondering if a shrug counted as a lie. In this case it probably did.

"I didn't know that he was," she said. "But my guess would be that it's for the same reason I need that murder book. We're trying to get caught up. We're working as fast as we can."

He met her eyes and held the look for a long time. She wasn't certain that she believed her, and she felt rotten for deliberately misleading him. But then, without prompting, he shoved the murder book back across the table.

"Okay," he said, still measuring her. "Okay. All you're doing is catching up. You need background. But I've gotta know what's going on. You walk into Pacific unannounced and ask for something like this . . . I want to know about it first from here on out. Okay?"

"Okay," she said.

Barrera leaned back in his chair, striking a match and relighting that cigar. "Now tell me what you did to this gossip reporter."

Lena's mind went blank. She didn't know what he was talking about.

"Dick Harvey," he said. "What did you and Rhodes do to him outside Club 3 AM last night?"

Dick Harvey. The memory clicked, but it seemed so long ago—like a month had been lost in a single day.

"He got past the line and broke into my car," she said. "We found him hiding in the backseat with a new set of auto jigglers."

"His attorney says that you roughed him up. He's taking pictures and posting them on Harvey's Web site."

"Taking pictures of what?"

"Cuts and bruises."

"Has Harvey been released?"

Barrera shook his head. "No, he's still in. His attorney took the shots during a visit. What did you do to the man?"

"He wouldn't get out of the car, so we dragged him out. It was by the book. We cuffed him and read him his rights. We thought he might be using. He tried to bite me, but he settled down. When we left, he was fine."

"Bite you?"

She nodded without a reply, then watched Barrera glance at his cell phone as if he was waiting for a call.

"They're saying that he had a video camera with him, Lena. That somehow whatever Harvey recorded that night is gone. You know anything about that?"

She knew a lot about it. Before they chained Harvey to the street-light, before the patrol unit arrived, Rhodes had taken the cameras they found hidden in the reporter's baseball cap and eyeglasses and erased everything on the drives. All Dick Harvey had from the night were memories. She was about to tell Barrera about it, but he didn't seem all that interested anymore. A bottom-feeder like Dick Harvey was the least of his problems right now. Especially if Harvey couldn't produce any video to back up his claims.

"I didn't think you knew anything," he said. "When I talked to Rhodes, he didn't, either. It's probably for the best."

"Where's Rhodes?"

"Following a lead in San Diego. Tito turned it up this afternoon.

Their case broke wide open. They should be back in three or four days. When was the last time you got any sleep?"

"I'm good."

"You don't look it," he said. "You eat? You want some Chinese food?"

"I had something a couple hours ago."

"Well then, go home and get some rest. I need tomorrow to be better than today."

She didn't say anything. She didn't take what he'd said as a slight. And for reasons she couldn't explain, she wished that Rhodes wasn't out of town. But after slipping the murder book into her briefcase and heading for the door, she turned back.

"Who is Dan Cobb?"

Barrera seemed surprised by the question and took several moments to think it over. When he finally spoke, his voice had changed and become more reflective.

"He used to be a good cop," he said.

"Then you know him."

Barrera nodded. "I know him. You're sitting at his desk."

"What do you mean?"

"You're sitting at Cobb's desk. You replaced him."

Time seemed to stop. Barrera was gazing at her from his chair on the other side of the table. Lena could feel the hairs on the back of her neck lifting away from her skin.

"What happened?" she asked.

Barrera looked at the cartons of Chinese food and pushed them away. "Cobb had personal issues," he said. "He went on leave and was reassigned. It's over now. Let's leave it at that."

She didn't want to leave it at that. But when Barrera's cell started ringing and he waved her out of the office, she walked onto the section floor and moved in behind her desk. It was made of oak, and like all the furniture on the floor, it was the same age as the building. She gazed at the file holder, the papers strewn across the top. She could almost see Cobb sitting in her chair.

And then a memory surfaced—something she had noticed when she was first promoted to the division and assigned the desk. Something she'd become used to because she saw it every day. She cleared the papers away from the right side of the desktop and found the mark on its surface—a small section of the oak finish that hadn't faded over time. It was a rectangle the size of a snapshot, just like the one she had seen taped to Cobb's desk earlier in the day. That discolored photo of the sun setting into an ocean behind a grove of palm trees; the shot he'd taken in Hawaii fifteen years ago.

She took a step back.

Cobb had been sent away on leave, demoted and reassigned. When he asked to see her ID this afternoon, he knew exactly who she was.

Not just the *new deal,* but his replacement.

21

Personal issues . . .

She could see it now. Cobb standing in front of the door with his hands in his pockets stirring change. When he'd asked to see her badge, Cobb had been playing her.

Lena blocked it out as she turned up the volume on her cell. It was Vaughan, calling back, and she could barely hear him.

"Where are you?" she said.

"Looking for you on the third floor. Barrera said you just left."

"I'm across the street in the garage," she said.

"Doing what?"

"Waiting on the next shift change. I'm trying to hitch a ride home."

"I'll see you in five minutes."

She walked down the aisle to the guard shack, pushing the keys to the Crown Vic through the slot in the window. There was no point in driving the car home. Beck had called and her TSX was en route from the Westside. After tonight she would be anonymous again. Invisible.

She told the guard that she'd left the car on the second floor and gave him the space number. The old man smiled, then looked past her and shrugged—the air conditioner in his shack was too loud to speak over. But even without words, she understood what he meant.

It was late and hot, and summer was three months early.

She gazed across the street. Vaughan had just exited the building and was headed for the visitor spaces in the VIP lot. As he reached what looked like a Ford crossover, he spotted her on the sidewalk and waved, then pulled his car around to pick her up. Within minutes they were cruising on the freeway toward Hollywood Hills. Lena settled into the leather seat, listening to the hum of the engine and studying Vaughan's face in the soft light from the dash.

"How bad was it?" she said.

"The press conference? We've got bigger problems than that, Lena."

"I was thinking about Higgins. I saw him at the coroner's office. He was shouting at someone on the phone. I thought it might be you."

Vaughan flashed a tired grin at her. "It wasn't me," he said. "I got it in person about fifteen minutes ago. We had a meet and greet in his office. When he was done, I thought I'd see if I could find you. I'm glad I tried."

"I met Cobb," she said.

"Higgins told me."

They were passing Echo Park. Lena glanced at the lake, then began to recount her meeting with Cobb in the interrogation room. By the time they reached the Beachwood exit and started up Gower Street into the hills, she had filled in Vaughan on most of what she'd read in the murder book. He seemed particularly interested in the photo Lena had found in the memory box by Lily Hight's bed. The picture of Jacob Gant that Cobb's investigation had missed. Vaughan saw it exactly the same way she did.

No one would keep a photograph of her stalker hidden beside her bed. Hight's claim that Gant had been stalking his daughter didn't make sense.

The road steepened as it twisted through the hills. When they rolled out of the last curve, Lena pointed out her driveway and Vaughan made the turn. She could see the TSX parked in front of the garage—the metallic-gray finish glistening beneath the outdoor lights. Beck had delivered her car as promised and left to make his next pickup in Burbank. The TSX may have been two years old, but looked new.

She turned back as Vaughan passed the garage and pulled to a stop beside the house. He kept the engine running—the air-conditioning—and seemed to be taken with the view of the basin below. It was a remarkably clear night, the lights from the city shimmering through the heat all the way to Long Beach.

"Would you like to come in?" she asked.

He loosened his tie, still gazing at the city below the hill. "Can I get a rain check?" he asked. "I've got the kids this week. I need to go home and give their nanny a break. Maybe spend an hour or two watching them sleep."

"I understand."

Vaughan became quiet. Lena could tell that he wasn't seeing the view anymore, but thinking something over, so she waited. After several minutes, he turned to her.

"When Higgins left the autopsy to ream me out tonight, he told me about Cobb calling Bennett. I thought it was strange. If Cobb had a problem handing over the murder book, why didn't he just say something to his supervisor?"

"I felt the same way," she said.

"And why was there any problem at all? From his point of view, the case should have been over a long time ago."

Lena nodded. "If it didn't end for him with the verdict, it should've ended last night."

Vaughan leaned against the door to face her. "There was this case in New York," he said. "Suffolk County, Long Island. Very similar circumstances, Lena. A seventeen-year-old was accused of murdering his parents for their money. The detective was a seasoned bull known for pushing suspects over the edge. The DA backed him up just like Higgins. The prosecutors went for the jugular just like Bennett and Watson. Unfortunately for the kid, he didn't have a defense attorney like Buddy Paladino. He ended up spending half his life in prison for a crime he didn't do."

"You said the circumstances were the same."

"The approach the detective took, the mistakes he made, remind me of Cobb. The family was wealthy, the kid adopted, and so the guy decided right off that the motive had to be greed. The kid begged to take a polygraph, but the detective refused. He thought his read was better than the science. Just like Cobb, he looked at the kid and knew."

Lena realized that Vaughan was talking about the Marty Tankleff case. Although it hadn't been in the news for a year or two, the case was too horrific to forget. Tankleff's mother had been found on the bathroom floor, stabbed to death and nearly decapitated. His father had been severely beaten and stabbed multiple times as well. After hanging on for a month in a coma, the man died and the murder count climbed to two. Lena imagined that the brutality of the crime affected the detective's judgment. After seeing the crime scene photographs of Lily Hight skewered to the floor, she had thought the same thing of Cobb. Both detectives jumped early. Both detectives locked in on their suspects without bothering to interview anyone who might have given them a deeper perspective and widened their view.

Vaughan looked her over. "You know what I'm talking about, don't you? You know the case."

"I read about it," she said. "Marty Tankleff was a minor. The motive didn't make any sense because he wouldn't have seen the money for eight years."

"Then you get where I'm going. The detective missed more than he saw. The entire prosecution team built their case on the way they wanted it to be. When they were confronted with the facts, overwhelming evidence that pointed to the real killer, they refused to acknowledge their mistakes. Everyone knows who murdered the Tankleffs, except for the people who should. And that's why the killer is still free."

"When I worked homicide in Hollywood, my partner used to call it 'tunnel vision.'"

Vaughan thought about it, his eyes still on her. "Your partner called it right. But this could be more than that and you know it, Lena. This is Los Angeles. We're dealing with different people. Different circumstances with a lot more at stake. And I don't care what they say or how loud they say it. I don't care how hot the fire gets. If Gant was innocent, I want the world to know that he was innocent. If Hight killed his own daughter, I want to make sure the asshole pays for it."

Lena moved her head into the shadows so that Vaughan couldn't see the expression on her face. He'd made the turn. They were on the same page.

22

Lena switched on the lamp and pulled a stool up to the counter. She had just found the nude photos of Lily Hight that had been pulled from Gant's computer in the back of Cobb's murder book. There were three—each one more disturbing than the next. Lena had stumbled upon them while searching through the binder for the interviews Cobb conducted with Gant before Buddy Paladino had been hired. The transcripts weren't in the book, but should have been. And she'd missed the photos on her first pass because they were mixed together with hundreds of shots taken by an SID photographer on the day Gant's house was searched.

Cobb's murder book had been slapped together. His work reeked of carelessness.

She took a deep breath and exhaled, then looked at the sixteen-year-old girl lying on her bed. The girl seemed to have left her innocence on the chair with her clothes. Lena caught the seductive smile on her face. The smoky eyes and tangled hair. The dark-red lipstick. The girl laid out in a woman's body that was fully formed, and undoubtedly, fully functional.

Unlike the crime scene photos, these images were never presented at trial. Somehow over the past year, they had never been leaked. As Lena considered what she was seeing, what they implied ran counter to everything she had ever heard about the victim. And as disturbing as they may have been, she was surprised that Paladino hadn't seen their value to his defense. Images of the teenager stripped of all innocence would have lent credibility to Gant's claim that he was having a relationship with the girl and not stalking her.

But there was something more here. Something about the photographs that she couldn't quite put into words.

Tim Hight murdered Jacob Gant. But his reasons for committing the homicide seemed so much more important than the crime itself. Was it as simple as an act of revenge? Or was it an attempt to mask some horrible truth that Gant had discovered? Was Hight trying to keep something buried that had almost leaked out?

Lena took a last look at the girl lying on the bed. The glint in her eyes. The heat that went with her long legs and curvy body. The seductive smile that now seemed so haunting.

But she was thinking about that piece of paper again. The one she kept that listed the reasons why she wanted to be a cop. Barrera was wrong on this. Digging into the past wasn't a step back. It was a move forward. It was the only move worth making.

She closed the binder and pushed it away. It was well after midnight and the house was still hot, still hovering at over 80 degrees. She could hear the air conditioner straining outside the window.

Stepping around the counter into the kitchen, she opened the freezer and let the cool mist brush against her face. The cloud of moist air didn't last very long. Only ten or twenty seconds, when what she really needed was an hour or two. When the frost finally vanished, she reached inside for the bottle of SKYY vodka and poured a drink.

She took a first sip, feeling the ice-cold liquid hit her stomach and glow. Peeling off her shoes, she opened the slider and walked outside to the pool. The moon was just beginning to climb above the horizon. She could see it directly behind the tall buildings downtown. Shafts of warm yellow light were spilling down the streets all the way to the ocean. Rolling up her jeans, she sat down and slipped her feet into the cool water. She took another sip of vodka, hoping that her view of the city raked in moonlight might overtake her memory of the photographs she had just seen. And then another sip, hoping that the drink might freeze up her mind and bring on a few hours of dreamless sleep.

And that's when she heard a car pulling into her driveway, the sound of tires eating up gravel. She wasn't too concerned about it until she got up and looked around the house.

The car was rolling forward with its headlights off. A white Lincoln.

She climbed up the steps onto the porch, watching the car coast to a quiet stop in the shadows. A man got out, and after spending several moments staring at her house, walked over to her car. Lena could tell that he was trying to avoid the outdoor lights. But when he leaned toward the driver's side window to peer inside, light reflecting off the glass struck his face and she got a good look.

It was Cobb.

She pulled herself together, moving into the living room and locking the slider. After switching off the kitchen lights, she killed the lamp by the couch and hurried through the darkness to the bedroom window. She could see Cobb walking toward the back of the house. Even worse, he had a flashlight in his hand and no longer seemed concerned about hiding in the shadows.

There was fear and anger charging through her body, but there was confusion, too. What could he possibly be thinking?

She rushed through the living room into the kitchen and looked outside. Cobb was by the pool with his flashlight and had found her drink. When he noticed the wet footprints she'd left, he panned the light across the concrete and up the steps to the porch.

He knew that she was home. And now he realized that she knew he was here.

Lena filled her lungs with air, her eyes riveted to his hardened face. He was standing perfectly still. He was thinking something over like a guy who still had a full bag of personal issues—like a rabid animal that walks toward you instead of running back into the woods.

Cobb started up the steps. As he shined his flashlight into the living room, Lena spotted her .45 on the counter and removed it from the holster. She pressed her back to the wall and inched her way to the corner. She could see Cobb peering through the slider. He looked extraordinarily pale—like a ghost with a goatee and two black holes for eyes. She could hear him fidgeting with the lock and trying to force open the door.

Lena had seen enough and inched the slide back on her .45. If Cobb got into the house, she had no reason to hesitate.

Minutes passed, her heart pounding in her chest.

But then he backed off.

She saw the kitchen bloom with light, then darken as he finally stepped off the porch. Returning to the window, she watched Cobb begin to circle the house with his flashlight. She followed his course from room to room. He moved slowly and often stopped to examine the windows on the second floor. When he reached the front door, he gave it a long look but eventually got back into his car.

Lena yanked open the slider and ran down the steps. She could hear tires digging up gravel again. Clearing the corner, she saw the white Lincoln back out onto the street. When Cobb finally switched on his headlights, Lena kept her eyes on them and followed the car's path through the curves until it vanished at the bottom of the hill.

And then her body shuddered. She noticed the sweat covering her face. The electricity in the air. She thought about what Barrera had said to her just a few hours ago. Thought about the words he'd used as she tried to catch her breath.

Tomorrow needed to be better than today. Even if it had to begin at Tim Hight's house.

23

She woke up with the sun in her eyes—on the couch and still in her clothes. When she noticed her .45 laying out on the coffee table, the memory of last night came back to her and she sat up.

Cobb.

He was more than a nuisance now. He had become a problem, one that seemed to be evolving. And she wasn't sure how to handle it. She didn't think a phone call to Barrera would stop the man. Based on what she'd seen of Cobb so far, a reprimand that came from the department or even his own supervisor would only feed his irrational behavior and light the man up.

Lighting Cobb up didn't seem like the way to go.

Deciding that the best move was no move, at least for now, Lena pushed the thought aside and headed to the kitchen. She needed to check in with Martin Orth at the crime lab before driving over to Hight's house, but it was too early to make the call.

Lena brewed her coffee by the cup with filter paper and the best beans she could afford. Setting the tea kettle on the burner, she switched the flame to low and left the room to shower and change. When she returned, she made toast and soft-boiled eggs and ate standing over the sink.

The meal revived her, but it was still too early to call Orth. Digging through her briefcase, she found the weekly planner she and Harry had discovered in Gant's room and removed it from the evidence bag. She sat down at the table by the windows, sipping coffee and leafing through the small book. By all appearances, Gant's planner was more of a journal than anything else. And it was short—something he had started after the trial, but stopped two weeks before his own death.

It looked like Gant had been trying to piece together the last ten days of Lily's life without much luck. Lena could see the problem immediately. Not many people would have been willing to talk to him or to help someone that they thought had committed a murder and walked away free and clear. According to one entry, Lily's best friend had agreed to meet him but had been followed by her father. After several attempts to reestablish contact, Gant received a phone call from someone identifying themselves as a cop and stopped trying.

Lena didn't recognize the girl's name from either Cobb's murder book or the trial. Julia Hackford. It seemed curious that she hadn't heard the name before and she wrote it down, then returned to Gant's journal.

Several pages were stained with blood, and Lena found more than one passage where Gant wrote about being attacked on the street, about his fear of going outside, and about months of bad dreams that began with his arrest. Advice that Paladino had given him during the trial was recounted here as well—thoughts that inspired Gant and seemed to give him hope.

Lena read through the entire book in about twenty minutes, then pushed it aside and gazed out the window as she thought it over. She knew that Cobb would have called the journal bullshit. That he would have said that Gant didn't keep up with it because his writings were nothing more than an attempt by a psychotic killer to recreate his self image as an innocent.

If it looks like I'm innocent, I am.

Most of the department would probably have agreed with him.

Yet, there was a certain authenticity to Gant's words. Like the photo of Gant found by Lily Hight's bed, it was a shift too decisive for Lena to ignore. She only wished that there would have been some mention of meeting and working with Johnny Bosco. Her gut told her that Bosco didn't do anything unless he was the primary beneficiary. As she glanced back at the journal, she decided that the omission could only mean that he came in late. That whatever went down between Bosco and Gant began within the last two weeks of their lives.

She checked the time. It was almost seven. As she picked up the phone to call Orth, she was still thinking about Jacob Gant's life since the trial. What it must have been like to walk in his shoes. How horrible it would have been to go through what he went through if he really was innocent.

Orth picked up after three rings.

"I was just about to call you, Lena."

"Good," she said. "Then you have something."

Orth was an SID supervisor and had played a key role in Lena's last case. They worked well together. Like everyone else at the lab, Orth had been caught up in the DNA evidence that went missing during Gant's trial. But Lena regarded the scandal as guilt by association. Orth's only involvement in the crisis was his position as a team leader. Lena had always known him to be a consummate professional and she trusted him completely.

"We've got something," he said. "The cocaine's a match. What you found at Hight's house mirrors what was found at Club 3 AM in every way. They are chemically identical, the cut made at exactly the same percentage. It's high-grade stuff, better than what we've seen in a long time."

Lena started pacing. "So, either Hight was in the room or they used the same dealer. What about fingerprints on those hundred-dollar bills?"

"No luck there," Orth said. "But we've got blood, Lena. We found it in the sole of Hight's left shoe."

"Enough to work with?"

"If he was in that room, we'll know about it. And that's a promise."

It wasn't the gun, but it was close. Maybe even enough to convince Hight that a confession was the easiest way out. If the blood from either victim wound up on his shoe, there could only be one explanation.

"Are you gonna be in your office this afternoon?" she said.

"I'll be here all day. What's up?"

"I want to show you something."

Another call was coming in. Lena glanced at the caller ID.

"I've gotta go, Marty. I'll see you this afternoon."

"See you then," he said.

She clicked over to the next call. It was Buddy Paladino, calling on her home line at ten after seven in the morning.

"It's a little early, isn't it?" she said.

Paladino remained silent for a moment. When he spoke, his voice was soft and low and smooth as silk.

"There's a rumor floating around town, Detective Gamble. All across the city, people want to know."

"What's the rumor?"

"That you've reopened the Lily Hight murder case."

It hung there—a heavy silence enveloping his words and radiating through the house. Lena moved to the counter, grabbed a stool, and sat down. She had helped Paladino with a personal problem last year, and knew that he was in her debt. But that didn't mean that he wasn't dangerous. It didn't mean that she could trust him or that she was safe.

"It's a bad rumor, Buddy. You shouldn't believe everything you hear."

"I think you're trying to mislead me. I can tell by the sound of your voice. I thought we had an understanding, Lena. That we were above all this. You scratch my back, I scratch yours—so to speak."

Vintage Paladino.

"Who did you talk to?" she said.

"A friend."

"Then it's not all over town?"

"No. Just you, me, and a friend. We're a small network. I just wanted to see how you'd take it. By the way, I could tell that you were lying to me. You're gonna need to work on your technique. It's not what you say. It's the way you say it."

Lena shook it off. "Maybe we could meet at your office," she said. "Later in the day."

"Later in the day. I like it."

"Fine," she said. "But I have a question before we meet."

"About what?"

"Tim Hight."

He paused a beat. "I'm listening."

"Hight and his daughter. Was there anything there?"

Paladino became quiet again. When he finally spoke, his voice had lost its polish and become exceedingly quiet and precise.

"I had three spotters in the courtroom, Lena. Three of the best analysts around. When I floated the idea that Hight molested his daughter, it was clear that no one on the jury wanted to hear that."

Lena got up and moved to the slider. The city was awash in new morning light. "Okay, so the jury didn't want to hear it. But were you fishing, or was it more than that? Did you have something real?"

"We'll talk in the office," he said. "Later in the day."

And then he hung up.

24

She drove across town to Hight's house in the TSX, listening to the V6 under the hood and thinking about what she hoped to accomplish in the next hour. She didn't mind doing this alone. There was a certain advantage to seeing Hight without a partner by her side, a chance that Hight might speak more freely. But as she pulled around the corner and spotted the patrol unit still on watch at the curb, she had to admit that she felt some degree of relief.

Lena parked in the drive and walked over to the car with her briefcase. Sitting behind the wheel was a uniformed officer she recognized from the day before and knew by name. Carmine Ruiz looked like he only had one or two weeks on the job, but that was okay with her.

"Is he in there?" she asked.

Ruiz fought off a yawn as he pointed to the sunroom. "He's been in there all night. He sits in that window chain-smoking in the dark. He came out once to tell me that he wanted his car back. I think he was drunk."

"I'm gonna need your help, Carmine. No big deal. Just come inside with me and wait in the foyer."

"You got it," he said.

They walked through the gate and up the path onto the porch. Before Lena could knock, the door swung open to reveal Hight and those bloodshot eyes of his. He stared at them for a while—back and forth and long enough to creep Lena out. But then, without a word, he stepped aside to let them enter.

"Are you sober?" Lena asked.

Hight nodded. "Close enough."

"I want another look at your daughter's bedroom."

The man seemed to need time to process her request, but eventually started up the staircase. Lena followed three steps behind, keenly aware of the distance between them. When they reached the landing, she gave him a good lead through the gloom until they reached the door.

"Where's your friend?" he asked.

"Officer Ruiz will wait downstairs."

"How much time is this gonna take? What are you looking for?"

"Open the door, Mr. Hight."

He turned the knob and gave it a soft push, the bright light from the bedroom spilling over them like the crest of a ten-foot wave. As Lena entered, she noticed Hight's hesitation to follow and watched him lean against the doorjamb.

"You lied to me yesterday, Mr. Hight. You said that you hadn't seen Jacob Gant since the trial. But that wasn't the case at all, was it? You've seen him many times over the last six weeks. And you had an argument with him on the day he was murdered."

He met her eyes, but couldn't hold her gaze—shifting his weight and looking down at the floor.

"Maybe I didn't understand the question," he said.

"Maybe. But it was a simple question, Mr. Hight. Tell me what the argument was about."

Hight shrugged. "I saw him hop over the fence. I told him to stay off my property."

"That's it?"

He nodded. "Pretty much."

"I don't believe you, Mr. Hight."

"That's your problem, not mine, lady."

"Is this the way your attorneys told you to act?"

"I didn't call them."

There was a touch of arrogance in his voice. Defiance.

"You can't do this alone," she said. "You can't do it because it is your problem. And it's a big problem. You need legal advice. It's your right."

He wasn't listening. He needed legal advice, but he needed a shower and a shave and a change of clothes as well.

Lena finally broke her gaze to take in the room. She could see finger-print powder on almost every surface and remembered the request she'd made as they waited for Paladino's press conference to end yesterday in the front yard. No matter how odd, their daughter's bedroom hadn't been turned into a tomb. Based on the large number of smudges, the room was obviously still in use.

"You spend time in here," she said.

Hight shook his head. "I haven't set foot in this room since Lily died. Once in a while I'll find my wife in here. I don't know what she does."

Lena found a pair of gloves in her briefcase and walked over to the chest of drawers. Yesterday she had been looking for a gun. Today was all about confirmation. When she spotted a camera in the top drawer, she pulled it out and hit the POWER button. Remarkably, the device fired up, but only to indicate that the battery needed to be charged and that the media card was empty. After ten seconds, the screen went blank and the power shut down.

"Your daughter liked to take pictures?"

"She wanted to make it her living," he said. "That photograph by the bed is one of hers."

Lena stepped over for a look. It was a landscape, a black-and-white image shot at the beach from atop a cliff. The lens was pointed straight down at the rocks and sand, the shutter snapped just as a wave reached the shoreline. What struck Lena most about the image was the sunlight sweeping across the rocks and sand from a low angle—the way the image was composed.

"Your daughter had an eye."

"Well beyond her years."

"What happened to the rest of her work?"

"Cobb had her computer taken away after Gant was arrested. When we finally got it back, I downloaded the images and erased the drive."

"Were they all landscapes, Mr. Hight? Or did she photograph people, too?"

Lena's eyes were on him, but Hight showed no emotion—no changes.

"A little of both," he said.

"Anything stand out?"

"Not really."

A moment passed, but she didn't think he'd bend. "The night she was murdered, where did you find her?"

"Right where you're standing."

Lena acknowledged the spot, then turned to the window and found the impressions in the carpet left by the chair. Pushing the chair over, she turned it toward the window and felt the feet fall into place. Through the window and across the drive she could see Jacob Gant's room and the chair still in place before his window.

"We like it better the way it was," Hight said.

"But on the night of the murder, the chair was here. And it had been that way for a long time. Long enough to break down the carpet."

"I guess so."

"When you had the room cleaned, did they do anything with the chair?"

"They didn't need to. Just the bloodstains over there by the bed."

"And the fingerprint powder," she said.

"Yeah, that, too."

Lena knelt down to examine the seat cushion, then flipped it over and studied the other side. When she found what she was looking for, she returned to the chest and opened the second drawer. She thought she remembered seeing it yesterday, but wanted to make sure—not the underwear of a girl, but the lingerie of a woman. It hadn't registered until now. The sheer bras and panties wouldn't have had any meaning to her before she'd seen the nude photos of Lily on her bed.

"What kind of a girl was she, Mr. Hight?"

He didn't respond. When Lena turned to check on him, she caught him staring. Not at the contents of the drawer—from his angle he couldn't see what she held in her hands. Hight was staring at her. At her legs and hips and then up to her chest until he reached her face and realized that she had been watching him measure her. Being caught in the moment didn't appear to faze him.

"What kind of a girl was Lily?" she repeated.

"Lily was everything they said she was and more. She was full of life. A dream come true."

"Did she see boys?"

"Most girls her age see boys."

"Was she involved with anyone?"

He paused to catch himself, but not soon enough. Lena saw through it.

"No one that I'm aware of," he said in a quieter voice.

"I'm curious about her best girlfriend. What was her name?"

"Julia," he said. "They were like glue."

"Julia Hackford—that's it. How come she didn't testify at the trial?"

"I asked about that."

"Who did you ask?"

"First Cobb, then Bennett and Watson."

"And what did they say?"

Hight shook his head. "Julia didn't know anything. There was nothing she could do to help."

"She lives close by, doesn't she?"

"Right around the corner in the blue house. Why?"

Lena didn't answer the question and moved to the bedside table. The drawer was filled with pads and pens and knickknacks—things that she had seen yesterday when they were searching the house for the gun. But what she was looking for now would probably be hidden in the back—something else that she would have glossed over before see-ing the nude photos in the murder book. As she fished through the contents, she spotted the small tube of K-Y jelly behind a deck of play-ing cards, then returned everything to its place and closed the drawer.

"What about Lily's cell phone?" she said.

Hight paused a moment, and Lena noticed something in his eyes—a spark, a glint—something that she hadn't seen before.

"What is it?" she asked.

He shrugged her off. "We looked for that phone everywhere. When Cobb spoke with the service provider and they agreed to help, he told us that he had everything he needed and we could stop."

"Did he ask you to keep the account open for a while?"

"Just in case somebody used it, but no one ever did. I checked the bill every month. No one used it to make or receive a call. Cobb told us Gant took it and threw it away."

"But that's not what came to mind when I asked the question, is it?"

"What does any of this have to do with what happened at the club? When am I gonna get my car back?"

"What were you thinking when I asked about Lily's cell phone?"

He gave her a long look, his face reddening. "Her account," he said. "Not the phone, but her account. It's still open."

"You call the number," Lena said quietly. "You listen to her voice."

Hight steadied himself against the doorjamb. As Lena looked him over, she sensed that she was witnessing something important. Hight keeping his daughter's cell-phone account open was anything but strange. She knew that most people who had lost a loved one did exactly the same thing. Most people wanted to call the number and listen to the outgoing message. They wanted to hear their loved one's voice. And they didn't need the phone to do it—just the account and phone number.

But Tim Hight wasn't like most people.

She wondered why he was doing it. She wondered if he didn't see it as some kind of punishment. Or if he wasn't lost in some sort of psy-chotic denial.

Her cell phone started vibrating. When she pulled it out of her pocket and saw Vaughan's name on the touch screen, she slid the lock open with her thumb.

"I've got something," he said. "Where are you?"

She could hear the excitement in his voice. The punch.

"What happened?" she said. "What is it?"

Vaughan covered the mouthpiece. The sound became muffled and she could hear him telling someone to close the door. When he came back on, his voice was quieter.

"I figured out why Cobb called Bennett first. They've got a history, Lena. They go way back."

25

L ily Hight and Jacob Gant.

The girl was sexually active, a willing partner—but there was also a certain kink to it. A kink to Lily. To Gant. To them. One that included nude snapshots and phone sex in a chair by the window every night.

And one that may have included Lily's father watching them from the darkness . . . and doing what?

The thought, the depravity, sent chills up Lena's spine. But even worse, how could Cobb have missed it? And what about Bennett and Watson?

The elevator opened and Lena started down the hall toward Vaughan's office. Within a few short steps, she became aware of someone shouting and realized that it was Steven Bennett's voice. Lena picked up her pace and turned the corner. Bennett was inside Vaughan's office with the door closed, and Vaughan's assistant wasn't at her desk. Lena noted the steam from a hot cup of tea by her computer—she must have just left. When she caught a glimpse of the newspaper on the desk, she rolled the chair away and moved in for a closer look.

It was today's edition of *The Los Angeles Times*, and by all appearances, two journalists had written an article on the Jacob Gant trial singling out Bennett, Watson, and Higgins as complete incompetents. According to the banner above the headline, this was part one in a series that would run for the next fifteen weeks.

Worse still, the article had been set above the fold on page one and ran through most of the first section of the newspaper. On page three, photographs of Lily Hight, Jacob Gant, and Johnny Bosco were encircled by cutout photos of Bennett, Watson, and Higgins, but also by the chief administrator and commanding officer of the crime lab, Howard Kendrick, a man Lena had only met in passing. Beside the graphic a large arrow pointed to pictures of both Lena and Vaughan, set above the caption: *District Attorney Jimmy J. Higgins & Company run for cover after serving up a fresh pair of scapegoats, or are they just the latest victims?*

Lena dropped the newspaper back on the desk.

If Higgins truly hoped to glue Vaughan's face to the scandal, it wasn't going to work. The DA and his protégés had been outed and would be circling the drain for the next fifteen weeks. But far more important to Lena, the series would boost Tim Hight's reputation as a father who did what he needed to do in killing Gant. Unbeknownst to the journalists, their examination and criticism of the trial would damage her case against Hight and hurt everyone.

Bennett raised his voice and began shouting at Vaughan again. Without hesitating, Lena pushed open the door and walked in on them. Bennett snapped his head at her, his face a deep purple, the veins in his neck jutting out thick as rope.

"Get the fuck out of this room," he said.

Vaughan banged his fist on the desk. "You need to chill, Bennett. Pull yourself together. No one's out to get you."

Bennett rubbed his hand over his scalp and appeared stunned, even crazed. Ignoring Vaughan, he charged across the room and didn't stop until he was in Lena's face. It took all her strength of will to hold her ground.

"I knew the two of you would fuck this up," he said.

Bennett looked like a man who was drowning. He was spitting the words out of his mouth, his lips were quivering, his cheeks dripping with perspiration. She could see the panic in those emerald-green eyes of his—rage mixed with fear.

Snake eyes.

"I knew you'd fuck it up," he said again. "You're talking to all the wrong people. You're asking all the wrong questions. You're fucking up my life."

Vaughan looked like he'd had enough and approached from the side. "Nobody's fucking up your life, Steven. You're gonna have a heart attack. You're gonna kill yourself, and it's not worth it. Get out of my office and calm down."

Bennett was still ignoring him, still zeroing in on Lena with his tail standing on end. He was easily a foot shorter than her, but meaty and strong. He took a step closer—nose to chin. Lena kept her eyes on him, her voice soft and easy and steady as a train on a new set of tracks.

"What's next, Bennett? You gonna hit me?"

At first, he acted like he didn't hear her or didn't understand what she had just said. But after a few seconds, he mouthed the words "fuck you" at her and took two steps back. Vaughan moved in beside Lena, with Bennett now glaring at both of them.

"Fuck you both," he said. "Just do your fucking jobs. Just do what you were told to do."

He stormed out of the office. As he passed the assistant's desk, he saw the newspaper, crushed it into a ball, and started punching it. Satisfied that the newspaper was dead, or at least mortally wounded, he kicked the desk chair and ripped the phone out of the wall—in a rant and repeating the words "Do your fucking jobs" over and over again through clenched teeth. When he finally caught his breath, he backed away from the desk like a madman and ran down the hall.

Vaughan turned to Lena. "You see today's paper?"

She nodded, but kept quiet.

"Let's get out of here," he said.

26

They walked through the park beside City Hall and found a bench underneath the trees. Across the street on the corner, the safety barrier between the sidewalk and construction area was being removed from the new building that would soon become LAPD headquarters. A handful of landscapers were planting palm trees along the curb while another team of construction workers power-washed the steps.

On the way over, Lena had brought Vaughan up to speed on what she had learned at Hight's house and the conclusions she was ready to make. She had given him a detailed picture of exactly where they stood, including Cobb's visit to her house last night. Vaughan didn't take it very well, but finally agreed that antagonizing Cobb any further wasn't in their best interest, at least in the short term.

"His case against Jacob Gant was based on a lie," she said. "Gant was not stalking Lily Hight. Cobb's first move was in the wrong direction."

"But I'm going through the trial, Lena. The transcripts, the video. What about Gant's anger? What about the messages Cobb pulled off the girl's service? Bennett and Watson read them in court."

"Gant said that they had a fight. It lasted for two weeks and then they made up. What if it's that simple? And Hight was never asked to provide an alibi, Greg. He was never a suspect. His story was never checked out. Never verified."

"You think Cobb knows he screwed up and that's why he's acting this way?"

She turned to him. "Do you think Bennett thinks he screwed up the trial?"

"I get it," he said. "Like that case on Long Island we talked about last night. They don't make mistakes. Everybody else does."

"You said they go way back."

Vaughan removed his jacket and loosened his tie in the heat. "When Bennett first came to the DA's office, he needed help, a detective with experience. Cobb gave it to him. They liked working together and became friends. I get the feeling Cobb was something of a mentor to him early on."

"Barrera told me that Cobb used to work out of Robbery-Homicide. Something happened, but he didn't want to talk about it."

"I didn't put it together until last night. When I got in this morning, I went online and started to remember things. Then I made a few calls."

"Remember what?" she said.

"They worked a lot of cases together. They had a lot of success."

"Okay, so what went wrong?"

"They worked together and then they stopped. Seven or eight years ago—around the time Higgins got into politics."

Lena tried to make the leap, pressing her memory for a murder case that stood out, but nothing came to mind. Vaughan gave her a look.

"It was a drive-by shooting in Exposition Park," he said. "A woman walking her grandson in a stroller by a vacant lot on Western Avenue. I think it was across the street from the library on thirty-ninth. Both were dead before the cops arrived."

Lena thought it over. Eight years ago there were a lot of drive-by shootings in L.A. But that probably wasn't the reason for her faulty memory. Her brother had been murdered eight years ago, and she had taken some time off.

Vaughan leaned closer, his voice becoming more gentle. "Elvira

Wheaten," he said. "The infant's name was Shawn. They didn't walk into the crossfire between two gangs, Lena. They were gunned down intentionally. Wheaten was trying to clean up the neighborhood and had a target on her back. Higgins was running for DA and needed headlines. By then, Bennett was his boy in the office. I'm surprised you don't remember."

"Me, too," she said.

"There was an eyewitness. A kid in his early teens. Wes Brown. He helped Cobb and Bennett identify the shooters in the car, but refused to testify against them in court."

Something about hearing Wes Brown's name seemed familiar. After a moment, she realized what it was. The young teenager had made headlines, too.

"Wes Brown was murdered," she said.

Vaughan nodded. "Three months after the trial and Higgins took office. Brown didn't testify in court. His identity was kept secret. The shooters never knew who made the initial ID, but somehow they got to him just the same. Three months later Brown was dead."

"But Higgins won the trial."

"It would have been a slam dunk with Brown's testimony, so he and Bennett had to work harder. I was in the office then. I remember them sweating it out—the trial and the campaign. But Higgins got his guilty verdict, milked it in front of the cameras, and ended up winning the election."

"And Bennett and Cobb had a falling out because Cobb couldn't get Brown to testify."

Vaughan nodded again. "Makes sense when you think about it. Bennett's not the kind of guy who would have cared about Brown's fear. He probably blamed Cobb for putting their case at risk and jeopardizing Higgins's campaign. Things happen when there's a lot on the line. Higgins took some heat when Brown was murdered as well. That wouldn't help mend any fences."

"So, Cobb loses his friend," she said. "His best connection in the DA's office."

"I think there's a divorce somewhere after that. Money issues. Darkness."

"Bennett didn't need him anymore."

"Until Lily Hight was murdered and Cobb got the case. Then it became the same thing all over again."

"Higgins wanted a third term, knew he needed headlines and another big trial to win. And Bennett wanted to look like a hero so he could run four years from now. All of sudden, they needed Cobb again."

Vaughan smiled at her. "When you asked Cobb for the murder book yesterday, who's he gonna call?"

"Steven Bennett," she said. "His on-again-off-again new best friend. The guy who can bring him back to the top."

"It's almost the same thing, only this time it didn't work out. The trial blew everything down."

"That and today's newspaper," she said. "Where's your car?"

"In the garage. Why?"

"Want to take a drive with me out to the crime lab?"

"What is it?" he said. 'What's up?"

"I want to take what's left of Lily Hight's clothing out to Orth."

Vaughan gave her a look and nodded. "Let's do it."

"Meet me at Parker in fifteen minutes," she said. "Wait in the VIP lot and stay with your car."

27

S he could see it now.

The entire case against Jacob Gant hinged on the DNA evidence taken from Lily Hight's body and underwear. For Cobb, Bennett, and Watson, the match to Gant convinced them that they had their killer. When the samples went missing in the lab, along with the victim's panties, Paladino was able to convince the jury that the lab results presented at trial couldn't be trusted because it was no longer possible to back them up.

You need verification, he would repeat over and over again. If you can't verify, then you can't vilify. And that means you can't convict.

Lena had seen the lab reports in Cobb's murder book. Although Paladino knew how to play a jury, she had no doubt that the semen samples the lab retrieved and analyzed were righteous—no doubt that the semen came from Gant and the results were reliable. But just like everything else, if Gant had been telling the truth, his semen should have been found with the victim. It didn't necessarily prove innocence or guilt to the beating and murder, and had no meaning other than what it was. Had Lily been raped and murdered after Gant left, everything would have looked exactly the way it did.

But for Lena, the case hinged just as much on the estimated time of death.

It was a small window—less than two hours long—with nothing tangible to back it up. From what she could tell, the calculation was based less on science or physical evidence and more on the statements made by Jacob Gant and Tim Hight. The time line began when Gant claimed to have left her and ended when Hight said he found her. The case hinged on that window because both men had been there.

Lena walked through the basement at Parker Center and gazed through the plate-glass windows into the property room. The storage facility was one of two in the system and had the look and feel of a dilapidated bank. There was a man filling out a form at one of the two tables by the door. Another waited at the counter, watching a female clerk—an old woman—log in his package behind the beige wire mesh. Lena knew that both men were detectives, but didn't recognize either one as she entered the room.

No one looked up. Still, she kept her head down and turned her back as she stepped over to the second table and began filling out a property request card. She knew that the evidence was tracked by computer. Anyone paying close attention would notice and could bring trouble for both her and Vaughan. But somehow she managed to push her fears aside.

She wasn't looking for blood, semen, or even saliva because they wouldn't be there. The crime scene photographs indicated that Lily's jeans and boots had been tossed into a pile three or four feet away from where the victim's corpse had been found.

What Lena needed were skin cells. The kind found beneath the surface of the killer's hands that would have been exposed if he stripped away Lily's jeans and boots with any force.

Force was the key issue—the main ingredient—because the cells needed to be alive at the time of the murder. Without force there wouldn't be enough DNA to detect a transfer.

As Lena completed the request card, writing the case number down and signing her name above her badge number, she couldn't help but think about the odds. It might have been the right thing to do, but it was a long shot. Even getting Martin Orth to agree to perform the tests was a long shot. It would mean working in secret, jeopardizing his career and putting himself at risk at a time when the crime lab was under so much scrutiny.

And for what?

She should have told Vaughan the truth. She should have told him that what came next was pure desperation. That this is what you did when you ran out of road—hoped that your victim's killer had been amped up enough to leave skin cells.

She turned to the counter and looked at the old woman behind the wire mesh. One of the two men smiled at her as he left the room. The second detective was dropping off an evidence packet. When he walked out, Lena slid her request card through the slot and waited while the clerk adjusted her glasses and entered the case number into a computer.

"Lily Hight," the old woman said finally. "Her daddy got the guy. What do you want with this?"

Lena saw suspicion growing on the clerk's face, her antenna rising out of what looked like a bad wig. She didn't need to justify her request, nor did she have any desire to. At the same time, the case could have been flagged and she didn't want the old woman to pick up the phone.

"Just cataloging evidence for my boss," she said, feigning drudgery. "More reports. More paperwork. You know how it is. I was hoping it hadn't been moved over to Piper Tech. That's all I'd need today—another drive across town in this heat."

The old woman bought it and grinned at her. "Got it, honey. Everything's still here. I'll be right back."

Lena watched the clerk walk down the long aisle and disappear around the corner. The storage room behind the counter was enormous and it would probably take a while.

It was the waiting that she found the most difficult. Standing in a room with plate-glass windows and a view of the hall outside. The fact that so many people were walking by. The basement corridor was the quickest route between the building and the parking garage across the street. Lena checked her watch, realizing that it was almost noon. When she looked up, she saw Barrera and Deputy Chief Ramsey and turned back to the counter. When the door opened behind her and she heard Barrera's voice, the dread hit her in a flash like dragon's breath.

"Gamble?"

She pulled herself together and turned. Barrera was holding the door open with Ramsey behind him in the hall. She didn't have time to think about what she was still showing on her face.

"Just wanted to give you a heads-up," he said. "That piece-of-shit gossip reporter's out. Dick Harvey. He was released this morning. It sounds like he blames you for his arrest and wants to get even. I wouldn't spend too much time watching TV."

Lena could hear footsteps behind her—the old woman starting back down the aisle. Timing was everything if life. She took a deep breath.

"Great," she said. "Thanks for the tip."

Barrera took in the room, picking up on something, then shaking it off. Lena was waiting for him to say something like, what the fuck are you doing in here? Instead, he told her to keep an eye out for Harvey, called him a rotten piece of shit again, and closed the door.

"That the boss, honey?"

Lena turned around as Barrera and Ramsey walked off. The old woman was standing behind the wire mesh holding an evidence box. She nodded at her and watched as she unlocked the window and pushed the box across the counter.

"Yeah," she said. "That's the boss."

28

It wasn't a very large box. As Vaughan pulled out of the lot heading for the freeway, Lena cut through the tape with a key and opened the carton. Inside she found an inventory of the contents and checked to see that everything was there. The girl's jeans, her boots, a belt, and a pair of socks—it didn't add up to much. A note attached to the list indicated that what remained of the teenager's other clothing—her T-shirt and blouse—had been frozen and placed in the vault at the lab because both items contained blood evidence from the victim's wound.

Vaughan reached the freeway and shifted lanes, steering the car east toward the San Bernardino Freeway. "If it's possible that the killer's DNA was transferred to her clothing, why didn't they send it to the lab before the trial?"

"I'm sure they did."

"Then why are we doing it again?" he said.

Lena tried not to show any doubt. "Because they weren't looking for what we're looking for. Think about what they already had. Gant's semen. His saliva. Why waste time and money when they already had everything they thought they needed? It wouldn't have made sense after they locked Gant in. They had their man."

"Right," he said. "I keep thinking that they knew about the lab screwup before the trial, not one week in when it was too late. But this clothing has been handled. It would have been examined for hair and fiber. The lab would have gone over every inch, looking for bodily fluids. After that, it was thrown in this box and sent to storage. What could be left?"

Lena didn't say anything; she was still wrestling with the same question.

What could be left?

She turned and looked out the window. The air was no longer transparent, the city barely visible through the brown haze. According to a weather report she had heard on the drive into town, the city would break another record as temperatures climbed to 117 degrees. She wondered when the heat would break—and when the case would break.

The drive out to the crime lab only took another ten minutes. As Vaughan parked, Lena glanced at the sign and admired the building. Officially named the Hertzberg-Davis Forensic Science Center, the new crime lab was set on the campus at Cal State University and housed the LAPD's Scientific Investigation Division as well as the Sheriff's Department Scientific Services Bureau. The facility was capable of handling evidence from more that 140,000 criminal cases every year—the people who worked here were dedicated to their jobs. The fact that the evidence went missing in one of the city's biggest cases was more than unfortunate for everyone.

Lena hadn't been out to the lab since the verdict. As she followed Vaughan into the building, she sensed something was wrong before they got through security and reached the elevators. It was the same odd feeling she had experienced yesterday morning as she entered Parker Center. When they found Martin Orth in his office and he looked up from his desk, she could see the concern in his eyes. He glanced at the evidence box she was carrying, then looked back at her. Was it concern? Or was it fear?

"What's going on, Marty?" she said.

He grimaced, pushing his chair away from his desk as he stood up. "Take a look across the hall," he said.

Lena turned with Vaughan and gazed through the glass window at the two men in the conference room. Howard Kendrick, the chief administrator of the crime lab, was seated at the table watching the second man pace along the far wall while talking to someone on his cell phone. Lena didn't recognize him. Although he appeared to be somewhere in his late fifties, it was obvious that he still worked out. He was sturdy and tall with wiry hair that had been dyed an unnatural reddish brown and looked like it might be a piece. His face appeared frozen, his rough skin stitched so tight across his cheeks, she couldn't get a read on him.

"Who is he?" she said.

Vaughan answered for Orth. "Jerry Spadell," he said in a quiet voice. "A former investigator with the DA's office. A shadow from Higgins's past. A goon."

Orth gave Spadell a last look, then shut the door and returned to his desk. "He might be with Higgins, but Bennett sent him over."

"What is it?" Lena said. "What's going on?"

"That story in *The Times.* They want us to go through the lab again and see if we can find those DNA samples that went missing. It's all for show."

Vaughan leaned against the windowsill. "Kendrick agreed?"

Orth nodded. "For what it's worth, I've never thought that we actually lost them. Just that someone mislabeled them. That's why it's a waste of time. The samples are invisible. You could be staring right at them and still not see them."

Lena pushed the evidence box across the desk. "We need a favor."

Orth read the label on the carton—his eyes changing as they passed over Lily Hight's name. When he opened the box, Lena started to say something but he waved her off.

"I already know what you want, Lena. The timing's not so good right now."

"It's a big favor," she said. "An important favor."

He met her gaze, mulling it over. "Let me ask you a question first," he said finally.

"Anything."

"Yesterday you had one of our guys dust Lily Hight's bedroom for prints. I'd like to know why."

She paused a moment, worried that she might have misread Orth. It was possible that he might not be the ally she thought he was. That he was about to repeat everything Barrera had said to her last night—that she was scaring the shit out of everyone. That her request to dust the room bordered on the ridiculous—and in the end, Steven Bennett was right. Just do the job you were asked to do. Get Hight for the double murders at Club 3 AM, and let go of the past.

She glanced at Vaughan, then back at Orth. "We had time to kill," she said. "Paladino was doing a press conference on the front lawn. We couldn't get out."

"But the crime scene was at Club 3 AM, not the house."

Lena shook her head. "There's something about the girl's room that's not right. I found things that shouldn't have been there. And there's something wrong with her father that has nothing to do with what happened the other night. If I wasted everybody's time, I won't apologize because I'd do it again, Marty. If someone has a problem with that—if someone complained—they should have called me, or even Barrera, not bothered you."

"No one complained," he said. "But you might want to stop by the Latent Print Section when you get a chance. I just got a call. They finished up this morning. Your reports should be ready in another hour."

Lena studied Orth's face, suddenly aware that she had missed something important. It wasn't criticism that the SID supervisor had in mind. Instead, she sensed an undercurrent of support. For some unknown reason, Orth was on their side and had every intention of—

"What did they find?" she asked.

Orth glanced at the door, then turned back to her and lowered his voice. "Jacob Gant's fingerprints," he said. "All over the room. The closet, the dresser, every handle on every drawer. And they're fresh prints, Lena. They're exceedingly clean. No doubt about it—Gant was in that room within the last two weeks of his life. And he was looking for something. You got any idea what it might have been?"

29

She didn't know what Gant had been searching for. But whatever it was, it probably got him killed. . . .

Lena scooped up Johnny Bosco's keys, slipped the chain-of-evidence form into her briefcase and left the building. While Vaughan had been anxious to get back to his analysis of the trial, she had spent the past two hours screening additional security videos pulled from Club 3 AM with a forensic analyst from the Photographic Unit. The analyst, Henry Rollins, had examined every image recorded that night.

Unfortunately, nothing had changed.

Tim Hight, a man who made his living working with cameras, had managed to avoid every lens in the building. The fire escape on the north side of the structure remained a blind spot and the most likely point of entry.

But Rollins had also given Lena an update on the street cam photo that captured Hight driving away from the club that night. The resolution of the image had improved significantly. To Lena, the shadow on the passenger seat was beginning to take on definition and look more like a gun than a flashlight. While Rollins agreed, he wasn't ready to commit and said that the enhancement process would give them a definitive answer soon.

After reviewing Jacob Gant's fingerprints for another hour with an analyst from the Latent Print Section, Lena was out of time and had to move on.

There could be no doubt that Gant had been in Lily Hight's bedroom within the past two weeks, and that he had entered and exited the room through the window. Lena remembered the tree outside, and wondered how often Gant made the climb while Lily had been alive. How many nights he'd spent in her bed.

For reasons she couldn't explain or even support, Lena's first thought upon hearing the news from Orth had been that Gant was looking for the girl's cell phone. But hiding a phone was different than hiding a photograph in a memory box. If the phone had been in the bedroom, she didn't think it could have remained hidden for so long. Too many people had been looking for it. An entire year had gone by. But even more, how could the victim have even managed to hide it? The killer had delivered a mortal blow. Once the screwdriver was driven into her back, nothing else could have occurred but death.

Yet, Gant had to have been looking for something. Something important enough to risk breaking into the house.

Tim Hight's house. Lily Hight's bedroom.

Lena crossed the street to the garage and got into her car. She hadn't had a chance to load the CD player or deal with her cell phone so she flipped on the radio and toggled down to 88.1 FM, a jazz station out of Long Beach. After adjusting the volume, she realized that she had dialed in at just the right moment and that the audio system in the car was worth the price of admission. She could see the playlist on the video display—the FM station was dedicating the next hour to Coleman Hawkins. Even better, the first cut was something she hadn't heard since her last case.

"Mighty Like a Rose."

As she pulled out of the garage, she let her thoughts drift down the road with Hawkins's sax and wished that Paladino's office was more than a twelve-block ride.

30

The law offices of Buddy Paladino occupied the twelfth floor of a
high-rise building on the 400 block of South Hope Street in downtown Los Angeles. The view from Paladino's desk encompassed the
entire city, included Dodger Stadium in the hills to the north, and
stretched out over the basin all the way to the beach. As Paladino offered Lena a seat and flashed that million-dollar smile that had become
the defense attorney's trademark, she noted the quality of his suit,
his manicured fingernails and close-cropped hair, the simple but ele-
gantly understated gold watch. The office itself followed the same basic
floor plan as the oval office in the White House. As far as Lena could
tell, the only difference was that Paladino had more money, didn't
have to justify what he spent, and had an interest in art rather than
politics.

Lena sat down on the couch facing the windows and gazed at the
sun hovering over the ocean. The fiery globe had turned red again as it
burned through the clouds of carbon monoxide, washing out Paladino's
entire office in a bright crimson light.

"I can't help but express my disappointment," he said in a smooth
and quiet voice. "Jacob's death could have been prevented. The LAPD

should have seen it coming. They lived next door to each other. Neither one could afford to sell their homes in this economy. It looks like the department dropped another ball, and it's gonna cost them. And it looks like Mr. Tim Hight's gonna get a big bill, too."

"We haven't made an arrest, and you've already started working on a civil case against Hight?"

Paladino settled into a chair, completely at ease. "You've been around long enough to know that the line between here and insanity is as thin as a thread, Lena. People cross it every day—back and forth like somehow it's okay now. There's something about that guy I find disturbing. The man's out there looking in."

"Then we can't talk?"

He didn't reply, but she could see him thinking it over.

"We need to talk, Buddy. As far as I'm concerned, this conversation isn't taking place and I'm not here. You've probably already guessed that we may even be on the same side. But that can't happen without your help."

Paladino remained quiet for several moments. When he finally spoke, he was gazing at the bands of scarlet light rippling up and down the wall, but only seeing his past.

"I was thinking about something," he whispered. "Something that happened a long time ago when I was in law school. My roommate had a good relationship with his father. His dad knew that we didn't have much money, so once a month he'd stop by and take us out to dinner. He was a very wise man—more than most—and I was jealous that I didn't have a dad just like him. One night he took us out for steaks and beer, and he said something I'll never forget. He told us that we needed to keep our eyes open. That there are a lot of nice people in this world— lots of nice people—but that doesn't mean they're good. Good is special. Good is very rare. You might only meet one or two, three or four, in your whole life. That's why you've got to keep your eyes open. You can't afford to miss one."

His eyes drifted away from the wall and lingered on her.

"Will you help me?" she asked. "Will you talk to me?"

He nodded slowly, and seemed ready and pleased to help. "What do you need to know?"

"Lily Hight's image," she said. "The way she was presented to the public versus the way she may have really been. They don't seem to jibe."

Paladino smiled at the memory. "They don't, do they? It made things difficult for both sides during the trial. A very delicate situation."

"Tell me about it."

"Lily may have only been sixteen, but she had a voracious appetite for sex. She liked it, and she liked Jacob. She had something going on. I never met her, so I can't really say. But you hear about women like her. The kind that can put a spell on a man. Jacob was infatuated with her."

"Why did it make the trial difficult? Why didn't you bring any of this out? You must have seen the nude shots of her that they pulled from your client's computer. It would have gone a long way in proving that Gant wasn't stalking her."

Rays of deep red sunlight struck Paladino in the face. Shielding his eyes, he got up and crossed the room to a glass display case. After retrieving what appeared to be a commemorative mug, he sat down on the second couch with his back to the window—the outline of his body aglow in crimson light.

"You've got to remember that Gant's trial had three parts, Lena. Everything that happened before the trial had just as much impact as everything that happened in the courtroom. Bennett and Watson set the table by introducing Lily to the public with family snapshots and home videos. And they did it well. Lily was seen as her father's daughter—completely virginal and full of life. A child like everybody else's child, the kind of child everybody wished they had—with one big difference. This child—this beautiful teenage girl—had been raped and murdered by a monster. Lily was presented as the ultimate victim—but always coupled with the terror that what happened to her could happen to your child, too."

"Bennett and Watson rode the wave of public opinion."

"They *planted* it. They cultivated it. And it worked. Lily's image as an innocent was forever defined. I had seen what happened when that Hollywood gossip show—what's it called?"

"*Blanket Hollywood,*" she said. "Dick Harvey."

"That's it. He's got a Web site, too. I had seen what happened early on when Harvey put it out there that maybe Lily and Jacob were having an affair."

"What happened? How did it play?"

"Her image as an innocent was already carved in stone. And she was dead. She couldn't defend herself. That's how martyrdom works. No one wanted to hear about what *might* be the real Lily Hight. What Bennett and Watson did worked like Teflon. Anything you might say that conflicted with that image bounced off and made Lily appear even more innocent . . . more vulnerable. Anyone pointing a finger at her—anyone who attempted to disturb that image—became a bad guy. Even Harvey understood that he had to switch directions and work the fallacy."

"What you're saying is that you couldn't afford to lose the jury."

Paladino shook his head. "I'd already lost them. We had always claimed that Lily and Jacob were seeing each other. That Jacob's semen was there because they had made love that night. That Lily was a willing partner. No one on the jury wanted to hear that. Juries see a dead body, hear the words DNA, and something happens in their heads. It's like they snap. It's like they can hear God talking to them."

"So, the jury never saw the nude photos."

"Three months before the trial everyone thought Jacob had taken those pictures from his window. But SID proved that the camera had been in her bedroom. All of a sudden, Jacob's claim that Lily had given him the photos could be substantiated, so no—the photos were kept away from the jury by both sides."

Cobb had managed to leave this information out of his murder book. Nowhere in any report was it mentioned that SID had confirmed that the nude photos had been taken by Lily Hight, and that Jacob Gant had been telling the truth.

Lena let the thought go and gave Paladino a look. Until now he had been holding the mug with both hands wrapped around the base. As he passed it over, she could see images of Lily Hight's face on the front and back, along with the words, IS JUSTICE REALLY BLIND? The mug had been part of the pretrial frenzy that engulfed the city, along with the T-shirts, posters, and wall paintings by street artists.

"You see what I'm saying, Lena? How do you beat what you're holding in your hand? The answer is, you can't beat it. No one can. The jury pool wasn't poisoned. The jury pool had been turned into drones. The louder you bang, the less they hear."

"You were losing this case," she said.

He nodded and flashed that smile at her again. "Big time. We had no chance. You want something to drink? A cup of coffee, tea, anything?"

"If you have coffee, sure."

While Paladino picked up the phone, she set down the mug and walked over to the window. The sun was just settling into the ocean. After a few moments, Paladino joined her and they watched as the city was transformed from a deep red to a dusky blue.

"Did Harry Gant tell you why your client was with Johnny Bosco?" she said.

Paladino nodded. "They thought they knew who really killed Lily. That's all he told me. That's why I called you."

"Okay, so what about Hight and his daughter? You took a big risk with the jury and floated the idea that he molested her. Your spotters confirmed that they didn't want to hear it. Were you fishing or did you have something real?"

Someone tapped on the door, then opened it. A middle-aged woman dressed in a chef's smock pushed a cart into the room. As Lena walked over, Paladino thanked the woman and she made her exit with a slight bow. On the cart, beside a coffee urn and two cups and saucers, were small bowls of white and brown sugar, several varieties of chocolate chips and mints, and a small pitcher of cream.

Paladino poured a cup and passed it to her. As he poured another for himself and returned to the couch with her, he said, "I wasn't fishing, Lena. At the same time, I can't confirm it for you. Hight's relationship with his daughter seemed unusual to me. Almost like it was too close for comfort. From what Jacob told me, Lily fought it and struggled with it like any other teenager would or should. What struck me was something Jacob told me he'd seen a week before the murder."

"You're shooting straight with me, right, Buddy? This isn't some kind of play?"

Paladino met her eyes and held the gaze without a word as he sipped his coffee.

"Okay," she said finally. "What did Gant see?"

"It was on a Friday night. Lily was struggling to get out of the car and ran into the house. Hight chased her inside."

"So what?"

"Jacob thought it looked like Hight was touching her in a way no father should. It was during the struggle in the car. The door was open."

"Touching her where?"

"He thought it looked like he was trying to kiss her—like he was grabbing her chest—but it was only an impression. He told me that he couldn't be sure."

"Those houses are right next to each other," she said. "Why couldn't he be sure?"

"Hight's driveway is on the other side of their house. There's that oak tree and it was dark. Jacob was sitting in a lighted room reading a book. Eyewitness testimony is shaky enough at noon from ten feet way. You know that as well as I do."

"But they were friends. They were doing it. Why didn't he make sure she was okay?"

"They were having problems—those voice and text messages he left over those two weeks were real. It took him a while to rise above all that. When he did, he went over but the car was gone. No one answered the door. The next day he saw her with her girlfriend and she looked fine. Things were still awkward. Nothing had changed between them, so he never had the opportunity to ask her what happened."

"Her friend being Julia Hackford. She never appeared in court."

"She didn't have anything to say. I got the impression that she and

Lily hung out together but didn't share much. That's another reason why I thought something might be going on with Hight. His daughter never really talked about her home life. Not with Hackford. Not even with Jacob. According to Jacob, she deliberately avoided it."

"So, you floated the idea at trial and pulled back."

Paladino moved over to the chair and picked up the commemorative mug. "My hands were tied. I couldn't present an alternative theory without hurting my client. Our backs were up against the wall."

"Until the DNA evidence went missing."

"That's right," he said. "Then everything changed. That's why I said that there were three parts to this trial."

"How did you find out the evidence went missing?"

"An anonymous tip. It came in at the end of the first week. I didn't really trust it, and we had already conceded that the semen belonged to Jacob. But I spent the weekend thinking it over. Not about how the lab might have misplaced the samples. I was more concerned about why. Why do you suppose that the only evidence that went missing was the evidence that pointed to my client? Everything else was still there. The blouse and T-shirt with Lily's blood, the screwdriver that became the murder weapon, the blood samples that the SID tech mishandled and dropped in the driveway outside their van. Why did the crime lab only lose evidence that pointed to Jacob?"

"You know that you could look at it another way, right, Buddy?"

"How's that?"

Lena shrugged. "You said it yourself. Your back was against the wall. The prosecution was killing you in one of your biggest cases. Your client's life was at stake. But you were the one who benefitted most by what went wrong at the lab, not them. So maybe you're responsible."

Paladino laughed, then got up and opened a cabinet. Inside, Lena could see a small bar that included a wine rack. Paladino selected a bottle of scotch and offered her a glass. When she shook him off, he poured a drink for himself and took a small sip.

"I knew it could break our way," he said. "But I wasn't there yet. I still wanted to know why. And I was no longer willing to concede that the semen they found was Jacob's. I wanted an independent lab to take another look."

"Which was your right, but impossible because the samples were gone. When you made the request in court, how did Bennett and Watson take it?"

"They said they weren't aware of the mishap, but I could tell that it was an act. And they were scared. Not where it shows, but underneath where it counts. When I saw that, I became even more suspicious."

"What do you think of them?" she asked.

Paladino took another sip of scotch, mulling it over. "Not much," he said. "Would it be too crude to say that Bennett can't keep his dick in his pants?"

Lena smiled. "It's only a rumor that they're having an affair."

"Only a rumor? Come on, Lena. The district attorney's office keeps a suite over at the Bonaventure so that they don't have to drive home during trials. I needed to talk to Bennett about a discovery issue a month before we got started, and was told that he and Watson were at the hotel having lunch. When I called the front desk, my call was redirected from the restaurant to the suite upstairs. Watson answered. You know how you can tell by the tone of someone's voice that they're laying down?"

"Yeah."

"Well, Watson was on her back."

They laughed together, but only briefly.

"I saw it as an asset," Paladino said. "The two of them being distracted like that was good for our side. I'm just surprised Bennett stayed with her this long. Despite his wife and kids, I've always read him as the kind of guy who thrives on variety. The kind of guy who can't go deep and needs a cheerleader by his side to keep telling him he's not an asshole."

Paladino's words lingered—his irritation for the man and his resentment were obvious. Lena went with the vibe and could see Bennett and Watson thinking that their slam-dunk case was set on automatic and had plenty of fuel. She could see them taking everything for granted while feeding on the media attention, the spotlight, the public's approval and good wishes. She could even see them fucking each other at the Bonaventure and thinking that this high-profile trial would push them over the top.

But in the end, Paladino was right. Steven Bennett couldn't go deep.

The defense wanted an independent examination of the semen found on Lily's body, and the two deputy district attorneys couldn't produce the evidence. And then everything began to unravel. Paladino saw his opening. But even more, Paladino saw the end. Jacob Gant wasn't on trial anymore. Bennett and Watson and the LAPD were.

Lena could still see Paladino standing behind his client in the courtroom. Still see his hand on Gant's shoulder. Still hear his smooth voice laying it out for all to see . . .

If you want to say somebody did something and get that printed in a newspaper, you need at least two sources to say it's so. That's what it takes to get a story printed in a newspaper. Two sources to say it's so. But we're not talking about a story in a newspaper. We're here in this courtroom today talking about matters of life and death. And what we need right now are two sources to say it's so. What we need right now is verification. If you're gonna put a young man away for the rest of his life—if you're gonna stick a needle in his arm, steal his life away and put him to death—you need to know exactly what he's done. You can't think you know, you can't hope you know, and you can't weigh the odds and make a best guess. You need certainty. Absolute certainty like the world is round and the sun rises in the east. You need verification. If you can't verify, then you can't vilify. And that means you can't convict.

"You okay, Lena?"

Her mind surfaced. Paladino had moved to the other couch and was looking at her with concern.

"I'm fine," she said. "I was thinking about something."

"You're not fine," he said. "The way I see it, you've got a big fucking problem. One that I can't help you with. Lily Hight was raped and murdered by a monster. He's still out there. And everybody in the DA's office knows he's still out there."

She wasn't sure if she heard Paladino right. "What are you saying?"

"Higgins, Bennett, Watson—they know, Lena. They've always known. Jacob Gant was innocent. They knew that before the trial."

A beat went by. Then another, more corrosive than the first. She gave Paladino a hard look. His smile was gone and she could tell that this wasn't a play or some kind of test. It was the reason that he had agreed to meet with her. The reason he had agreed to talk. As the implications began to surface, she tried to find her voice but it came out broken and scuffed.

"What you're saying is crazy, Buddy."

"Actually, I would have used the word *insane*."

He got up and walked over to his desk. When he returned, he passed a file to her from across the table.

"We didn't just ask for a polygraph, Lena. We begged for one. When they kept refusing, I hired someone to perform the test. Someone I thought carried weight with the department. Someone I thought the district attorneys office would listen to. Someone everyone trusts."

Lena ripped open the file and skimmed through the report. When she saw that the polygraph had been performed by Cesar Rodriguez, that feeling of dread became overwhelming. Until his retirement last year, Rodriguez had been known as the best forensic psycho-physiologist in SID. In the midst and horror of the Romeo murder case a few years back, Rodriguez had been hand-picked for the job of weeding out the innocent from their list of suspects.

Paladino may have been saying something, but Lena wasn't listening anymore.

She was reading the report, chewing up the results in big, horrific chunks. Rodriguez had asked Jacob Gant fifteen questions. And in each case Gant's answers showed no signs of deception. The questions were specific and included everything anyone would have needed to know. After examining the data, she paged back to Rodriguez's conclusions: Jacob Gant was in love with Lily Hight. He was angry and jealous for two weeks, but for only two weeks. He had made up with her on the afternoon of her death. He had made love with her early that evening.

And never once had he ever hurt her, hit her, raped her, or stabbed her. When he left her that evening, Lily was alive and standing in the kitchen.

Had Lena been handed the results of this polygraph, she would have cut Gant loose and never thought about him again. Any detective she had ever worked with would have done the same thing.

She looked up from the report at Paladino. He was trying to rein in his anger. Trying to cope with his rage and hold everything in. Still, it was there—underneath, where it counts.

"You showed them this report?" she said.

"Yes," he said quietly. "I sent all three of them copies."

"When?"

His jaw tightened. "Six weeks before the trial."

31

They'd known . . .

Lena walked out of the Rite Aid at Fifth and Broadway, ripped open a pack of Camel Lights, and lit one. As she drew the smoke into her lungs, she could feel her body resisting. But it wouldn't work. Not tonight. She took another hit, bigger this time, then released the smoke and climbed into her car. After jacking the AC all the way up, she cracked open the window and reached for her cell phone.

They had known that Gant was telling them the truth. They had gone to trial knowing that they were prosecuting the wrong man. An innocent man. Someone who had lost his mother in a homicide at the age of fourteen. Someone who had lost a second time with the rape and murder of Lily Hight. Someone who should have been cut loose and held free of suspicion. Someone who had gone through enough and deserved to be handled with care.

And then there was the malignancy. The blowback. Everything that cut to the bone.

Because of them and only them, Jacob Gant had been someone who'd spent the last six weeks of his life being chased and beaten by packs of angry dirtbags. Because of them, Gant had been someone who ended up dead in a nightclub bathroom with both eyes shot out of his head.

Someone with a soul. Someone trying to find the real killer. Someone lost in the wind.

Lena took another drag on the smoke, the main wheel in her gut making the turn of turns.

Paladino had sent Higgins, Bennett, and Watson the results from Gant's polygraph six weeks before the trial. By now Lena knew enough about all three of them to understand how it played out. Like Paladino had said, what happened before the trial had just as much impact as what went on in the courtroom. Higgins, Bennett, and Watson had seen the media frenzy, the city swept up in emotion over Lily Hight's murder. They had worked the press corps hard. Although interviews had been ruled out by the judge, their message was ever-present and they remained the subject of countless news stories in print and on radio and TV.

But now they were faced with admitting that they had committed the fuckup of all fuckups. Gant didn't do it, and they had the wrong man. If the keepers of the keys kept a list of the biggest fuckups in the city's grand history of fuckups, all three of them would have been catapulted to the top of the list—shoo-ins to make the Fuckup Hall of Fame.

She could see them sweating it out. She could see Higgins working with his consultants to come up with some sick plan. All three standing at the edge of the cliff and staring at the rocks below. All three sitting on top of the fuckup list.

Lena could see it.

They were too far in to pull out. Too far gone to fess up.

A moment passed. A long one. She noticed the cigarette burning between her fingertips, took a last hit, and flicked the butt onto the street. Sliding open the lock on her cell, she found Vaughan's number at the office and made the call. He was still there, and picked up on the first ring. But when she began to give him an update—when she began to give him the news—he cut her off in a voice that sounded more than strange.

"I can't talk now," he said. "Let me call you back. Five minutes."

He hung up before she could even say okay.

Lena sat in the car, trying to keep her imagination at bay. She was parked in a metered space on West Fifth Street with plans to drive out to Johnny Bosco's place in Malibu for an initial look that she should have done yesterday. It was getting late, but she didn't want to move until Vaughan called back. Except for the pharmacy on the corner and the Mexican place across the street, most of the businesses on Fifth had already lowered their security grilles. Magic hour had passed two hours ago and the city was making its transition from the people with jobs who inhabited its streets during the day to the people with shopping carts who roamed the sidewalks at night.

She held everything in and waited, sipping bottled water and trying to keep her eyes off the clock on the dash. When Vaughan finally called back, his voice still sounded off and she realized that it was fear.

"Something's happened, Lena. They went through my office when we were out at the crime lab. They went through everything."

Lena closed her eyes. "What did they take?"

"That's the problem," he said. "I can't tell. I have video from the trial. The transcripts. Background notes. Some of Bennett's files. The trial map and supporting evidence. That's all still here, but in what form? I haven't had time to go through everything. If they took something small—a letter or a report—there's the chance I'd never know."

Lena noticed the background noise from Vaughan's phone—the sound of a bus lumbering up the street. Vaughan had left the office to call her back using his cell.

"Where are you?" she said.

"Outside the building. There's something wrong with the phone in my office."

"You think they're listening?"

He paused a moment and she could hear someone he knew say hello in passing. When Vaughan came back on, his voice was still peppered with anxiety.

"I found something in the handset," he said finally. "I left it there.

I'm no pro, but I'm sure they've planted more than one. What am I missing, Lena? This has got to be about more than a couple of asshole deputy DAs blowing a trial."

Lena didn't reply, searching for the best way to tell Vaughan what she was thinking. The math was simple. It began with Cobb—the way he slapped together the murder book and the information he chose to leave out. She remembered the way Watson had looked at her in the meeting room and now realized that her read on the woman had been all wrong. There was Bennett's outburst in Vaughan's office today. The bug Vaughan found in his phone. And then there was that goon they saw at the crime lab this afternoon—Jerry Spadell, supposedly launching another search for the missing DNA samples. All these separate events working in concert had to be considered, then cut against the fact that every one of them knew Jacob Gant had passed a polygraph and the case never should have gone to trial.

Lena could guess how it added up.

It was all about darkness now, keeping everything hidden and lost. And now it was about survival as well. In the end, Lena decided to tell Vaughan everything she knew.

32

Cobb took a big bite out of his second chicken taco, squirting guaca-
mole and taco sauce all over the Bud Light sign hanging in the window. After washing the taco down with just maybe the best sweet tea
he had ever tasted, he wiped the spill off the sign with his thumb and
gazed through the glass.

He was inside a hole-in-the-wall Mexican place called El Rancho—
on his tired feet and using the Bud Light sign for cover.

Gamble was talking to someone on her cell. She'd been parked in
front of that Rite Aid for more than twenty minutes—burning gas on
her way to nowhere. Cobb had been following her ever since she left
Parker Center. Although he had no clue what went down in Buddy
Paladino's office, it had enough octane to it that Gamble's first move
was to buy a pack of smokes.

Cobb was just across the street. So close that he could count her
eyelashes from here—read the tea leaves and tell her future from here.

All things being equal, she lit up that Camel like she needed it.
Cobb took it as a sign that she was on the ropes. That the fucking
new deal was having a bad day and couldn't make the cut. That he had

guessed right about her—that he had known who she was the minute he set eyes on her.

He finished the taco and tossed the paper wrapper in the trash. When the girl behind the register asked if he wanted another, he checked on Gamble's status and ordered two more to go. Then he returned to his place behind the Bud Light sign and peered up the street.

Loser No. 2 was in a white van parked one block up on the other side of Broadway. He, too, had been following Gamble ever since she left Parker, but was unaware of Cobb and looked too stupid to figure it out.

All the same, Cobb found the man curious. He was a busy little guy in a sweat-stained suit. And he wasn't just keeping an eye on things. He was shooting video of Gamble. Cobb glanced at her still talking to someone on the phone, then looked back at the van. Every once in a while he could see a reflection in the rear window, the kind made when headlights from a passing car spike a camera lens hidden behind tinted glass.

Cobb had caught a glimpse of the little guy's face when he parked the van outside Paladino's office. He seemed familiar, but Cobb saw the cuts and bruises on his left cheek and kept drawing blanks. Either way, Loser No. 2 looked like a dickweed.

He heard the girl behind the register call out to him. Tossing two bucks and change on the counter, he grabbed the bag and moved to the door. When his eyes zeroed in on Gamble, she was just switching on her headlights and looked ready to roll.

It was okay, he told himself. As long as his knees didn't lock up, he had plenty of time.

He waited for her to pull into the street, then walked as fast as he could manage over to his Lincoln parked two cars back. Before jumping inside, he gazed down the street and found her car in traffic. West Fifth was a one-way street with access to the 110 Freeway. She was shifting lanes and heading for the entrance about four blocks ahead. He could see the white van just pulling in behind her.

Cobb tossed the bag of tacos on the passenger seat, jerked his car

into traffic and made the green light at Broadway. Within a few minutes he was cruising three cars behind the white van on the 110, travel-
ing south. Traffic was heavy and tight, no one moving over 50 mph.
Gamble had remained in the right lane and was making the transition
to the Santa Monica Freeway for a return trip to the Westside. Cobb
settled back in his seat, keeping his eyes on them and trying not to let
his mind wander.

But he couldn't pull it off. He couldn't get Buddy Paladino out of his
head. Gamble had spent the better part of two hours in his office. Why?
What could they have said to each other that took so much time?

He played through a list of possibilities in his head. None of them
worked in his favor. He wolfed down those tacos, thinking everything
over from different angles and breaking into a sweat. Images of his own
demise surfaced—some of them violent and bloody. Images of being
tortured flashed though his mind as well—accompanied by mass quan-
tities of pain. By the time he came out of his trance, he could see Gamble
and Loser No. 2 peel off the freeway, heading north on the Pacific Coast
Highway. He slowed some, giving them room as they passed through a
number of signal lights. But then the road cleared, and Gamble picked
up speed. It was a sudden burst of motion, like a jet at the end of a run-
way thrusting forward to reach air speed.

The white van dropped back and finally pulled over and gave up.
Cobb tried to keep his eye on her taillights, but she was stretching the
car out—a V6 with 280 horses and 254 pounds of torque—he'd looked
it up.

She must have spotted them. She must have known that they were
there. She must have decided to end it once she found enough road.

Cobb checked his speedometer. He was doing ninety and still couldn't
carry her bags. He wanted to hit something. Smash something. When he
looked back at the road, her taillights had vanished into the night. She
was gone.

33.

Johnny Bosco's house in Malibu was on the 29000 block of Cliffside Drive overlooking Dume Cove. It was a big modern job on a narrow lot, the rooms put together like blocks, the exterior painted three or four shades darker than the sand the blocks sat on. As Lena made her approach, she noticed a gold Chrysler 300 in the drive and passed the house by.

She had expected Bosco's place to be empty. She wasn't sure why because it made more sense that someone would be here. Still, it threw her.

She turned the car around and kept things slow, taking another look. The lights were on in the room closest to the water, and she could see the flicker from a television in the same room. But that was about it. The rest of the house remained dark, and no one had bothered to turn on the exterior lights.

Lena pulled into the drive and got out. She could smell the ocean in the cooler air and was grateful for the breeze. As she walked up the steps, she noticed that the front door had been left partly open. The door was made of glass, the view limited to the foyer. But she could hear two men talking over the sound of the TV, and rang the doorbell.

She waited a good ten seconds. When no one responded, she opened the door and noticed that the men had stopped talking and the TV had been turned off. She called out in a firm voice, identifying herself as a police officer. When the men inside switched off the lights, she backed out and returned to her car.

She moved with determination and purpose.

She grabbed the flashlight out of her briefcase, and wrote down the plate number on the Chrysler. But when it came to making a call for officer assistance, she hesitated. Malibu was serviced by the Sheriff's Department, not the LAPD. The station was a long way off in Agoura Hills. If their response began from there, it would take them too long to get here. She thought it over for all of about five seconds. Then she made the call and gave the deputy Bosco's address.

After that, it was play as you go.

She jacked the slide back on the .45, moved up the steps, and entered the house. For several moments she didn't move, letting her eyes adjust to the darkness and trying to quiet her rapid breathing. Once she settled down, she listened to the house and concentrated on the silence. Her flashlight was small enough that she could hold it against the grip of her gun. She switched it on, moving through the foyer quickly.

When she hit the corner, she noted the open floor plan and realized that Bosco's house had been ransacked. She could see CDs and DVDs strewn all over the couch and coffee table. While the kitchen remained undisturbed, the contents of a closet beside a large flat panel television had been dumped on the floor.

The two rooms took up most of the first floor, faced the ocean, and included a massive fireplace. Lena worked her way through the darkness. The silence remained steady and true. But when she reached the staircase, she sensed something had changed, and stopped.

She could hear the waves crashing against the rocks below the cliffs. The sound seemed too loud and too clear.

She turned around, bolting through the living room. One of the sliders was cracked open. Switching off the flashlight, she looked outside and saw two men running across the lawn. The property extended all the way to the edge of the cliffs and was fenced in.

Lena raced off the terrace into the yard. Both men were peeking over their shoulders and appeared panic-stricken. She could hear their deep and rough breathing. She could see their short and choppy steps. When they finally reached the wooden fence, they made a leap for the top and used their feet to help push them over. Unfortunately for both, they were big men—too big for the climb.

Lena switched on the flashlight and raised her gun.

"Stop," she said, "or I'll shoot."

The two men froze—still hanging from the top of the fence with their feet dangling above the ground. It was dark and windy. A dog was barking from somewhere in the neighborhood. Lena moved closer, shining the flashlight on them and measuring them. Several moments passed before one of the men finally spoke, his voice strained.

"I can't hold on any longer," he said. "I need to drop down."

"Me, too," the other one said.

"Then drop," she said. "Drop and turn around with your hands raised. And think real hard about what you're doing. You guys pull anything, you're both dead."

She stepped back far enough to give herself room if she needed to fire her weapon. She hoped that they weren't stupid. Hoped that they wouldn't force her to do something she didn't want to do tonight. She watched them drop to the ground. It was all of about two feet, but they had to steady themselves against the fence. And they were taking too much time doing it.

"Turn around," she said. "And raise those hands."

They hesitated. Lena could feel her heart pounding.

"I said, raise those hands."

Time ticked by. She couldn't see their hands. They were stupid. They were fucking around. She pulled the trigger, driving a .45 slug into the fence one foot above their heads. Both men almost leaped out of their skins. Then slowly, as the sound of the gunshot faded over the ocean, both men raised their hands and turned around.

Lena's heart almost stopped.

It was the district attorney of Los Angeles standing beside that goon he'd brought back from the dead. Jimmy J. Higgins and Jerry Spadell. And the ocean breezes hadn't been very kind to Spadell. That bad dye job turned out to be a cheap toupee after all, and it was flapping up and down on his buffed head like a bird with a broken wing.

Higgins took a step toward her. "Lower your gun, Detective. This farce is over."

Lena grimaced, feeling the anger well up from a place so deep inside her that she wasn't sure she could control it. Higgins was two or three light years past being a piece of shit. She jerked the muzzle at him and he stopped.

"I'll tell you when I'm ready to lower the gun, Mr. District Attorney. Let's go into the house and talk. Same rules apply. You guys do anything stupid, and I'll shoot."

Her body was going numb, the situation over the top. But she could tell that she wasn't showing it. Her voice didn't break and her hands were rock steady. She turned to Spadell, who seemed too quiet. He was staring at her with those eyes he'd brought back from the other side. And he was a scary-looking guy when you got this close—mean and rough.

"Do you realize what you're doing?" Higgins said, shaking with fury. "Do you understand who I am?"

Lena jerked the .45 at him again. Spadell's eyes were still on her.

"Do what the woman says, Jimmy. Let's go inside and talk."

Higgins hesitated—thinking it over and incensed—but finally started walking back to the house. Spadell fell in line, with Lena keeping a safe distance. As they passed through the slider and entered the living room, Lena switched on the lights and steered them over to the fireplace.

"Okay," she said. "Now put both hands on the mantel and take two steps back."

"I'm the fucking district attorney, you bitch."

"I know exactly who you are," she said. "Now lean against the mantel and step back."

Spadell gave Higgins a look. "Do what she says, Jimmy. Do it."

The two men grabbed hold of the mantel and stepped back until their bodies were at a forty-five-degree angle to the floor. Lena wasn't too concerned about Higgins, but she knew Spadell would be carrying so she frisked him first. She found the piece holstered behind his jacket—an old .38 that had the look and feel of a throw-down gun.

"Is this thing registered?" she said.

Spadell shook his head. "I don't remember."

"Somehow I didn't think you would."

He looked back over his shoulder and winked at her. Lena slipped the revolver into her jacket, patting him down quickly and tossing his keys and wallet on the floor. When she found a case containing a set of lock picks, she slipped it into her pocket with Spadell's gun. Moving over to Higgins, she took a moment to reel in her anger before frisking him as well. Higgins remained livid, his neck and face swelling out of his shirt collar like a hot-air balloon in the middle of a long burn.

"So, what were you doing in here?" she said.

"Fuck you," Higgins said.

Lena ran the barrel of her .45 between his legs, knocked the muzzle against his balls, and watched him take it. She couldn't believe what she was doing or who she was doing it to. Couldn't believe what was roiling through her veins.

"What were you doing here?" she repeated.

"Bosco was my friend," he said, his voice seething. "I left something here. We were looking for it."

Lena glanced at the way they'd tossed the room. "Oh, yeah?" she said. "Did you find it?"

Too exasperated to speak, Higgins shook his head.

"What did you leave? What were you looking for?"

"Stuff," he said. "Personal stuff. It's none of your fucking business."

"Did you use a key to get in?"

"Of course we used a key."

"Where is it?"

"I think I left it on the table by the door."

Lena smiled, but there was no pleasure in it. "That's what I would have done, too," she said. "Only there isn't a table by the door here."

"Then maybe it fell out of my pocket when we were in the back-yard."

"Maybe that's what happened," she said. "The key fell out of your pocket when you were running away. If you had a key, why were you running away?"

He stammered. "I have no fucking idea."

"I agree," she said. "You don't have a clue."

Lena had already tossed his wallet and keys on the floor, but felt a large roll of cash in his pants pocket. Higgins flinched slightly as she wrapped her hand around the money and pulled it out. It was a roll of fresh hundred-dollar bills—the same kind that Johnny Bosco used to keep in his pocket before he was shot in the back. She went through the cash as quickly as she could. Higgins was carrying five grand.

She grimaced at the discovery, then picked up his wallet and opened it. Inside she counted three twenties, two fives, and ten ones. It didn't take much to put it together. The district attorney of Los Angeles had found the five grand in Bosco's house and stolen it.

"You're so dead," he whispered through his teeth. "So fucking dead."

Lena dropped the wallet on the floor. "You need to watch what comes out of your mouth, Higgins. Especially when you're speaking to a police officer holding a gun. Things can happen."

"But you're not gonna be a police officer after tonight."

"Turn around," she said. "And keep it slow."

Higgins and Spadell made the turn and looked at her holding the gun on them. A long, dark moment passed. Lena had never entertained more than her share of bad thoughts before tonight. She'd never spent too much time thinking or fantasizing about revenge. But in this moment she could feel a certain joy overtaking her anger and disappointment for who Higgins turned out to be. She could see herself pulling the trigger and dumping both bodies off the cliff. The problem was that they were big men. Too big to get over the fence.

"Pick up your things," she said. "Grab your stuff and get out."

Higgins had his eyes on the roll of cash she was holding.

"That's my money," he said.

"Not anymore, Higgins. Tonight it's the price of admission. Five grand in one-hundred-dollar bills. Now get the fuck out of here."

"Your ass is grass, bitch. You understand what I'm gonna do to you?"

Spadell gave Higgins a jab with his elbow. And Lena didn't care about who Higgins was or what he thought he could do to her. She watched them pick up their keys and wallets, and noticed Spadell hesitate slightly when he saw that she had kept his case of lock picks. He gave her a look without saying anything. The Grim Reaper was a quiet man.

Lena stepped back to let them pass. She could hear a siren in the distance. The Sheriff's Department on their way.

While she waited, she looked at the CDs and DVDs tossed all over the couch and coffee table and tried to make sense of what had just happened.

What had Higgins and Spadell been looking for?

Her eyes moved to the DVD player. It was playing something, but the TV had been switched off. She looked around for the remote, found it on the floor, and hit the POWER button. When an image rendered on the screen, she understood what she was seeing, but not why.

Higgins and Spadell had been screening video recorded by the security cameras at Club 3 AM. Each frame included the camera's location, along with the time and date. Curiously, the date on these images went back nearly fifteen months.

Lena ejected the DVD, noted that it was labeled with a Sharpie, and slipped it into the paper sleeve she found on the player. She skimmed through the DVDs stacked on the coffee table. Each one was labeled the same way. When she checked the dates, she realized that every week was accounted for from eighteen months ago to the present.

But why?

As she began to gather up the DVDs, she heard footsteps in the foyer and turned just as a pair of deputy sheriffs burst into the room with their guns raised. The one on the right looked young and nervous and began screaming at the top of his lungs.

"Stop," he said. "Or I'll fucking shoot."

34

Lena rolled past the gate at Club 3 AM and pulled around the building. The place was closed tonight with only two cars in the lot. It was a safe bet that the Toyota pickup belonged to the guard she'd just passed, and that Dante Escabar drove the Ferrari.

As she parked and walked up the steps around the fountain, it felt like she was on a timer.

Once the sheriff's deputies had cooled down, she identified herself and told them that she had walked in on a robbery. She left most of their questions blank, claimed that she didn't see the intruders but thought that the DVDs in the living room might be related to her own investigation. It wouldn't help though. Because the Sheriff's Department serviced the address, getting the DVDs into Henry Rollins's hands at SID would not be seamless. It could take time. And it could become complicated. Because celebrities were involved, privacy issues could surface and attorneys representing the club could slow things down. But even more, at a certain point in the very short term, Deputy Chief Ramsey would be calling her. Given the story Higgins was probably telling him, there was the chance that Ramsey might become aggressive and have her picked up.

She reached the top step and found Escabar holding the door for her. After she entered, he pulled the door closed and locked the place up. Then he led her into the bar and offered her a stool.

"How's your night going?" he said. "How's business?"

She could hear the sarcasm in his voice, and watched him step behind the bar and pour a bourbon over ice. He was wearing black leather pants, and his hair was pulled back into a ponytail. Even in the dim candlelight, his face seemed paler than the other night and it looked like he wasn't getting much sleep.

Lena grabbed a stool and sat down. "I just caught the district attorney of Los Angeles burglarizing your dead partner's home in Malibu."

Escabar smiled at the thought. "What was he looking for?"

"You tell me."

"Could have been anything."

He reached for his pack of cigarettes. Beside the pack Lena noticed a 9-mm Glock with the safety switched off. She watched him light up, then return the pack to its place beside the gun.

"You staying?" he asked. "You want something to drink?"

"No thanks. I'm on a short leash tonight."

He met her eyes and pursed his lips. For a brief moment he seemed amused.

"Does Higgins spend a lot of time here?" she said.

"He isn't a regular, if that's what you mean. Once or twice a month. Sometimes more."

Lena gave Escabar a long look. "They weren't really friends, were they?"

He took a drag on the cigarette and shrugged.

"Come on, Dante. Bosco and Higgins weren't friends."

Those pursed lips were back. "I guess you could call it a matter of convenience."

"But that's all over now," she said. "That's why you left the cocaine upstairs. You hate Higgins. Anything you can do to embarrass him, you'll do."

She had been thinking about it on the drive over. Higgins breaking into Bosco's house could only mean one thing. Escabar's gun on the bar felt like verification.

"Let's just say that we come from different worlds," Escabar said. "I don't need Higgins the way Johnny did."

"It's obvious that your partner had something on him. And now Higgins is searching for it. He was going through video taken from your security cameras here at the club. DVDs that your partner kept at home. Did Higgins use drugs? Is that what Johnny had on him? Video of Higgins doing coke?"

"I can't answer that because I don't know."

"Why are you holding back?"

Escabar glanced at his gun and lowered his voice. "Because the world is a scary place, Detective Gamble. Because crime is what the powerful say it is. You could be a Wall Street motherfucker who stole fifty billion dollars—but that's okay because the government says it is. Shit, they'll do everything they can to bail you out. But try stealing a frozen dinner from a market on Pico Boulevard because you're starving to death. If it's strike three on a three strike count those fucking assholes will put you away for twenty years and use it as a cheap talking point to get into politics. So don't ask me about holding back. Crime is what the man says it is. Nothing more and nothing less—and I don't have Johnny's clout. Things are different now."

Escabar's voice faded into silence. There was a certain sadness to it.

"Are you afraid of Higgins?" she asked. "Has he threatened you in some way?"

"Not at all. I just don't want to get chewed up in the grind."

"If you're not worried, why is that gun on the bar?"

He shrugged without an answer, then took a bigger pull on that glass of bourbon.

"Why did Bosco keep security videos at his house?" she said.

"You sure ask a lot of questions, Lena Gamble."

She coaxed him on with a look.

"Because of our clients," he said finally. "Because they're celebrities. We need a record of what happens in the public areas of the club. It's like an insurance policy. Johnny had backups made and moved them to a second location, just in case something happened here like a fire or another earthquake. He probably should have put them in a vault somewhere, but he didn't."

"Higgins was searching through the last eighteen months."

Escabar gave her a look like he didn't know or couldn't guess what that meant.

"Are the DVDs at Bosco's house a complete backup?" she said.

"Johnny handled that, not me."

"But everything's here, right?"

"Sure," he said. "What are you getting at?"

"Just two questions," she said. "Two loose ends. You respected your partner. You admired him. Your life changed when you met him and he gave you a job. Johnny Bosco was bigger than life. An L.A. success story. The front man for a club that catered to everybody who's anybody in the business. An exclusive club where people with clout met other people with clout. So, why would he have risked any part of his world and agreed to help Jacob Gant when everyone in the city thought Gant murdered Lily Hight and got away with it? Why would Johnny Bosco have agreed to help Gant when the result would have embarrassed the district attorney and everyone connected with the trial? Like you said, their relationship may have been only one of convenience. But that doesn't mean it wasn't necessary. Because Gant was involved, because a teenage girl is dead, Higgins would have been embarrassed publicly with no way back. So tell me, why was your partner willing to put everything on the line?"

Escabar remained silent, his wheels turning. "Are you trying to say that Gant didn't kill the girl?" he said finally. "That Johnny knew?"

Lena nodded slowly. From the look on his face, she could tell that he was hearing it for the first time. Something shocking enough to deaden nerves. But she could also see him putting it together. The next logical step.

If Johnny Bosco knew that Jacob Gant was innocent, so did the district attorney.

"How can I help?" he said.

"The security videos we found tonight are probably gonna be tied up for a while. I need to know what's on them. Maybe it's nothing. Maybe it's more than that. Maybe it's a lot more than that. But you're here every night. You know everyone involved better than anyone else. I'd like you to go through your footage and let me know what you find. I'm gonna guess that you'll know what it is when you see it."

"You want me to start eighteen months back?"

"I'm more concerned about the month leading up to Lily Hight's murder. After that, sure, make a pass through all eighteen months. I need you to work quickly though."

"I understand," he said. "I'll do it for Johnny."

He killed his drink, and Lena could tell that he was still tossing something over in his mind. As she studied his face, she wasn't sure that she could trust him. And when it came to Higgins, she still thought that he was holding out on her. But she didn't have much choice. Not with her cell phone vibrating in her pocket. It was after 11:00 p.m. and she could see her supervisor's name flashing on the touch screen. Somehow she doubted that Barrera was calling just to check in.

"You cool?" Barrera asked.

His voice was stuck in neutral. She couldn't get a read on him.

"I'm good," she said.

"You need to come in, Lena. We're burning the midnight oil down here. Sixth floor, Deputy Chief Ramsey's office."

"I'm on my way."

"Good," he said. "Sooner is better than later."

35

Ramsey's door was open, the overhead lights switched off, his office illuminated by a couple of table lamps spread about the room. Lena tried not to show any surprise when she saw Vaughan sitting at a small meeting table. Ramsey was behind his desk watching Barrera type something into a notebook computer. She had expected to see Higgins, but he wasn't here.

Ramsey pointed to a chair without saying anything, his steel blue eyes pinned on her. The silence was overwhelming. The weight of the air made it hard to breathe. She glanced over at Vaughan, who nodded at her almost imperceptibly. As his eyes moved slowly but deliberately across the room, Lena followed them to the phone on the credenza behind Ramsey's back. The line light was burning. Someone was listening over the speaker phone. She didn't think that it would be Higgins. And while it might have been Chief Logan, still on the East Coast recruiting students for SID, it could easily have been something much darker. She took a quick look around the office, wondering if Internal Affairs had hidden a camera somewhere.

Ramsey leaned over his desk. "Mr. Vaughan has already informed us that Jacob Gant passed a polygraph six weeks before the trial. Did Paladino use one of his people?"

"No," she said. "One of ours."

"Who?"

"Cesar Rodriguez."

Ramsey grimaced like he'd just eaten bad food, then rubbed his hand over his shaved head. As Lena gazed at his rough face, he seemed both worried and amped up—a combination that on any other night would have made him all the more frightening. But not now—not with so much on the line.

"Well, let's have it," he said. "What happened in Malibu, Gamble?"

She decided not to dwell on the consequences and just get it out of her system. Tell them what happened and worry about defending herself later. She got out of the chair and started emptying her pockets on Ramsey's desk. Her voice was low and scratchy, but didn't crack.

"The district attorney broke into Johnny Bosco's house with the help of a man named Jerry Spadell," she said. "They used this set of lock picks to get past the front door. I wasn't there long enough to see how they beat the alarm system. But Spadell looked like the kind of guy who could handle the job. I found this .38 on him and I don't think that it's registered. I found five grand in Higgins's pocket. I think it's Bosco's money, and that the district attorney stole it from the house."

Ramsey traded looks with Barrera. "Higgins didn't mention the money."

"I didn't think he would," Lena said. "When I identified myself as a police officer through the front door, both he and Spadell tried to make a run for it."

"He didn't mention that either," Ramsey said.

Lena sat down at the table with Vaughan. She couldn't get a sense of where things were going. She had expected her termination to be quick and decisive. Expected to hear Ramsey's smoked-out voice raging in her ear. No matter what the circumstances, she had fired her weapon at the district attorney. Most politicians have a thing about being shot at. It's not just a matter of form.

Ramsey got to his feet, glancing at Lena and Vaughan as he moved to the window. "Okay," he said. "Here's my take. The city is in fucking strife over the murder of a teenage girl. Not only did we blow the fucking trial, we got the wrong fucking guy. And now the wrong fucking guy and another guy with clout are both fucking dead. Aside from what's happening with Higgins and his bullshit band of clowns, that pretty much sums up where we're at, right?"

Lena glanced at Vaughan and they nodded.

Ramsey turned to Barrera. "You ready?"

Barrera gave him a look, then spun his computer around. "You're being followed, Lena. Dick Harvey's been on your back all day. And he's shooting video. It's on the Web, and it's on TV. Every part of your day until tonight when you lost him on the Pacific Coast Highway."

She remembered seeing a white van, but not the driver's face. Something about the van had made her feel uneasy, so she'd decided to give the new car a run once she found enough road.

Barrera pointed to the monitor. The *Blanket Hollywood* Web site was broadcasting her day with commentary by Harvey. The shot of Lena entering Buddy Paladino's office seemed to be playing over and over again with pictures of Lena and Paladino matted in graphic boxes over the building. Harvey's wild speculation was just as endless. When the Web site cut to a shot of Lena talking to Vaughan on the phone from her car, Vaughan's picture faded up beside Lena's.

"How did he know Lena was talking to me?" Vaughan said.

Ramsey waved his hand through the air, indicating that he wanted the computer shut down. "Harvey knew it was you because he hired a lip reader. Gamble used your name."

Vaughan traded looks with Lena, then turned back to Ramsey.

"How much of what we said did he get?"

"Not enough to reveal what you two were up to," Ramsey said. "Most of the time Gamble's mouth was below the dashboard. But I heard enough to know that this shithead is a real problem. And it's been my experience that guys like this don't stop. They just keep coming. Harvey wants to think that he's been wronged. He spent that night in jail convincing himself that he was wronged. He's itching for a lawsuit and the publicity that would come with that. So both of you guys are on notice, okay?"

Vaughan nodded again. Ramsey pushed Spadell's revolver aside and sat on the edge of his desk.

"Now I want to talk to Gamble alone," he said. "If you guys would excuse us."

Lena watched Vaughan and Barrera get up and head for the door. Vaughan turned back to her and shot a look of support her way, but Barrera closed the door. And then she was alone with Deputy Chief Albert Ramsey. Alone and waiting for him to deliver the blow. He was still seated on his desk, still staring at her with those hard eyes of his.

"I saw you smoking a cigarette on Harvey's Web site," he said finally. "Where's the pack?"

She patted down her jacket and found the pack in her pocket. Ramsey tapped a cigarette out and lit up with a lighter he kept in his top desk drawer. He took a hard first pull on the thing, then paused a moment before he blew out the smoke.

"You gonna have one?" he said to her.

Lena shook her head. "No thanks."

Ramsey sat down at his desk and pulled the trash can closer. After tapping the ash into the can, he turned and gave Lena another long look.

"Higgins said that you hit him in the balls with your gun tonight."

Lena felt the pull in her chest and struggled to find her voice. "I just gave him a tap," she said finally.

"Why?"

"He'd lost his focus. He needed to know that I was there."

"You ever do that kind of thing before?"

"No."

"Then why did you do it tonight? Give me the real reason, Gamble. No bullshit. I've got X-ray vision. I'll see through it."

Lena moved to the window. She could see their new building. Tonight it was all lit up and looked like a work of art.

"Why'd you do it, Gamble?" Ramsey repeated. "Higgins is the district attorney."

"Because I was angry," she said, looking him in the eye. "Because they took Jacob Gant to trial for no reason. Because they didn't have the brass to back out and say they were wrong. Because I could see Gant's dead body on that bathroom floor with two bullets in his head. Because the guy who murdered Lily Hight is still out there. I was thinking about a lot of things, Chief."

Ramsey took another deep pull on the cigarette. "Let me see your piece," he said.

Lena drew her gun from its holster, gave it a quick check and passed it over. Ramsey ejected the mag and examined the weapon.

"Why do you carry a .45?" he asked.

"I like it."

"Higgins told me that you fired a shot into the fence just above their heads."

"I didn't know who they were at that point."

"I understand that. But when you figured it out . . . when you saw Higgins and Spadell standing in front of you with their hands raised . . . when you were thinking about what they did to Gant and you had all that shit in your head—I want to know whether or not you thought about shooting them. Did you, Gamble? Did you think about putting them down?"

She hesitated, guessing that Ramsey was hoping to trap her. When she finally nodded, something bloomed across his ruined face. Confirmation of some kind. She wondered when he would get to the part where he asked for her badge. It felt close.

"What stopped you?" he said.

"I'm a police officer. I took an oath."

Ramsey jammed the mag into her gun and passed it back to her. She wasn't sure what was happening anymore. She walked back to the window, steadying herself against the sill.

"Okay," he said. "So they went to trial knowing that they were prosecuting the wrong man. Now they're doing their best to cover everything up. But why do you think Higgins was at Bosco's house? What's he looking for that a security camera could pick up?"

She had asked Escabar the same question. Stray thoughts surfaced like how the mob had been able to keep J. Edgar Hoover, the director of the FBI, in their pocket for so many years. As it turned out, they'd managed to take a photograph of Hoover performing oral sex on another man—his assistant at the FBI and his longtime companion. The more she'd thought about it, the more sense it made. Johnny Bosco wasn't a mob figure, but would have had similar needs. He ran Club 3 AM, a place where on any given night, a VIP could be driven to excess, get into trouble and need a free pass. Higgins already had a reputation for keeping celebrities, even trust fund babies, out of jail. It had come up during Lena's last case when a TV actor driving drunk crashed his Land Rover, killing his friend in the passenger seat. It had come up even more recently when countless actresses charged with possession walked away free and clear.

"What do you think, Gamble? What's Higgins looking for?"

"I can't say with any certainty, Chief. But he's been keyed up about that pile of coke we found from the very beginning."

"And about Bosco's reputation with drugs," Ramsey said.

"He worked on you, and he tried the same thing with the medical examiner during the autopsy."

"What's Higgins doing at an autopsy?"

"That's what I mean," she said. "It's unusual."

Ramsey flashed a wicked smile. "He's using," he said. "And Bosco recorded it. He wanted something on Higgins just in case he ever needed to force the issue."

"It's possible," she said. "Escabar told me that Higgins shows up just short of once a week."

"He's a casual user. And Bosco was his provider. Bosco would've given him the shit for free to get that kind of an insurance policy." Ramsey crushed the head of his smoke inside the trash can. "What about Tim Hight? How close are you to putting him in the murder room at the club?"

"SID found blood on his shoe. Enough to work with. We should have the results soon."

"But you've got nothing on him for killing his daughter."

"Not yet."

"Other than the fact that the sky's falling and you're the one holding the bag, you got any other issues, Gamble? Anything I should know about?"

"Dan Cobb," she said. "He's in this thing with Bennett. They've got a history. They go way back."

"Vaughan told us about it before you got here. I know Cobb. I remember when he used to work here."

Ramsey pulled another cigarette from Lena's pack and lit up. When he noticed the light on the phone, he stared at it for a long time, then switched it off. Several moments passed in silence. As he joined her by the window, she could see him taking in the breadth of the city and thinking it all over. More time passed before he finally spoke, his voice low and raspy and shot for the night.

"There comes a point in every decent cop's life when they've gotta do what they've gotta do," he said. "That point started for you tonight. It started in Malibu when you stood up to an asshole like Higgins. I only wish I'd been there to fucking see it. I hope I dream about it tonight. I hope I see it in color. You get my drift, Gamble?"

"I think so," she said quietly.

"I want you and Vaughan to keep going. I want you to take it as far as it goes."

She met his eyes. Her head was spinning.

"Let the chips fall?" she said.

Ramsey nodded. "Let 'em fall, Gamble. We don't need to advertise what we're doing. The arrests will speak for themselves."

"How's Higgins gonna take the news that I'm still around?"

Ramsey glanced over his shoulder at the roll of hundred dollar bills on his desk. "It doesn't matter anymore," he said. "He didn't mention the five grand, and you did. I'll make sure he knows that I sent the bills over to SID for prints. If Bosco's turn up on the money, Jimmy J. Higgins is dead."

36

Green lights work both ways, she thought. They open the road ahead. At the same time, they force you to move forward—perhaps entering territory that you're unfamiliar with, territory that comes with a price and no guarantee that you'll make it back.

She found Vaughan waiting for her in the lobby. As they exited the building together and she walked him to his car in the visitor lot, he seemed jazzed that Ramsey had cut the strings and that they were finally free to work the case wherever the evidence took them.

"I need you in the morning," he said.

"What is it?"

"Tim Hight's producer is a guy named Pete London. He's agreed to talk to us. They've worked together on and off for the last twenty years."

"How did you get him to agree?"

"He called me this afternoon. It sounds like he wants to get something off his chest. He's producing a reality TV show for one of the music channels. Hight directed the show for about a year, then stopped sometime after his daughter's murder."

"Did he fire Hight?"

"He wouldn't talk about it over the phone. All he said was that they were shooting at a house in Venice. He gave me the address and he's expecting us to show up tomorrow morning by eight."

Vaughan hit his clicker, unlocking the car and opening the door. As he turned back to her, their eyes met and he took a step closer.

"I can't believe what you did tonight," he said in a quiet voice. "Taking Higgins on like that. You know if it ever got out that you caught Higgins with his pants down, your picture would be on every deputy DA's desk in the building."

She smiled, and Vaughan laughed and gave her a hug. Then he climbed into his car and lowered the window.

"You're okay, right?" he asked.

She nodded. "Where do you want to meet up in the morning?"

"I live in Rustic Canyon. It's a five-minute drive to Venice. If you come by early enough, you can meet the kids."

"Sounds good," she said. "See you at seven-thirty."

"I'll text you the address."

Then he laughed again and drove off.

She couldn't put her finger on it. His eyes, his face, his body, or his person. All she knew was that something had happened. When he hugged her, something changed and she became very aware of his physical presence.

She was driving on the Hollywood Freeway, heading home. The wind was up—a bone-dry wind spewing clouds of dust from the desert into the city. The clouds were so thick and dirty that Lena could hear the particles beating against the side of her car.

She lit a cigarette. She was trying to concentrate on the road, but she kept thinking about Vaughan. She couldn't be sure, but she thought that she might have rubbed her breasts against his chest. If she did, it wasn't something deliberate and it didn't last very long. If she did, it just happened and he might not have even noticed.

She took another drag on the cigarette and tried to put the thought out of her mind. At the moment, her life had enough drama. And the idea of becoming the next Bennett and Watson, in any way or any version or any variation thereof, was something she would never let happen.

So why did the churning in her stomach suddenly feel so good?

The Beachwood Drive exit was a hundred yards up. Moving into the right lane, she glided onto the ramp and continued until she reached Gower Street. Then she made a right turn, hit a green light, and started the climb into the hills. To her amazement, the dust cloud had a ceiling, and she pierced it as she reached the crest. Passing through a series of turns, she spotted her driveway on the right, but kept moving when she caught a glimpse of a car that had pulled off the road behind the bluff.

It was a white car. A white Lincoln.

As the image of the car hidden in the darkness rendered in her mind, she realized that she had used up all her fear and anxiety over the past six hours. The only thing left was irritation and curiosity.

She continued up the road to the next house and pulled into the drive. The house was empty due to a bank foreclosure, and like the next house up, had been that way for more than a year. Lena cut through the yard on foot, following the coyote paths through the trees and around the bluff at the edge of the hill. When she stepped out of the brush, she found herself by the pool facing the back of her house and ducked behind a bush.

Cobb was just making his exit.

She could see him trying to squeeze through a window onto the roof above the porch. His movements appeared awkward and she could hear him straining. When he finally made it out, he slipped on the shingles and slid down the roof before catching himself just above the edge.

He took a moment, pulling himself together and looking back at that open window. Lena could tell what was going through his mind and watched as he crawled back up the roof and managed to get the window closed. The process took time and seemed like a painful ordeal. And when he had finally completed the task, he lost his footing again and slid back down to the edge. He took a few minutes to rest, this time staring at the concrete and flagstone below. Once he was ready, he dangled his legs over the edge, searched for the rail with his feet, and climbed down. Then he stepped off the porch and headed up the driveway, huffing and puffing, and wiping his sweaty brow with what looked more like a rag than a handkerchief.

Lena moved into the yard, watching Cobb vanish in the darkness and waiting to hear him drive away. Once she saw the headlights pass, she jogged back through the brush and returned with her car.

In spite of the hour, she was wide awake when she unlocked the front door and switched on the ceiling lights. Her eyes moved through the living room, searching for changes. She didn't think that Cobb had wired the place up because he wasn't carrying any tools. But as she reached the table by the slider, she saw the file beside Gant's journal and noticed that the papers inside were askew. She pulled the chair out, feeling the seat with her fingers and noting its warmth. Then she reached underneath the lamp shade and touched the lightbulb. It was still hot.

Cobb had been sitting at the table. And he'd spent time here.

She didn't know what to make of it. His behavior seemed so outrageous. So risky and bold.

She sat down in the chair and tried to see the table from Cobb's point of view. Gant's graphic novel appeared to have been pushed away, while the file and journal were front and center. Inside the file, Lena found her notes and a copy of the chronological record she had started the night after Bosco and Gant were murdered. Both her notes and the journal would have been new to Cobb. Information he could take back to Bennett.

Her cell phone started vibrating. Checking the touch screen, she saw Sid Kosinski's name and recognized the number from the coroner's office.

"Sorry for calling so late, Lena, but I just walked out of the operating room."

The signal was bad. Opening the slider, she stepped outside onto the porch.

"What is it, Sid?"

"Maybe it's nothing, but the detective who worked the Lily Hight murder was down here about three hours ago."

"Cobb?"

"That's him. He wanted to look at my notes from the autopsies we did on Bosco and Gant. He seemed nervous. And he was asking a lot of questions. What made it feel so odd was that most of his questions were about you."

Lena sat down on the wall. "Did you show him anything from the case?"

"Of course not. But that doesn't mean that he didn't see what he wanted to see."

"Why's that?"

"He's got friends around here."

"What kind of friends?"

"From the old days," Kosinski said. "When he used to work out of Robbery-Homicide."

She decided that she didn't really want to meet any of Cobb's friends. She felt numb and looked out over the hill. The cloud of dirty air had filled in the basin up to the rim, concealing everything in the city except for the upper floors of the Library Tower downtown. The moon was up, lighting the cloud's surface and making it appear solid enough to walk on.

"You still there, Lena?"

"I'm here, Sid. Thanks for the heads-up."

"It's probably nothing, right? Cobb coming down here? It's probably nothing."

She looked back at the dust cloud and shivered in the heat.

"Right," she said. "It's probably nothing."

37

Vaughan lived on Hillside Lane, a short drive up through the canyon from the beach. Lena could see the house half a block ahead, but pulled over when she noticed a woman with blond hair walking out the front door with two young children and their nanny. Vaughan followed them out, opening the doors to his crossover and helping with the car seats. All three adults were laughing about something. Once the kids were finally strapped in, the blonde got behind the wheel and Vaughan waved as she drove off in his car.

Lena didn't know what to make of what she was thinking or feeling right now. All she hoped for was that when she looked at Vaughan or Vaughan looked at her, things would be back to normal. She didn't want to sense something *extra* going on. She needed assurance that what was happening in her mind was only happening in her mind, and not part of the real world.

She pulled up to the house. Vaughan walked over and poked his head in the passenger side window.

"You just missed the kids," he said.

"I'm sorry," she said. "Where's your car?"

"My ex-wife took it for the day. Hers is in the shop. When it's fixed, they said they'd deliver it to my office. We'll switch back later. You don't mind driving, do you?"

"Not at all."

"Let me grab my briefcase."

He smiled at her. She caught the glint in those light brown eyes of his. Switching the radio over to KNX, she hoped that the news station might distract her and make things easier. But her efforts proved unnecessary. Once Vaughan got in the car, he spent most of the drive talking about what they had discovered yesterday. He couldn't comprehend how two deputy DAs were able to step before a judge and look him in the eye knowing that they were trying the wrong man. The fact that they had the district attorney's blessing made it all the more difficult to absorb. When Lena glanced over at him, she could see how revitalized Vaughan had become. She could see the transformation in his posture, in his face; the confidence and energy that comes from the thrill of the chase.

The drive took less than ten minutes. Vaughan checked the address and spotted a parking space a block off.

"Better take it," he said.

Lena backed into the space, and they walked up the sidewalk to the corner. The house on Strongs Drive was easy enough to spot. A camera crane sat on the front lawn, and movie lights had been mounted outside the windows on the first floor. As they got closer, Lena realized that the house was backed up against the canals. She could see a large hot tub off the rear terrace. Beside the house was probably the only vacant lot in all of Venice. Two trailers were here, along with a grip truck, a catering truck, and several long tables with chairs set beneath a large tent. Both lots had been secured with yellow tape as if they were crime scenes. On the street, two off-duty cops leaned against their black and white cruisers providing security.

Lena gave Vaughan a nudge. "What's the name of this show?"

"I keep forgetting the title. It's one of those crappy reality shows. I see them when I'm looking for the cartoon channel for the kids. They put six losers in a house, shoot them talking about nothing, and somehow it sells."

Lena noticed a small sign stapled to a telephone pole. The word *Lowlife* was printed across the top with an arrow pointing toward the house.

"That's it," Vaughan said. "That's the name of the show. *Lowlife.*"

It was one more reason on a list of a hundred other reasons why Lena seldom found anything worth watching on television. But she didn't say anything. As Vaughan spoke with a young production assistant, Lena identified herself to the off-duty cops, then turned and followed Vaughan underneath the tent. Pete London was sitting at one of the tables, sipping coffee, and editing a script with a blue pen. When he noticed them enter, he stood up and they shook hands.

"Thanks for coming," he said. "I appreciate it. Would you like coffee? Something to eat? The catering truck never closes. The food's pretty good on this one."

Both Lena and Vaughan thanked him but declined, and everyone sat down. London pushed the script aside, cradling the paper coffee cup in his hand. Remarkably, he looked like he could have been Tim Hight's more polished brother. His hair was the same mix of blond and gray, but longer and better styled. Dressed in jeans and a light cotton shirt, he was on the lean side, wore glasses with tortoiseshell frames and seemed too cerebral, too intelligent to be producing a reality TV show called *Lowlife* for one of the music channels that no longer had any interest or influence in music.

"I've been reading about the murders at Club 3 AM," he said. "And I'm very concerned about Tim Hight. He's my friend, and that's why I called you."

Lena glanced at Vaughan, then turned back to London. "Have you spoken with him?" she said. "Did he tell you what happened that night?"

"No," London said. "He won't take my call. We haven't talked for a long time."

"Since you let him go?"

A beat went by before London finally nodded. Lena tried not to show her disappointment. Vaughan picked up the slack.

"Why did you fire him?" he asked.

"I didn't want to," London said. "He took a month off after Lily was murdered. When he came back, he was different. I tried to overlook as much as I could. But at a certain point, no matter how much sympathy I may have had for what he was going through . . . it just wasn't working and I had to let him go."

"What about before that?" Lena said. "What about his relationship with his daughter?"

"What are you talking about?"

London obviously thought of Hight as a friend. Lena tried to work through the subject as gently as possible without sounding too vague.

"Did you ever notice anything odd? Anything out of the ordinary?"

"They were close," he said. "But not that kind of close."

"How do you know?" Vaughan asked.

"Because I've worked with him for most of my life, and I know who Tim Hight is. I produced *Prairie Winds,* his best motion picture. We spent three months living in tents and working in conditions that would break most men. Believe me. You do time like that with a guy and you run out of secrets. You walk away knowing each other like brothers."

"You're not upset, are you?" Lena said.

"Not at all. I know that you have to ask questions like this. It's part of your job. If I can help, I'm happy to do it. But you've gotta understand something. Tim might be drinking and smoking and doping it up, but all of that started *after* Lily's murder, not before. It isn't part of who he was. He loved Lily. He was ruined by her death. Ruined by the way she died as much as the death itself. I don't know what losing a child would be like, what demons are haunting the guy. All I hope for is that he gets help."

"I'm guessing you knew Lily and spent time with her as well," Lena said.

London looked away for a moment, eyeing the memory. "Tim was a great father. He used to bring her to work as often as he could. She liked cameras. She had real talent and got along with everyone on the set."

"What about Jacob Gant?" Vaughan asked. "Did Hight ever talk about him?"

London nodded. "He was worried that Lily was growing up too fast and that her friendship with Gant was more than a friendship. Gant was in his mid-twenties, right? Lily was only sixteen. I mean, that kind of thing worked for Elvis. But in the real world, what dad wouldn't be worried?"

Lena had been watching London. His story presented Tim Hight as a loving father. From what she could tell it was perfect. Everything about it was perfect. Everything except for the way London was cradling that paper coffee cup in his hand. Ever since they had begun the interview, London had been rotating the cup and swirling the brew. And that's why nothing about the moment was perfect. It was supposed to be a cup of coffee, but London was treating it like a glass of bourbon.

Lena glanced around the tent and didn't see anyone, then turned back to London. "Do you know what happens to people who try to mislead or interfere with police officers investigating a homicide?"

London froze up. Vaughan seemed just as surprised by the question.

"Do you know?" she repeated.

London didn't say anything, still appearing shocked and trying to collect himself.

"If you want us to pull your phone records, I will," she said. "But if you make me do it, if you waste more of our time, things aren't gonna work out so well for you."

London didn't respond, but something was beginning to show on his face. Vaughan appeared to notice it as well.

Lena checked the tent again. Two people were standing by the catering truck, so she lowered her voice.

"When was the last time you spoke with Hight? And please don't say that it was when you fired him, because all three of us know that's not true."

London couldn't look her in the eye. "Yesterday," he whispered finally. "We talked yesterday."

"And he put you up to this?"

London nodded. "He said he needed some help. I thought I owed him."

"Did you go over the things you told us today?"

"We talked about it. He had some ideas."

"What else did he say?"

London paused, barely able to get the words out. "He said that you think he did it. That he murdered Lily."

38

It was the kind of case where with every new seam, every half step forward, she hoped for the best but got pushed back. It had been that way from the very beginning, from the moment she walked into Club 3 AM and discovered that one of the two dead bodies was Jacob Gant. And it had been that way with Pete London and the story he'd told, written and directed by his friend Tim Hight.

On the drive over to the Westside this morning, Lena had been listening to KPCC, an NPR station broadcasting out of Pasadena. The host of the program was interviewing a baseball player at spring training in Clearwater, Florida—a slugger who had been averaging nearly fifty home runs a year and was considered to be an automatic first-ballot pick for the Hall of Fame once he retired. What struck Lena most about the interview was the player talking about how he'd dug his way out of a hitting slump last August. After a long series of strike-outs, he began to realize that the longer the slump went on, the more the percentages began to move in his favor. The longer he went without a hit, the more likely he was to break out of it at any moment and find the zone.

Lena watched Vaughan search through a stack of DVDs piled up beside his computer, and along side a single pair of headphones. He'd pulled a clip from Gant's trial that he wanted to show her, but they couldn't watch it in here with the sound up because of what Vaughan had found in his phone. Lena understood all too well that she wasn't qualified to sweep a room for electronics. But after watching Bobby Rathbone search her house last year, she knew a few things to look for. The bug Vaughan had found in his phone was the obvious one. Unfortunately, it looked to her like there were at least three more in the room.

"Let's go," he whispered under his breath.

Vaughan slipped the DVD into his pocket and they walked out, heading around the corner for another office at the end of the hall. As Lena entered, Vaughan followed her in and closed the door.

"It's okay," Vaughan said. "He's away on vacation."

"Your office is wired, Greg."

Vaughan rolled a chair over to the computer and switched it on. "I know," he said. "I've been coming in here to use the phone."

"I'm not talking about what you found in your phone. I counted three more, and I'm not even a pro."

He stopped and looked at her. "Where?" he said

"The surge protector that your computer is plugged into. That was easy because I found one exactly like it at my place last year."

"Where are the other two?"

"The wall plate covering the outlet above the credenza, and another just like it facing your desk. Both are wired for video and sound. If you look in the middle of the plate you'll see what I mean. That's not a screw holding the plate to the wall. It's a small camera."

Vaughan sat back in the chair, stunned. "They're watching. They can see what I'm doing."

"The signal's probably not strong enough to reach the street."

"It wouldn't need to," he said quietly. "Bennett's office is right upstairs."

He let out a deep breath and seemed to be letting the worry get to him.

"Show me the clip," she said.

He nodded, then snapped out of it and loaded the DVD into the computer. When a menu rendered on the screen, he scrolled through a long list of files, found the clip and hit PLAY.

The clip began with a shot of Jacob Gant sitting beside Buddy Paladino in the courtroom. Lena moved closer for a better view. There was something about seeing Gant alive again. Something about seeing him at that table knowing what she knew about him now. Something about the determination showing on Paladino's face. Something about knowing Gant was about to run out of luck and time, and about to be kissed by fate.

"This isn't it," Vaughan said. "Another half minute."

Lena became aware of the audio track. It was Debi Watson's voice. She was asking someone—

"Here it is," Vaughan said. "This is it."

The video made a hard cut to Cobb sitting on the witness stand. He was holding one of Lily's boots, which was found behind her body by the bed. And as Watson threw him one question after the next, he seemed confident and perfectly at ease. He was dressed in a gray suit that looked so well tailored, Lena guessed that it had been purchased for this court appearance. Had she been sitting in the jury box, she would have been impressed with who he was and how he spoke.

"Detective Cobb, how many homicides have you investigated?" Watson was asking.

"I'm not sure I could give you an exact number. I've been working homicides for twenty-five years."

"Would you say that the number of cases you've investigated is over one hundred?"

"Yes," Cobb said.

"Over two hundred?"

"Unfortunately, yes."

"So you would call yourself an experienced detective," Watson was saying. "A veteran detective. Someone extremely familiar with any or all crime scenes in a homicide investigation. You know what they look like. You know how they operate. Crime scenes have been your place of work for the last twenty-five years."

Cobb glanced in the jury's direction and said "Yes" with a polite smile.

"So let's get back to this crime scene. A few minutes ago you said that you could tell by looking at Lily's body that she had been sexually assaulted before her murder. Specifically, what did you see?"

"Her underwear had been hiked up around her waist," he said with authority. "I could see blood on her thighs. And it wasn't coming from the chest wound. It was coming from between her legs."

Watson let Cobb's last line settle in for the jury. She took the boot that Cobb had been holding and pretended to examine it. After a short time, she handed the boot back to him.

"Her jeans had been stripped away from her body," she said finally. "Her boots and socks—everything tossed into a pile. Where did you find them in relation to Lily's body?"

The video had cut to Watson, who expected a quick answer—but it never came. When she turned back to Cobb, she seemed annoyed. The size of the image on the computer monitor was small. Still, Lena thought it looked like Cobb had lost his composure and broken out into a heavy sweat.

Watson repeated the question, but Cobb remained silent and began fidgeting in his seat.

"Detective?" she asked finally. "Is there something wrong, Detective?"

Cobb stammered. "Excuse me," he said. "But may I have a glass of water?"

The monitor went blank, the video clip over. Vaughan turned back to Lena.

"After he drinks the glass of water, he's fine. It cuts back to a wide shot, but you can tell he's okay."

Lena sat down beside the desk. "So what are you saying?"

"I don't know," Vaughan said. "Something happened, and I don't think he was having a heart attack."

"You think he was stalling when he asked for the water."

Vaughan shrugged. "Maybe, but why? Watson's got a nice rhythm going. Paladino is giving her a pass and not objecting. Cobb's talking about his experience and looks as cool and relaxed as any detective I've ever seen. And then in a single instant, it's like his mind needs a reboot. He can't speak. He's just been asked a routine question, and he can't answer it. He can't find the words. Once he has a minute to pull himself together, he's fine for the rest of the day."

"Maybe they didn't spend a lot of time coaching him."

"In a case this big—are you crazy?"

"Maybe he didn't rehearse," she said.

"Impossible. And for the same reason, Lena. Too big a case."

"Maybe the whole thing was scripted. Maybe he lost his place."

"But every trial is scripted. If he'd lost his place, or even forgotten where the clothing had been found, he could have glossed over everything until Watson repeated the question and he was okay again."

Lena's cell phone chirped. When she checked the touch screen, she realized that Martin Orth from SID had tried to reach her five minutes ago. Her phone was searching for a signal that kept drifting in and out.

"I've gotta make a call," she said. "How do I dial out?"

Vaughan pushed the desk phone closer. "Nine," he said. "Who?"

She met his eyes. "Orth."

Lena entered the number on the desk phone. When Orth picked up, she could tell by the sound of his voice that something had gone wrong.

"It's the blood on Hight's shoe," she said.

"Not the shoe, Lena. We're not there yet. Maybe later today or to-morrow."

"Then what is it? What's wrong?"

Orth hesitated for a moment, his voice weak. "It's the girl's jeans," he said finally. "You were right. They were removed with force. Enough skin cells to leave a DNA trail."

Lena glanced at Vaughan. Flipping the handset up, he leaned in close enough to listen.

"You've got the results?" she said.

"I've got them, but I think you should sit down."

Lena traded looks with Vaughan, ready to burst. "I'm with Greg," she said. "Tell us, Marty. Who was it? Jacob Gant or Tim Hight?"

"That's the thing, Lena. That's why I told you to sit down."

"Who murdered Lily?" she said. "Who did it?"

Orth took another moment to compose himself. When he was ready, he said, "That's the thing, Lena. It's not Gant and it's not Hight. It's a third man."

39

A third man.

It had been there all along. Right in front of her eyes. A crime scene photo stuffed inside Cobb's murder book. The photographer from SID had snapped pictures of the entire house on the night of Lily's murder, including the sunroom where Tim Hight sat every night. But just as Pete London had told them, Hight's slide to the bottom of the hill didn't occur until *after* he had lost his daughter.

Lena sat at a table on the terrace over at the Blackbird. The heat was so oppressive, the air so foul, that she had the space to herself. Hot coffee wasn't much of a help, nor was the cigarette she'd just finished. Still, she struck a match and lit another as she stared at the photograph.

Hight's chair wasn't in the sunroom. Nor did she see a police scanner, an ashtray or an oversized glass of vodka set on the sill. Instead, Lena saw a Pilates machine, a floor mat, and a room filled with house plants.

She closed her eyes and lowered her head.

Hight wasn't who she'd thought he was. Hight was the man Pete London had stepped up to defend.

A loving father who measured his daughter's height on her birthday every year and marked her progress on the pantry door. A father who encouraged his daughter's talent with a camera and took her to work with him as often as he could. A father who had been worried that his daughter was growing up too fast.

A loving father who had been ruined by his loss.

Lena had misread everything.

Everything.

While Hight may still have been responsible for the murders of Bosco and Gant, she doubted it. The killings were about what Gant had found. What he had seen. What he'd brought to show Bosco. The killings were about Lily's murder and the third man.

But it got worse. Much worse.

Martin Orth had given them more news.

After reexamining Lily's jeans, a small amount of semen was found inside the clothing just below the zipper that had been missed during the original investigation. DNA analysis revealed that the semen belonged to Jacob Gant and proved that he had been telling the truth all along. He'd had sex with Lily early in the evening. When they'd finished, Lily got back into her jeans and they went downstairs to the kitchen.

The polygraph had proven a lack of deception on Gant's part and should have been enough to end it. But finding his semen inside Lily's jeans proved that her rape and murder had been an entirely separate event. Had the semen been found the first time around, it would have prevented every domino since the night Lily was murdered from falling down. Lives would have been spared.

There was no gray to it. No question marks. No blank spaces. Everything was in black and white now.

A sixteen-year-old girl was dead—a teenager growing up too fast with a voracious appetite for sex. Johnny Bosco wanted to help. Johnny Bosco wanted to—

She leafed through her notes looking for the Death Investigation Report. Dante Escabar's contact information would be listed in the second box down because he'd reported the murders, discovered the bodies, and identified Johnny Bosco's corpse. She found his cell number and punched it into her phone. Escabar picked up on the first ring, his voice no longer littered with sarcasm.

"I know why Johnny wanted to help Jacob Gant," he said.

"I think I do, too," she said quickly. "You might not be safe."

He laughed at her. She remembered the gun he kept.

Lena cleared her throat. "When was Lily at the club?"

"The cameras picked her up twice," he said. "Both were Friday nights. One and two weeks before her death. She's sitting at the bar."

Lena was thinking about the man Gant had said he'd seen struggling with Lily on the Friday night one week before the murder. Paladino had told her that Gant couldn't be sure of anything because it was too dark and too far away to see clearly. When he'd gone over to the house to check on Lily, the car was gone and no one answered the door.

"Was she with anybody, Dante?"

"She came with a girlfriend the first time," he said. "They didn't stay very long. But one week before the murder she came alone. She was talking to a guy. Touchy-feely stuff. They left together."

"Can you see his face?"

"He's standing beside her, not sitting. His face didn't make the shot. I'm burning you a copy right now."

"Keep the doors locked," she said. "I'm on my way over."

He laughed again. "They're always locked, Detective Gamble. See you when you get here."

40

Something about the way Escabar laughed hit her in the gut. The tone. The edge. The grim feeling followed her as she hurried across the street into the garage. She found Vaughan's cell number on her recent call list, and felt some degree of relief when he picked up.

"Where are you?" she asked.

"Downstairs," he said. "They're delivering my ex-wife's car."

She gave him a three-sentence update that ended with the words, "Lily Hight left Club 3 AM with a guy."

"I've got wheels," he said. "I'll meet you there. I'll only be five minutes behind you."

She blew through a red light—that grim feeling sitting beside her in the passenger seat. Once she'd pulled onto the 101 Freeway, she slid into the far left lane and decided to call for backup. The Hollywood Station was just a few blocks south of the club. The dispatch operator took the information down, then repeated it to her.

Probably nothing, but would you please send a first response unit to the club.

Probably nothing, but would you hurry.

It took Lena twenty-five minutes of hard driving to reach Holly-wood. As she approached Club 3 AM, she didn't see the guard in his booth and the gate was open. She turned into the drive and pulled around to the back of the building. And then her heart sank. The Toyota pickup was here, and so was Escabar's Ferrari, but no one else. She could hear sirens in the distance, but it sounded like they were moving in the opposite direction.

She gave the building a hard look, then hurried up the steps to the main entrance—that grim feeling still as close as a shadow. She tried the front door, wrapped her hand around the handle, and gave it a slow pull hoping that the place was locked up.

But when the door opened, she took the shock and knew. . . .

She stepped inside the foyer—everything dark and quiet. Digging into her pocket for her phone, she found Escabar's cell number and pressed CALL. Two or three seconds later, she heard his phone begin ringing from somewhere upstairs. She could hear the haunting sound travel through the dark building. She could hear the eerie silence when his voice mail cut in and the ringing finally stopped.

She tried to compose herself.

Her eyes had adjusted to the darkness and she could see a body on the floor. It wasn't very far away. She noticed a light switch on the wall and flipped it on. The switch only handled a row of dim floor lights lead-ing to the staircase, but provided enough illumination for Lena to pick up detail.

She moved toward the body slowly and knelt down. A green trash bag had been pulled over the man's head and tied around his neck. From the shoes and slacks he wore, Lena knew that she was looking at the security guard. She started to check his pulse, her response on auto-matic, but looked at his face pressing through the plastic bag and stopped.

Few people die pretty. . . .

She turned away, trying to catch her breath. She heard something behind her—the door opening, the foyer flooding with light. It was

Vaughan, and he looked frightened and nervous. As he moved in beside her, he couldn't seem to stop staring at the dead body.

"I called for backup," she said quietly.

"There's a bank robbery on Sunset," he whispered. "I heard it on the radio."

Lena spotted the pistol on the guard's belt. "We can't wait," she said. "Do you know how to use a gun?"

Vaughan shook his head and seemed jittery. "I'm a lawyer," he said.

Lena pursed her lips. They were in a tough spot, yet she couldn't help acknowledging to herself that there was something about Vaughan that got to her. Something she liked a lot. She shook it off, grabbing the guard's pistol and lifting it out of the holster. Even in the dim light, the Beretta .40 glistened as if brand new. The hammer was half-cocked with the safety engaged. Readying the weapon, she passed it over and met Vaughan's eyes.

"Whoever did this is probably long gone," she whispered. "Can you handle this?"

He nodded at her with determination. "I'm ready."

Lena drew her weapon, then pulled out her cell and hit the REDIAL key on the touch screen.

Vaughan shot her a wild look. "What are you doing?"

"Calling a dead man," she said.

After several moments, Escabar's cell phone started ringing again and Vaughan understood. They moved quickly through the darkness, rushing up the stairs and following that ghostly sound down the hall until it stopped. Lena pressed the REDIAL key again and they continued pushing toward the sound. When they reached the corner, she realized that Escabar's phone was ringing from Bosco's office and broke into a run.

She found him on the floor beside the desk—one round through his forehead, and two more through the center of his chest. His mouth was open, his teeth jutting out. But even more striking, she could see what looked like fear permanently frozen on his face. His gun was on the floor beside his right hand. She turned to check the wall and spotted a bullet hole in the plaster by the door. Escabar had managed to get a shot off, but aimed too high and missed.

"Something's happening with the computer," Vaughan said.

Lena stepped around Escabar's corpse, her eyes dancing between the computer monitor on the desk and the television mounted over the fireplace. The screens were connected, the images identical.

"Files are being deleted, Lena. Look at the size of them."

She checked the screen, searching for a CANCEL option. When she found the button, she clicked it and sat down at the desk.

"Media files," she said. "The security cameras."

"Are we too late?"

"Not necessarily," she said.

"Escabar told you that he made a copy?"

She nodded, her wheels turning, "He was burning it when I called."

There was a stack of blank DVDs on the desk, but nothing else. The drive in the computer was empty. Lena searched through the desk drawers but found nothing there as well. After giving Escabar's corpse a quick check, she turned back to the monitor and tried to think it through.

There were a number of programs that Escabar had opened. Each one had been minimized and parked at the bottom of the screen. As she read the icons, she realized that Escabar had burned a copy for her without closing the program. Clicking the icon, the software opened and a graphic box popped up.

Would you like to make another copy?

The program had recorded a mirror image of the project and saved it. She glanced at Vaughan unable to speak, then loaded a blank disk into the computer and clicked YES. The next five minutes idled by in the key of slow—the anxiety was overwhelming. But after the drive stopped churning, Lena highlighted the disk and a video image began rolling on both the monitor and the television mounted over the fireplace.

"My God, it's her," Vaughan said.

Lena stood up and walked over to the television, mesmerized by the image.

She was sitting at the bar with a glass of white wine. She had on that red lipstick, and was wearing a black dress without a bra. There wasn't much to the dress, and her breasts were loose and only partially concealed. The bar was lit entirely by candlelight, and Lily seemed to glow more than everyone else in the darkened room. A man dressed in a pinstripe suit was standing beside her, his head lost in the shadows above the frame. But Escabar had called it right. Lily was laughing with the man and rubbing her fingers over his hand.

"Does she look sixteen to you?" Vaughan asked.

Lena shook her head and offered a sad smile that didn't last very long. Nothing about Lily Hight looked like a teenager on the Friday night one week before she was raped and murdered. The sheen of her blond hair. The glint in her eyes. Her spirit and beauty and magnetic smile. On this night, Lily looked like the kind of woman no man could walk away from.

Lena tried to push through the shock and concentrate on the man Lily was with. There wasn't much to see, and the camera angle was more than frustrating. She thought he might be wearing a wedding band, but when Lily finally lifted her fingers away, the man cupped his hand and lowered it below the bar. His pinstripe suit appeared expensive. As he turned and pressed his chest into Lily's bare shoulder, Lena's eyes zeroed in on the left lapel of his jacket.

"There's a mark on his lapel," she said.

Vaughan moved closer to the screen and squinted. "I've got it. I see it."

"Some sort of flaw in the material."

"You think it's from a pin?"

It seemed obvious to her now. The more she looked at it—but then the shock returned and that anxious feeling swam back through her chest: Lily was gathering her things. The man was helping her off the stool and taking her away. And with only two short steps they were out of the candlelight's reach. Lily wasn't glowing anymore. She was passing through the shadows with the man in the pinstripe suit leading her to the door.

41

Lena lowered the visor and reached for her sunglasses. She was driving east on the San Bernardino Freeway, and the sun was beginning to rise directly in front of her. It looked like the freeway was burning at the horizon line—like the road was taking her on a straight shot into the flames.

She wondered if it wasn't a warning of some kind.

Martin Orth had more news. He wanted to see her. Apparently, the news was so "good" that they couldn't talk about it over the phone.

She hadn't slept well last night. She'd dreamed about Lily. She'd dreamed about her in that black dress. Lena had been sitting at the bar beside her, trying to get a bead on the guy who was hitting on her. She could see them holding hands. She could see his pinstripe suit. But every time she looked up at his face, his head was gone. Not missing like it had been forgotten by an artist or framed out by a photographer. The man's head had been cut off. She could see blood rushing down his shirt and cascading all over his hands. She could see Lily cleaning her fingers with a napkin.

It wasn't the kind of dream Lena really wanted to stick with her. She had woken up three or four times—jolted out of her sleep in a cold sweat. But after fifteen or twenty minutes passed, she couldn't help drifting back into the stream. And each time she'd find herself sitting at that bar again, watching Lily walk out of the club with her killer.

Lena looked at the pack of Camel Lights on the dash, but fought the urge to light one. Within fifteen minutes she had reached the crime lab, passed through security, and was walking down the hall to Martin Orth's office. Because of the early hour, there weren't many people around. About halfway down she noticed a fragrance in the air—a new building smell that seemed to permeate the hall. The scent worked like a time machine and brought back memories of being a girl in the second grade and walking to class on her first day of school. Memories of going to work with her dad, a welder who worked on high-rise buildings and forever changed the skyline in Denver.

Why was she thinking these thoughts? Why was she dreaming these dreams?

She found Orth at his desk. He was staring at his Mr. Coffee coffeemaker and trying to appear patient while it sputtered and brewed. He looked a mile or two past tired and more than ready to drink the entire pot on his own.

"Okay," she said. "Tell me what I need to know."

Orth's eyes moved away from the coffeemaker and found her by the door.

"You can arrest Hight," he said. "The blood on his shoe came from Gant. No doubt about it. Hight was at Club 3 AM the night Bosco and Gant were shot. Hight was in the room."

Lena sat in the chair by Orth's desk. His eyes had moved back to the coffeemaker, and there was something wrong with his voice.

"I'm not arresting Tim Hight for anything," she said.

"Why not? The DNA proves that he was there."

And so did the cocaine that they found at his house, the street cam photograph of Hight driving away from the club, maybe even the hundred-dollar bills. But that's all any of it proved—that Hight was there.

Lena had been chewing it over ever since Orth gave her the results from Lily's jeans linking her murder to a third man. There had to be

another explanation for why Tim Hight was at the club the night Bosco
and Gant were shot and killed. After remembering Gant's brother telling
her that Gant and Hight had argued earlier in the day, she'd put it together and thought she knew what the argument was about.

Gant had to have told Hight that he was on the brink of discovering
who really murdered his daughter. Gant would have blurted it out in
the heat of the moment.

He didn't kill Lily, and he and Johnny Bosco were going to prove it
tonight.

Hight never would have believed him, and so the argument would
have progressed. But Hight would have kept an eye on Gant. And
Bosco's involvement would have worked on him over the course of the
day. When Gant took off to meet Bosco, Hight might have been stew-
ing on it long enough to follow him.

"Hight's the one," Orth said. "But you don't look like you're buying
it, Lena."

"I'm not," she said. "We're way past that, Marty."

Orth started laughing. It came from deep inside the man and there
was a certain madness to it. Lena had never seen him act this way before. She didn't know how to take it and even thought that he might be
losing his mind.

"You want a cup of coffee?" he asked.

"No thanks."

Orth started laughing again as he pushed himself out of his chair,
poured his brew into a Dodgers mug, and returned to his desk.

"What is it, Marty? Are you okay?"

"I'm fine," he said, sipping his coffee. "Better than fine. You don't
want to arrest Hight, and that's a good thing, Lena. A real good thing.
But it's crazy. Life sure gets crazy sometimes."

"What's crazy? What's happened?"

He looked at her for a long time. "The gun that killed Bosco and
Gant," he said finally. "We didn't need the one Hight bought to make
a match."

She leaned forward. "Ballistics got a hit."

He nodded and seemed nervous. "A big one, Lena. The kind that always seem to come at four-thirty in the morning. You ever hear about a woman named Elvira Wheaten? It was a drive-by shooting in Exposition Park. Must have been eight years ago. Her infant grandson got killed, too."

It felt like all of the air in the room had been sucked through the vents into the basement. Something inside Lena stiffened.

Bennett and Cobb's last big case together.

She nodded at Orth, but she didn't say anything. The hairs on the back of her neck were beginning to rise. She could see it—all of it—before her eyes.

"The gun that killed her," Orth said. "That's the gun the shooter used to waste Bosco and Gant. And that's why life's so crazy, Lena. We checked with Property. It's a nine-millimeter Smith. It should have been there. It should have been in the box, but it wasn't. Just like the blood evidence that went missing during the trial. Déjà-fucking-vu."

Lena tried to concentrate on her breathing.

"Did you check the property request cards?" she asked quietly.

"Uh-huh."

"Give me the name of the last person to fill out a card."

42

Cobb lived in a rundown apartment building beside Fiesta Liquors and the Rancho Coin Laundry on Vineland Avenue between the two runways at Bob Hope Airport in Burbank. As Lena studied the motel-styled building from her car, it seemed more than obvious that Cobb's fall had been a brutal plunge straight to the bottom.

Cobb wasn't staring into the abyss. He lived there.

The building offered a five-foot fence with a broken gate as its only means of security. Lena didn't see a parking lot and circled the block looking for the white Lincoln. Most of the cars she passed didn't appear roadworthy and in fact looked like they had hit bottom a few years back as well. More than a handful were jacked up on cinder blocks with their wheels ripped off and their windshields blown out. After Lena had made a second pass by Cobb's building and gained some assurance that he'd left for the day, she pulled into the lot at a Mexican supermarket two blocks south and headed back on foot.

She was on automatic pilot now. Out of patience. Out of understanding. Out of everything. She knew that if she touched the wheel with her hands, the fucking plane would crash. If she examined what she was doing too closely, the crime she was about to commit, she might realize that the plane was already going down.

She approached the building, checking the numbers on the doors. She could see Cobb's apartment on the second floor at the end.

She took the steps at a brisk pace. Most of the windows she passed were open and she could smell corn tortillas and hot oil burning. She could hear the mix of different languages—mostly Spanish, but Russian and Armenian, too. When she reached the last apartment before Cobb's, she was startled by an old Mexican woman sitting by her window. The woman's face appeared more ancient than old and remained expressionless. Even as their eyes met, there was no recognition of the moment. Just two blank eyes staring forward.

Lena hurried down to Cobb's door, gave the bell a ring, and looked over her shoulder as she waited for no one to answer. The old woman had moved her chair so that she could watch her.

Lena turned back to the door, examining the deadbolt and slipping the picks out of her pocket as quickly as she could. Cobb's deadbolt seemed to match the quality of the building, and Lena guessed that it probably turned toward the hinges. Inserting her tension wrench, she applied only the slightest pressure and began working the pins with a short hook. She could feel them clicking into place. Within ninety seconds she'd hit the last pin and the tension wrench began turning. When the door popped open, she checked on that old woman again. She was still watching her. Still working that dead stare.

Lena entered Cobb's apartment, closing the door and throwing the deadbolt. She didn't want to spend too much time here. Fifteen minutes at the most. Maybe ten with that woman out there watching.

She had learned how to pick a lock from a serial burglar she'd arrested while working in Hollywood more than five years ago. Jonathan Redgrave graduated from Stanford with an MBA, but spent the next thirty years of his life working nights and becoming a very wealthy man. She knew from the time they'd spent together in an interrogation room that a successful burglary came down to just three essential components. First, the score had to be worth the risk. Second, you needed to know how to enter the location without being detected. And third, and most important of all, you needed a backup exit just in case everything went to shit.

Cobb's apartment was a small, sparsely furnished one-bedroom. She checked the windows. The best way out if things went to shit was through the one in the bedroom, but it would require a twenty-foot drop onto concrete. Lena slid open the window and played through a possible escape in her head. Once she had it down, she decided to search the place in reverse. She wouldn't begin in the bedroom the way most pros do. She'd work her way toward it.

The living room and kitchen were a single fifteen-by-twenty-foot space that probably hadn't seen a fresh coat of paint in fifteen years. The couch was pushed against the wall, and an old kitchen table made of steel tubing and Formica was placed before the window with two chairs. She noted the computer—and the receipts and loose change and unopened mail. It looked like Cobb used the table as a desk and the wall beside it as a combination filing cabinet and bookcase. Stacks of files and papers were piled on the floor by an old TV.

Lena switched on the computer. While it booted up, she rifled through the files stacked against the wall. Everything she saw appeared to be related to Cobb's personal finances. Skimming through a recent bank statement revealed that most of Cobb's paycheck was going to his ex-wife. What money remained bought a life here on Vineland Avenue beside a liquor store and a Laundromat.

Lena shook it off and glanced at the computer. It was up, but it wasn't her priority. She checked her watch. Five minutes were gone. She needed to move faster.

The kitchen drawers and cabinets held no secrets, nor did the refrigerator or freezer. On the sill over the sink she noticed a photograph set in a cheap plastic frame. From a distance she thought that it might be a shot of Cobb with his wife and children before things fell apart. But when she picked it up, she realized that it was the photograph that came with the frame. The people in the shot were models representing an American family that still had a piece of the American dream. They wore big smiles and appeared well rested and well fed.

She set down the frame, wishing she hadn't seen it, then checked the cushions on the couch and returned to Cobb's bedroom.

She could feel the weight of the clock on her back. She could still see that old woman by her open window in her head. But worse, she could hear her burglar friend telling her that she'd broken his second rule, and it was an important one.

She ripped through Cobb's chest—one drawer after the next—disappointed that the gun wasn't here. She lifted the mattress, and looked beneath the bed. Moving to the closet, she checked the top shelf, searched through Cobb's clothing, and bent over for a quick look at the floor. And then she stopped.

It wasn't the gun. It was a blue binder hidden behind a shoe box.

She pushed the shoes away and grabbed it. When she read the table of contents—when she saw Lily Hight's name at the top and noted that the binder was overflowing with paperwork she had never seen before—she didn't stop to think it over.

She held it tight and closed the door.

Then she hustled into the living room for a quick look at Cobb's computer. The hard drive revealed nothing out of the ordinary. But as she checked his bookmarks and skimmed through his email, she slowed down some.

It looked like Cobb was a frequent visitor of the dating Web sites. Lena counted at least one hundred e-mails from a woman calling herself Betty Kim. Picking an e-mail at random, Kim was describing her body and what she wanted in a sexual relationship. She called herself "hot," left nothing to the imagination, and wanted to send Cobb a couple of nude photos. In his reply, Cobb stated that he loved eating sushi and going to the movies. He agreed that she sounded hot and would like to see the photos as soon as possible.

Lena's mind shot to the surface.

She could hear that old woman shouting at someone in Spanish.

When the shadow of a man moved across the curtains, she felt the rush of adrenaline and shut down the computer. Cobb was home. She could hear his key in the lock. Grabbing the murder book, she fled into the bedroom and tossed the binder out the window. Then she climbed outside, clinging to the sill, and grinding to push the window closed.

She heard the front door open. She heard Cobb's voice through the glass. She made the drop and hit the concrete hard. But she was on automatic pilot now. Out of patience. Out of understanding. Out of everything except bullets.

A jet flashed through the sky with its landing gear down, the noise deafening, the ground shaking. Lena grabbed the murder book and ran up the street as fast as she could.

43.

She hung up the phone and turned to Vaughan.

"It's a TracFone," she said. "There's no name attached to the number. The phone hasn't been used since."

They were working in that corner office at the end of the hall, the one that wasn't wired for picture and sound. Cobb's murder books were laid out on the table side by side. They had begun by pulling Lily's cell-phone bills from both binders for comparison, and unfortunately, they didn't match. Someone had been calling Lily the week before she was murdered. The calls began the day after she left Club 3 AM with the man in the pinstripe suit and continued with frequency during the week.

"When was the last call made?" Vaughan asked.

"Early evening on the night she was murdered. They spoke for seven minutes."

"The guy she met at the club," he said. "The killer."

Lena nodded, glancing at the cell-phone bill that had been in the murder book Cobb had given her. "So why isn't this number listed on this bill?"

The answer seemed obvious. They were dealing with a group of desperate people. People who felt cornered and had been willing to manipulate and manufacture evidence. People who didn't want her or anyone else in the future to see that phone number. They were dealing with a man like Dan Cobb who had filled out a property request card from a case he worked eight years ago because he needed a gun. The same 9-mm Smith that was used to murder Bosco and Gant. And in all probability, the same gun that put three holes in Escabar and was used to coldcock his guard before that trash bag went over his head and the man smothered to death.

Vaughan opened his briefcase and pulled out a thick file. "That's not the question, Lena. The question is, what did Bennett and Watson use in court?"

Leafing through the papers, he found another copy of the cell-phone bill and set it beside the other two. Most of the numbers had been blacked out with a Sharpie—the bill featuring only those calls that came from Jacob Gant. But even a permanent marker couldn't cover the text underneath once they turned the bill into the bright light. The number from the TracFone had been removed.

A moment passed like they'd hit a gap in the universe. They were dealing with a dirty cop and a triad of dirty prosecutors.

Lena lowered her voice. "You want to bet that the copy Paladino received didn't include this phone number, either?"

Vaughan still appeared stunned. "No," he said slowly. "I wouldn't take that bet. I think the same thing's going on with the e-mails Gant sent the girl."

"How?"

"I was reading these while you were on the phone. They don't match, either. The version in the murder book Cobb gave you makes Gant sound like an angry man who's threatening to hurt Lily. The version from the binder you found in Cobb's closet reads like Gant was worried about her and offering help."

Vaughan set the two e-mails down. While Lena read them, he returned to his briefcase and found the version Bennett and Watson had used in court. As Lena examined the third document, she couldn't help thinking about how much this ripped at her faith and trust.

"They submitted an edited version," she whispered.

He gave her a look. "You ever hear of the Michael Skakel case?"

She nodded. "Ethel Kennedy's nephew. He was tried for the murder of Martha Moxley. They were kids. She was fifteen at the time."

Vaughan pulled a chair over and sat down. "The prosecutor took audio recordings of Skakel talking about masturbation and his fear of being seen and edited them to sound like he was confessing to the murder and afraid he might get caught. When Skakel appealed his conviction, the judge turned out to be just as ignorant, just as morally challenged as the prosecutor."

Lena reached for the murder book she had taken from Cobb's apartment. The binder was stuffed with hundreds of documents that weren't included in the book she had received from the detective just a few days ago. As she paged through the binder, she saw something she recognized and stopped. It was a copy of the polygraph results Paladino had sent to Higgins, Bennett, and Watson. But there was something stapled to the back of the report. It turned out to be a letter addressed to Bennett. A letter from Cesar Rodriguez, the forensic psycho-physiologist who had performed the polygraph on Gant. As Lena started reading she began to realize that Rodriguez was making a plea to Bennett on Gant's behalf. According to Rodriguez, there was no indication whatsoever that Gant had anything to do with Lily Hight's murder. In all his years working for the LAPD's Scientific Investigation Division, Rodriguez had never seen a case so clear-cut and was willing to champion Gant's cause and put his reputation on the line.

It was a plea that Bennett obviously saw fit to ignore.

For Lena, reading Rodriguez's letter burned in her chest like a white-hot sun drying up rain before it could hit the ground. Trial attorneys playing with the facts like politicians running for office happened every day. She knew that. But this was something different. Something beyond sleazy. Something beyond sick.

"I want to meet with Bennett," she said.

"Why? You look pissed off, and these people are dangerous. I don't want to scare you, Lena. But all of a sudden, we're sitting in the same seats Bosco and Gant sat in."

She shook her head. "I need to see him about something. Would you call him for me? I don't have his number."

Vaughan gave her a long look, but finally picked up the phone and dialed Bennett's office.

"Tracy, it's Greg," he said into the phone. "Is he available? I need to talk to him. It's important."

Vaughan listened to Bennett's assistant for several moments, then thanked her and hung up.

"What happened?" Lena asked.

"He's not in his office," he said. "He went to lunch."

"Where?"

"Tracy said he's with Watson."

"Do you have his cell number? Where are they?"

Vaughan shot her another look, then lowered his voice. "She thinks they're at the Bonaventure."

The security director at the Bonaventure didn't look like he wanted to play ball. Lena had asked him to use his pass key to open a tower suite on the twenty-fifth floor. It was clear to Lena that he knew the suite was leased by the district attorney's office. It was just as clear to her that he had a good idea of what was going on inside. The only tangible card she held was that Roy Romero had spent twenty years carrying a badge and had been a good cop.

"I'll get fired," he said. "And I like this job. I like it a lot."

"Whose to say anyone's in there?"

He raised an eyebrow at her. Romero had more than a good idea. He knew.

"No offense, Detective. But are you really sure that you want to go in there? Seems like it could get you into some trouble, too."

"No one has to know who pushed the card key into the door, Romero. Now are you gonna cooperate and work with the department? Or are you gonna prevent a detective from carrying out police business?"

"Police business?" he said sarcastically.

She liked the guy, but didn't let on. After a few moments, he nodded in futility and motioned her over to the elevators.

"I've always hated Higgins," he whispered under his breath. "The DA to the stars. The guy's a piece of shit. And these two blew that trial like a couple of fricking ingrates shooting blanks."

An elevator ride at the Bonaventure offered a view of Los Angeles like no other. If Lena hadn't been thinking about the road she'd traveled over the past few days, she might have seen it. Instead, her mind was filled with a long series of stark images. She could see the bodies piling up; the lives of the victim's families and friends ruined and left behind. By the time the elevator opened on the twenty-fifth floor, all she could see was Steven Bennett's bullshit face.

Romero led her down the hall. When they reached the suite, he gave her a last-chance look, then pushed his card key into the door. The light on the lock turned green and the bolt clicked.

"You're in," he whispered. "And I'm fucking out of here."

Lena watched him hurry back toward the elevators as she entered and closed the door. She paused a moment, listening to them in the bedroom. The thrashing of sheets, Watson moaning, Bennett panting like a dog. As she crossed the living room, she spotted Watson's bra and pantyhose on the couch, Bennett's boxer shorts on the floor.

She reached the bedroom and looked past the door. Bennett was on top, grinding it out with his mean little head buried between Watson's breasts. In the past, Lena had always made a conscious effort to avoid looking at her breasts. She had heard the rumors—she couldn't tell if they were real or not . . . and she didn't care. But as she stood just outside the room, she couldn't help but notice their unnatural shape and size and tendency to defy the planet's gravitational pull. They looked like a pair of balloons filled with helium ready to fly off and pop.

The image dissipated quickly, and she walked over to the bed as if she were entering Bennett's office and everything was copasetic.

For Lena, the moment was unfolding in slow motion. She could hear Watson gasp and shriek. She could see Bennett in panic mode—frantically pushing himself off Watson's body, kicking his legs, and fighting to cover himself with the sheets. When Bennett started screaming, she opened her jacket and rested her hand on her gun.

"Are you fucking out of your mind?" he said.

"Probably."

"Get your hand away from that gun."

Lena shook her head. "No."

Those green eyes of his were big and glassy. And the hair on his body was as thick as fur. She could see fear pulsating through his entire being. He didn't know if he was safe. Lena knew that she had picked the right moment. The least likely moment.

"I'm just trying to understand something, Bennett. I needed to see you."

"Fuck you, you stupid bitch. Make an appointment."

Watson slapped him. "Stop it," she said. "And get this over with."

Lena took a step closer. "I'm trying to understand why the two of you destroyed evidence in the Jacob Gant trial. Why you deleted it, rewrote it, manufactured it, and corrupted it."

Bennett's demeanor changed. His eyes hardened. He was speechless.

"That's right," she said. "I know what you did. And that's why I needed to see you. That's why it couldn't wait. I don't understand why you went to trial when both of you knew for six weeks that Gant should have been cut loose. I'm trying to understand why anything that pointed to a more probable killer was ignored or suppressed or altered to look like it wasn't even there. I'm trying to predict what's gonna happen to everyone involved when the story gets out. All stories get out, Bennett. No matter how many people go down."

It hung there. All of it out in the open.

Bennett traded a long look with Watson, then turned back.

"That little prick was guilty," he said.

"Is that what you keep telling yourself, Bennett? Is that your mantra? Does it help you sleep at night?"

"Gant murdered Lily Hight, you bitch. He deserved what he got. He deserved to die by her father's hand."

It's what she expected to hear. What she wanted to hear. The corporate line. It had two necessary components. First, Gant murders Lily. Second,

Hight murders Gant in an act of revenge. It was clean and neat. It had a beginning and an end. Something that everybody could live with.

Except that it didn't work anymore. On any level. Not after Escabar was murdered.

But she needed to hear Bennett say it. She needed to be sure. She gave them a last look, hiding beneath the sheets. Then she closed her jacket and walked out, feeling dizzy. Sometimes the truth did that.

45

Sitting for a moment in her car, she still felt light-headed. She had broken into Cobb's apartment, walked in on Bennett and Watson's lunchtime love fest and shown her hand, spent the rest of the afternoon and early evening at her desk bringing her own murder book up to date.

She needed to eat something and get some rest.

She checked her rearview mirror as she drove through the hills on her way home. No one was following her. She'd kept an eye out for Dick Harvey, but hadn't seen him all day. She hoped that the gossip reporter had moved on to another story.

The radio was still tuned to 88.1 FM out of Long Beach. They were playing Robert Glasper's "Of Dreams to Come"—and she found the piano music more than soothing. As she pulled into her drive and parked, she listened until the jazz piece ended.

She walked into the house, dumping her briefcase on the couch and heading for the kitchen. But as she stepped around the counter, she noticed the light blinking on her telephone. She checked the caller ID, but didn't recognize the number. When she listened to the message and heard Debi Watson's voice, she pulled over a stool and sat down.

Her risk had paid off. Watson wanted to talk.

But even better, the deputy DA sounded anxious and had left her home phone number. There was the chance that she had something real to say.

Lena checked the time and entered the number into the handset. After four rings, Watson's service picked up so she left a message that included her cell number. Returning the phone to its cradle, curiosity began to work on her and she hoped that Watson would call back tonight. She glanced at her briefcase, her energy returning. But as she climbed off the stool, time seemed to shoot forward and break in half before her eyes.

She heard a loud *pop*—then shielded her face as a wave of shattered glass burst through the air and crashed into the room. Ducking out of the way, she turned just as a cast-iron chair from the terrace bounced off the living room wall. But she didn't turn back quickly enough. She didn't see Dan Cobb charging through the broken slider as much as she knew it was him.

He hit her hard. He blindsided her with all his weight, and tackled her to the ground.

Lena smashed onto the hardwood floor and felt the air rush out of her lungs. He was on top of her now. He pulled her gun away and tossed it by the couch, pressing his hand over her face and pushing her head down.

She forced herself to breathe. After two quick gasps, she drew in more air, then rocked her body onto her side and tried to squirm out from underneath. She kicked him in the stomach and chest, kept her feet moving, and tried to pull herself away. She reached out for the side table, but Cobb batted it away with such force that the legs broke off as it hit the floor.

He grabbed her by the waist, rolled her onto her back, and reeled her in. He was on top of her again, grunting and groaning and using his body weight to keep her arms and fists still. He was pulling her hair and gripping her head and slowly working his way downward.

She felt his hands close around her neck. His grip tightened and began squeezing the life out of her. She looked for her gun—tried not to panic—and saw it on the shards of broken glass. She knew it was too far away.

She looked at his face, the sweat beading on his forehead. His nose looked broken—his goatee framing his clenched teeth.

"You corrupt piece of shit," he was saying. "You corrupt piece of—"

She started choking. She tried to find his fingertips. Tried to pry them—

"You broke into my fucking place. You stole my files. My fucking murder book. My fucking murder—"

His grip tightened. She was dizzy again. He lowered his face into hers. They were nose to nose now. She could feel herself—

"You're the new fucking deal all right," he said. "A total fucking fraud. A liar and a cheat, a thief and a dirty fucking—"

She tried to find her voice. When the words came out, they broke up like a bad cell signal.

"Kill me, Cobb. But it won't make any difference."

His rage seemed to double. "It'll be better."

"It won't make any difference because they know."

He laughed at her and banged her head into the floor. She tried to pull his hands away. She couldn't. She thought that she might already be dead. Everything seemed upside down.

"They know you did it," she said. "They know you shot Bosco and Gant."

He let go of her neck.

She didn't know why.

She started coughing and tried to catch her breath. Cobb was still on top of her—his chest heaving, his face an inch away like they were lovers. Those wild eyes staring through her.

"They know you did it, Cobb."

"How?"

"The gun you used. It matched up."

"It matched?"

"That drive-by case you worked with Bennett and Higgins. Eight years ago in Exposition Park. Elvira Wheaten and her grandson. You pulled the gun from Property. They have your request card. You did it. All four of you assholes are guilty. You kill me and they'll hunt you guys down like animals."

His eyes were still on her, still measuring her as he chewed it over. He looked crazed and still couldn't seem to get enough air. After a long stretch, he rolled off of her body, then reached out and grabbed her gun, his mind a million miles away.

"They didn't make girls like you when I was growing up," he said.

"Screw you."

"We need to take a drive."

"So you can shoot me?"

"No," he said. "So you can see something."

"See what?"

"You tell me when we get there."

"You're a piece of shit, Cobb."

He handed over her gun and struggled to get to his feet. "No, I'm not, Gamble. I'm the guy who tipped off Paladino, and made sure that Jacob Gant's DNA got lost in the fucking lab."

46

She was sitting in the passenger seat of his Lincoln. Cobb had asked her to call ahead to make sure Martin Orth would be at the crime lab. Once she had confirmation, Cobb called a sheriff's deputy he knew to come over and fix her sliding door before the coyotes moved in.

Maybe the world really was spinning upside down. Maybe she'd crossed over and died on the living room floor.

She looked at him behind the wheel—his wild eyes pinned to the road. Another dust storm was blowing into the city thick as smoke. The freeway kept vanishing, then coming back.

During the silence, she tried to make sense of it all.

Cobb had turned on Bennett, Watson, and Higgins, and given Paladino the anonymous tip. First, Cobb had railroaded Gant, but then he'd given him the only chance he had at a NOT GUILTY verdict.

She tried to make sense of it, but she couldn't.

He seemed so jittery. He kept checking the rearview mirror. He said he wouldn't talk to her until they reached the crime lab. He wanted Lily Hight's clothing brought to a room where they could be assured of privacy. He said that they would need a foam mannequin that matched Lily's height and form as well. As Lena made the request over the phone,

Orth's voice sounded just as strange as it had this morning. Still, he agreed to the favor and told her that he would have everything ready by the time she arrived.

The drive through the dust cloud took forty-five minutes. They found Orth waiting by his office door. Orth seemed more than surprised to see Cobb with her. But after a moment's hesitation, he led them down the hall to a room with sinks and lab tables that hadn't yet been furnished with equipment.

Lena glanced at the mannequin, then stepped over to the lab table where Orth had laid out the girl's clothing. Cobb walked by her and picked up Lily's boots. Feeling the weight of them in his hands, he passed them over to Lena.

"Tell me what you see, Gamble. And then maybe we'll talk."

Orth didn't seem to understand what was going on. Nor did Lena, although she immediately remembered the clip Vaughan had shown her of Cobb on the witness stand. He had been holding one of Lily's boots when he lost his composure and said he needed a glass of water. She thought it might have been the right boot, but wasn't certain.

She set the left boot down on the table and began with the right. Nothing about the boot seemed out of the ordinary. The leather wasn't scratched or stained. The lining remained free of any marks.

And then she turned it over. She picked up the left boot, glanced at the sole, then discarded it.

Lily Hight's right ankle had been broken during the attack. And now she could see how it had happened. The sole of her right boot wasn't just worn. It looked like someone had blasted away the rubber with a high-speed grinder.

She could feel Cobb's eyes on her. She knew that they had never left her. When she looked up at his face—his hardened, brutal face—he nodded slightly and it felt like an electric shock working across her shoulder blades.

"Lily was trapped in the passenger seat of a moving car," she said. "She was trying to get out. Trying to escape. That's how she broke her ankle. In a moving car."

Orth took the boot for a look of his own and seemed stunned. Cobb sat down on a stool and began rubbing his knees.

"I was on the stand when I noticed," he said. "I saw it and knew that I'd fucked up. But we need to make sure of something, and I couldn't do it after the trial without people noticing."

"Make sure of what?" Orth asked.

Cobb didn't answer the question. Instead, he asked the SID supervisor to dress the mannequin in Lily's T-shirt and blouse and place it in a sitting position on the table. Lena suddenly realized what Cobb was up to.

It was all about the screwdriver that the killer had plunged into Lily Hight's back. It was all about the holes the murder weapon punched through her clothing—a T-shirt that would have clung to her skin, and a blouse that was loose enough to move. It was all about the fact that when her back was straight, the holes in the two pieces of clothing didn't match up.

Orth shook his head and gasped as he noticed.

Then Cobb began pushing the mannequin forward an inch at a time from the waist. When the holes in the two pieces of clothing finally merged into one, it was clear to everyone in the room.

Lily Hight had been leaning away from the killer with her foot out the door of the car when he plunged the screwdriver into her back.

"My God," Orth said.

47

Vaughan walked out of his house, took three steps, then spotted Lena standing in front of the white Lincoln parked in his driveway and stopped dead in his tracks. His body locked up. He looked afraid and uncertain.

"What's going on, Lena?" he said quietly. "Are you okay?"

His eyes were zeroed in on Cobb behind the wheel. When they rocked back over to her, she nodded. She'd made a mistake. She should have called him on the drive over and told him what happened. She gave him the bottom line as quickly as she could.

"Cobb's the one who tipped off Paladino," she said. "Lily wasn't murdered in her bedroom. The crime scene was staged."

Vaughan didn't move. "What are those marks on your neck? Are you sure this isn't some kind of trap?"

"It's not a trap, but things aren't cool. We need to talk, Greg. Let's go."

He seemed reluctant, but climbed into the backseat nonetheless. When Cobb offered his hand, Vaughan shook it without saying anything—his eyes big and glassy and still absorbing the shock.

Cobb drove south on the Pacific Coast Highway heading for Tim

Hight's house. While they drove, Lena gave Vaughan a detailed briefing on what had happened at the crime lab. Vaughan took it in with
some reservation until Lena mentioned Lily's right boot. He had seen
Cobb's performance on the witness stand with his own eyes, and now
the reasons behind it were clear.

The drive took less than fifteen minutes. As Hight's house came
into view, Cobb pulled over to the curb and switched off his headlights. The moment reminded Lena of the first time she and Rhodes
had set eyes on the two houses. Every window in the Gants' house radi-
ated a warm incandescent light. But for the glow of a police scanner in
the sunroom, every window in Hight's house was dark.

"You see the head of his cigarette," Cobb whispered.

Lena nodded. "I see it."

"He just sits there," Vaughan said. "Listening to his scanner and
staring at Gant's house. Why do you think he does it?"

"Because he knows," Cobb said.

"Knows what?"

"The killer's still out there, Vaughan. The one who took his daughter away. He loved her."

Lena glanced at Cobb. "We can put him in the murder room at the
club. He saw what happened to Gant. He's known all week."

"Why hasn't he said anything?" Vaughan asked.

"Same reason I didn't," Cobb said. "He's probably scared. I am."

Vaughan moved closer to the window. "So where did you find the
blood?"

"In the driveway by the back door," Cobb said.

They were talking about something Orth mentioned before Lena
and Cobb left the crime lab. The possibility that SID hadn't mishandled the evidence, and that the blood found its way to the driveway as
the killer moved Lily's body into the house.

But Lena wasn't really listening to them. She was thinking about
the gun the killer was using. The gun she'd originally thought Cobb
had pulled out of Property. The 9-mm Smith that had been traced back
to the drive-by shootings of Elvira Wheaten and her grandson eight

years ago. Before tonight she had attributed the use of this weapon to what she considered Cobb's poor judgment and lack of self-control.

Before tonight when she found out who Cobb really was.

Now she realized that the killer had to be using this particular gun for a reason. The question was why? Why would anyone use a weapon that he knew could be identified so easily? And who walked into Property calling themselves Dan Cobb and filled out that request card? Who walked out with the gun?

Higgins couldn't have pulled it off. Bennett seemed just as unlikely. And Lena had seen Debi Watson's swollen boobs. No one would have mistaken her for Dan Cobb.

But Jerry Spadell was different. Way different.

Spadell had been out of the loop for years, yet still would have known how everything worked. The Property Room was open 24/7, the clerks were civilians. He would have had access to Cobb's badge number through the DA's office and known how to make a counterfeit ID. He would have timed his visit for late at night. But even more, Spadell knew how to use a gun. Lena imagined that he had more than enough experience to handle whatever was asked of him as long as the money was good. And Spadell had that grizzled look of a guy who knew how to pull the trigger and not look back.

She wondered if that's what they were really dealing with now.

A man who raped and murdered Lily Hight, then hired Spadell to kill four more people in order to clean things up. The man Lena had caught with Spadell breaking into Bosco's house in Malibu. The man who was searching through security videos from Club 3 AM, and ran away when Lena knocked on the door.

The district attorney of Los Angeles County.

Jimmy J. Higgins in a pinstripe suit.

The flow stopped—the inner dialogue. She didn't like it. Something about it didn't feel right. Not yet anyway. Not without an answer.

Why that gun?

Her mind surfaced. Vaughan was saying something about Bennett, Watson, and Higgins leaving an electronic trail on their computer network. E-mails that had to be there but were buried in the system. When they quieted down, Lena turned to Cobb.

"Why that gun?" she said. "Why is the killer using a gun he knew would be traced?"

She could see him tossing it over, but he didn't say anything.

"Why?" she said.

"I've been thinking the same thing, Gamble. And there's only one answer."

"What's that?"

Cobb gave her a look. "He wanted it to be traced."

"But that's not an answer."

"I know," he said.

A sudden burst of bright light flooded the interior of the car. Lena checked the rear window and saw a white van rolling through the curve slowly. As the van idled by, she turned and watched the driver park in an open space five cars up the block. After several minutes, the door opened and Dick Harvey hopped out carrying a small video camera.

He looked up and down the street, but didn't see them. Cobb's Lincoln never would have registered. And he seemed too preoccupied by Tim Hight's house. He was staring at the sunroom—Hight's silhouette and the bead of light from his cigarette still visible in the dim light cast from his police scanner.

Lena traded looks with Cobb and Vaughan, but no one said anything.

Harvey was taking a second look around the neighborhood. Satisfied that no one was around, he slipped through the gate and into Hight's yard. Lena watched as he zigzagged his way through the shadows and finally reached the window. After adjusting the lens, he brought the camera up to his eye.

Hight was suffering. And Harvey wanted the shot for another episode of *Blanket Hollywood*. Thus was the credo of the lowlife. The worldview of modern scum as seen on every TV network every night.

48

Debi Watson hadn't returned her call, and Lena worried that the more time the deputy DA took to think it over, the less likely she was to open up and talk. In spite of the hour, Lena had left a second message on Watson's service when she returned last night and a third this morning as soon as she got up. If she didn't hear back by noon, she decided to show up at her office and force the issue.

Lena hadn't slept well last night. She couldn't stop thinking about that 9-mm Smith. She agreed with Cobb. The killer was using the gun because he wanted it to be traced.

But the question was why? And it was feeding on her.

It seemed more than obvious that it had something to do with what happened eight years ago.

Lena had spent the morning reading about the drive-by shootings of Elvira Wheaten and her grandson. She hadn't remembered the case when Vaughan first mentioned it to her. But she remembered the eyewitness, Wes Brown, who had been murdered three months after Bennett and Higgins won the trial and Higgins took office. At some point it dawned on her that her memory had been jogged for a reason. Wes Brown had a brother who owned a small record label. She didn't know

Reggie Brown, but she knew people who did and managed to get his phone number.

Although Brown agreed to talk to her and even lived near Lena in the hills above Sunset, he refused to meet in any place other than the exact spot where his brother had been gunned down. That spot happened to be in a small park across the street from the empty lot where Wheaten and her grandson had been killed. Apparently, there were two picnic tables underneath the trees. Reggie Brown's little brother had been playing chess at the table closest to the street on both days. And that's where she could find Reggie in forty-five minutes.

Her cell phone chirped. Vaughan had sent her a text message. He was at Parker Center working with Keith Upshaw from the Computer Crime Section. They were just getting started. Upshaw had played a key role in the Romeo serial murders a few years back. He was young and brilliant, an ex-hacker that Chief Logan had recruited after speaking with a judge who didn't want to see Upshaw go to jail. If anyone from the DA's office deleted their e-mails thinking that they were history, Lena knew that Upshaw would find them and bring them back to life.

She checked her watch, grabbed a bottle of water, and headed out the door. The location in Exposition Park was a half-hour drive south on Western Avenue. But Lena wanted to avoid the traffic in Koreatown. After twenty minutes working surface streets, she made a left turn and started to cut back to Western. The neighborhood changed and she could see the long line of young African-American men standing at the curb waving down cars. She didn't need to look at a street sign to know where she was. The street was nicknamed the Avenue of the Ghosts because the young men were as thin as stick figures, and their warm brown complexions had been bleached out to a pale gray from a life on crystal meth. They looked like skeletons—horrific Halloween displays that packed guns, dealt crank, and had no chance of finding their way back.

The sight was more than unsettling and she was grateful when she saw Western Avenue ahead and finally reached the park nestled in between a library and an elementary school.

She found Reggie Brown sitting at the picnic table smoking a cigarette and drinking sweet tea. He looked like he might be twenty-five, and was dressed in a pair of black slacks, a red T-shirt, and a Rolex that he wore loose like a bracelet. As Lena approached the table and introduced herself, she didn't sense any animosity at all.

"I checked you out," he said. "You're David Gamble's sister. We've got the same thing goin' on, huh?"

Lena shrugged and sat down. "You tell me, Reggie. I'm working with a detective—Dan Cobb—do you remember him?"

"Of course, I do. DC. That's what we used to call him."

"I know that it's been eight years. That you might have forgotten details."

He took a hit on his cigarette. "I haven't forgotten anything, Lena Gamble. And I never will. I lost my brother just like you did. Have you forgotten anything?"

A moment passed with Lena not sure how to put it into words. "Something happened," she said finally. "Something that's come up in a murder case this week. Something that might point back to eight years ago."

Brown paused a moment to consider what she was saying. His eyes were bright and expressive.

"I don't know what you're dealing with now," he said. "But you're right about one thing. Eight years ago something happened, and his name was Steven Bennett. I'm surprised Cobb didn't tell you. He knows as much as I do."

She looked away, trying not to show any surprise. Why would Cobb hold out on her after last night?

"Tell me about Bennett," she said.

"He's a motherfucker. A world-class motherfucker. Wes was sitting at this table. The empty lot's right over there across from the library. He hears the shooting and hides underneath the bench. He sees Mrs.

Wheaten go down. He sees the faces in the car as they drive off. He hears them laughing. My brother knew what he had to do. He helped Cobb ID every one of them."

"But then he wouldn't testify in court," she said. "He couldn't come out in the open. It would have been suicide."

Brown grimaced at the thought. "Snitches wear stitches," he said. "Wes knew it. I knew it. Cobb knew it."

"But Bennett didn't?"

"That's why he's a motherfucker, Lena Gamble. Bennett knew it just the same as everybody else. The difference was that he didn't care."

"He kept the pressure up," she said. "He wouldn't take no for an answer."

"He'd call three or four times a day. And he wasn't asking anymore, okay? He was telling. He was screaming at Wes. He was threatening my brother with jail time."

It hung there. In the heat of the day. Lena could feel the rage building inside her. She wished Vaughan was with her to hear this.

"But your brother didn't give in," she said finally.

Brown pushed his tea aside. "The trial comes and goes, and it turns out they didn't even need Wes. Bennett and Higgins win the thing outright, and Higgins becomes the next DA. The crisis in the neighborhood is finally over. No one knows what Wes did. Everything's fading into the past."

Lena could sense what was coming—what had to be coming—from the expression on Brown's face.

"But it didn't fade into the past," she said quietly. "After the trial—after the election—Bennett called back and told your brother that it wasn't over."

Brown nodded, lowering his head and wiping his eyes as the memory welled up before him. When he spoke, his soft voice shook in agony.

"It happened the next day," he said. "They waited until everybody could see. Bennett sent a cop to the house. When he saw Wes with his friends, the cop flashed a big dumb-ass smile at him, tipped his hat as if to say thanks, and drove away. Two hours later, Wes was sitting right where I'm sitting. Wes was doing what he liked best, sitting here and playing chess. Me and my mom don't think he saw it coming, okay? He was still holding a piece in his hand. Still making a move when they gunned my baby brother down."

Brown dropped his cigarette on the grass and didn't move to pick it up. His eyes were turned inward, lost in the past.

"Did Bennett ever call back?"

Brown shook his head. "No," he said. "He never did. But last year I saw him at Club 3 AM. Once in a while I'd go. Once in a while he'd be there. I'm not sure how a guy like Bennett gets in, okay? But somehow he did. He'd sit there at the bar and stare at me like he wanted me to know that it was him. Like he'd taken Wes away from us and there was no way anyone could ever prove it. Those green eyes of his. A friend of mine who served in Iraq called them desert eyes . . . snake eyes. They don't move and they don't blink. They just push through you and shoot back."

"Is that all you ever saw him do there?"

"I'd watch him try to hit on chicks," he said. "But all they ever did was look at the piece of shit and laugh. He stopped coming after a while. Maybe Johnny Bosco told him to get lost. I asked Bosco about it more than once."

Lena dug into her pocket for a cigarette and lit up. The sun was in her eyes and she moved to the other side of the table and sat beside Brown in the shade. She looked at the fence around the park, at the empty lot on the other side of the street.

When Bennett couldn't bully an eyewitness into risking his life, he fingered him and had him killed. There was a theme to the man. A method. A sense of repetition. And finally, an answer to the question, why that gun?

49

She was cruising down the Avenue of the Ghosts, but her mind was fifteen miles up the road, so she didn't notice those stick-figured teenagers getting loaded and waving down customers from the curb.

She didn't want to get ahead of herself, didn't want to let her imagination play with the facts or get too revved up. She needed to reach Debi Watson. She needed to get the woman to talk. And she needed to do it as fast as she could.

But she had a bad feeling about it now.

Before leaving the park, Lena had tried calling Watson at her office and was told by her assistant that the deputy DA hadn't come in today. When she pressed the young woman for more information, she was told that Watson hadn't called in sick and wasn't answering her cell or home phone. Her assistant said that she was worried about her, and had given Lena her address on Norwich Drive in West Hollywood.

Before the dread could get a decent grip on her, Lena made a hard right and picked up speed heading for Venice Boulevard. She was still waiting on Cobb. Two blocks later, he finally picked up his cell.

"How did you get this fucking number?" he said.

"You're a police officer, Cobb. You're in the directory. Now why didn't you tell me about what Bennett did to Wes Brown?"

Cobb didn't say anything for so long that Lena thought her phone had died. She checked the battery, then the signal—then he came back on.

"The 9-mm Smith goes back to what happened eight years ago, Cobb. Bennett had your eyewitness killed. Why didn't you say something?"

"Because I'm not sure what it means," he said.

He was trying to keep his voice down. Lena didn't like it.

"Where are you?" she said.

"I'm outside Bennett's house keeping an eye on things. He took the day off and seems agitated."

"If you're not sure what it means, why are you following Bennett?"

"I wasn't," he said. "I was on Higgins. He and that friend of his stopped by here about an hour ago. When they left, I got curious and decided to stay."

"Can you see Bennett?"

"He's standing in his driveway arguing with his wife. They've been at it for half an hour. They're every neighborhood's favorite couple, Gamble. They're screamers."

"What are they arguing about?"

"She knows he's cheating on her. Apparently she's not happy about it."

"Are you in your car?"

"No," he said. "There's a hill across the street. Lots of trees with an elevated view of the whole property. Bennett has bucks. He lives on North Rockingham off Sunset. How's a deputy DA make that kind of cash?"

Lena had reached Venice Boulevard and could see San Vicente just ahead. She began weaving through traffic and using the shoulder when she got stuck. With any luck, she was ten minutes out.

"You need to listen to me, Cobb."

"Listen to what?"

"I'm gonna tell you what the gun means."

He went quiet again. She couldn't tell if he was avoiding the issue or needed to shut down because of what he was doing.

"I'm back," he whispered. "Tell me what you think it means."

"You're being set up, Cobb. You're the way the killer gets away with this. Somehow he found out that you're the one who tipped off Paladino and wrecked the case. When Bosco and Gant got too close, he used that gun. When Escabar found the video of Lily at the club, ballistics is gonna tell us that he used it again. You've got a target on your back. You're not safe."

It hung there for a while, the target on Cobb's back.

"You might be right," he whispered finally. "But is it Bennett or is it Higgins? I always thought Reggie got it wrong. No question that Bennett was abusing his brother on the phone, but Higgins was the politician, Gamble. Higgins needed to win that trial, not Bennett. How do we know Bennett isn't just some mean little prick doing whatever Higgins tells him to do? How do we know it wasn't Higgins who sent that cop over and got the kid killed?"

She thought about Jerry Spadell again. "We don't," she said finally.

"And what about the target on your back? What about the target on Vaughan?"

She didn't have an answer. She couldn't be certain. She needed to get Debi Watson to talk.

She blew through a red light and turned onto Melrose, then made another right on Norwich and started picking out street numbers. Watson's house was halfway up the block on the left side—a two-story Mediterranean covered in ivy with palm trees nested beside the gardens and a eucalyptus shading the front yard. She pulled into the drive and parked before the garage. On any other day she would have looked at Watson's house as something of an oasis. But today, all she picked up on was the darkness. The bad vibes.

"Any chance you've seen Debi Watson today, Cobb?"

"Bennett's with his wife," he said. "What's wrong with your voice?"

Her eyes made a second pass over the house—slower than the first. It seemed so still. So quiet.

50

Up the street Lena could see two men cutting a lawn. A young woman was pushing a baby carriage down the sidewalk toward the shops on Melrose.

She turned back to Watson's house, rang the bell, and checked the front door. No answer. Moving quickly across the front yard, she stepped into the garden and peered through the living room window. When she didn't see anything amiss, she continued around the house until she had examined every window and door.

Privacy was no longer an issue. If someone saw what she was doing and called 911, Lena would have welcomed the company. Still, the quickest way in was the deadbolt on the back door.

She fished out her tension wrench and short hook and took a few deep breaths to steady her nerves. The lock was so old that she could hear the pins clicking over the din of the neighborhood. Within forty-five seconds, she felt the wrench begin turning and gave the door a push.

She was standing in a small mudroom. The alarm hadn't been armed, and she could hear the sound of a television cutting through the stillness. Stepping into the foyer, she noted the ceiling fan rotating slowly above the living room and a dining area that hadn't been cleaned up from last night. There were two place settings on the table, along with two glasses of red wine that had only been partially consumed. She lifted the bottle up to the window light and saw that it was empty. When she set it down, she spotted the TV in the corner tuned to CNN and became aware of an odor. Some sort of cleaning product with a strong artificial scent.

Grapefruit, maybe. It seemed so odd and out of place.

She stepped back into the foyer, turned the corner, and entered the kitchen. There was a bucket filled with water on the floor. A mop leaned against the wall, and she saw a pile of rags and a bottle of Mr. Clean by the sink. When a phone started ringing, she flinched but caught herself. She spotted the cell phone on the breakfast table by Watson's handbag but didn't touch it. Leaning closer, she read the caller ID and realized that it was Watson's office number. Her assistant was still worried, still trying to reach her boss.

Lena noticed the sun beginning to set outside and took two more deep breaths as she switched on the overhead light. It wasn't working anymore. The churning in her stomach wouldn't go away, the bad vibes following her from room to room.

She turned and looked on the other side of the refrigerator. There was a large cutting board on the counter and a set of hand forged chef's knives from Japan. A photograph of Watson with a little girl riding a swing was leaning against the backsplash. On the wall beside the door, Lena found another alarm panel and realized that the door opened to the garage.

And on the floor—when her eyes finally drifted down to the tiled floor—she saw the blood that hadn't been entirely cleaned up. The drag marks leading into the garage.

She took the jolt but steadied herself. Stepping around the blood, she opened the door and looked at the white Audi in the darkness. She took a whiff of the air and knew with certainty that her conversation with Debi Watson wouldn't involve many words.

She hit the light switch, scanning the room for a corpse. The floor was clear and she gave the car a long look. Returning to the kitchen, she opened Watson's handbag and fished out her keys. Then she stepped over the drag marks, hit the clicker, and tried to keep cool.

The car beeped and the trunk popped open.

The air in the garage changed quickly, becoming sour and harsh. Lena covered her mouth and nose and hurried around the car for a look.

And then she stopped.

She could see Watson's body in the small trunk. Her face. Her curly blond hair. The dried blood that had trickled out of her mouth. The two bullet wounds piercing her abdomen and chest. She was wrapped in clear plastic. Her eyes were open, her palm pressing against the plastic as if she'd still been alive when she was packed up and left in the darkness. Nothing about her death looked easy.

Lena staggered back into the kitchen, the gruesome image still with her as she closed the door to the garage.

She took a moment to collect herself, then another before picking up Watson's cell phone for a look at her recent call list.

Her last call out had been to Lena at 6:25 p.m. last night. Bennett had called her a half hour before that and the two had spoken for a couple of minutes. The next calls made to Watson's cell phone began at 10:00 a.m. this morning from her office, and continued every hour until just a few minutes ago.

She set the phone down and thought it through.

The disposal of Debi Watson was still a work in progress. She was certain of this. The killer had wrapped her up and placed her in the trunk because he intended to dump her corpse somewhere else. But even more telling, the killer hadn't finished cleaning up. The bucket of water, the fresh rags beside the bottle of Mr. Clean, the mop leaning against the wall—it seemed clear enough that he had every intention of returning. Because there were no signs of forced entry, it was a better than good guess that Watson knew her killer. That they shared dinner together last night with a bottle of wine. That the killer could come and go as he pleased because he had a set of keys. And that he would be back sometime tonight to finish up.

Could there really be any doubt?

She hit the stairs for a look at the master bedroom. On the chest of drawers was a photograph of Watson with Bennett. It looked like they had taken a day off and traveled south to the racetrack in Del Mar. They were sitting at a table with cocktails. Although Watson's smile looked genuine enough, Lena couldn't help thinking that even in this setting, Bennett appeared mean and vicious.

She set the picture frame down and stepped into the bathroom. There were two sinks. She saw the hair dryer and makeup, then spotted a shaving kit on the counter and moved down to the far sink. Nothing stood out as she sifted through the items except that the kit seemed so needlessly full. Checking the cabinet underneath, she found a number of empty baskets. From the stains in the webbing, she could tell that the baskets once held toiletries and that Bennett was making his move and packing up.

She could feel the tension building in her shoulders, a fresh load of adrenaline making a jagged run through her body.

She glanced at the large bed, noted the silk sheets, then yanked open the closet doors. The racks were filled entirely with Watson's clothing. There was no room for sharing here. When she checked the drawers, she didn't find anything that might belong to Bennett.

She hurried down the hall, found the guest room, and switched on the lights. As she entered, she saw two boxes of cleaned shirts on the bed and several pairs of men's dress shoes by the chair. An open suitcase was set on the trunk by the window. She pulled the closet doors open and counted five business suits on the rack, along with one that was wrapped up and had probably come from the dry cleaners with the two boxes of shirts on the bed.

She was overdosing on the moment now. Choking on it.

She started to pull the plastic away from the suit. Slowly at first, then ripping at it with her fingers when she saw the pinstripes. Her face flushed with heat, her eyes reeling back and forth across the fabric until they zeroed in on the left lapel and found the mark.

51

Cobb's mind was beginning to skip through time again.

He'd spent the last hour gazing at the sunset and daydreaming about a ribeye steak, a glass of Cutty Sark, and a night under the sheets with Betty Kim. After wasting the day watching Bennett fool around in his garage, Cobb thought he deserved a reward of significant proportions. If it came down to a single choice, he would have saved the food and whisky for later, and picked door number three. Betty Kim. But it was a Friday night; he knew his life was on the line, and he saw no reason why he didn't deserve all three.

He dug the bottle of Tylenol out of his pocket and gave it a shake, but only one caplet fell out. Grimacing at the empty bottle, he popped the pill and knocked it back with what was left of his bottled water. His back hurt. He'd spent most of the day hiding in the brush overlooking Bennett's McMansion with his elbows pinned to the ground.

He raised the field glasses up to his eyes, found Bennett in his four-car garage, and adjusted the focus.

The man was still washing his fucking car—a gray BMW with tinted glass. He'd been at it for hours. It didn't make sense to Cobb—taking a day off from work and devoting it to a car. Especially on a day when his wife took off with the kids. A day when everything inside the man should have been ripped and scratched.

His cell phone started vibrating.

Cobb looked at it on the ground, saw Gamble's name on the touch screen and smiled at the thought of her. He liked the idea of knowing her and working with her. He liked the idea that his first impression of her had been the wrong one. He liked the fact that the movie inside his head had stopped playing ever since he realized who she really was. That he wasn't alone anymore. That the dead bodies he could see piling up when he closed his eyes had stopped staring at him and stopped taunting him.

"Where are you?" she said.

"Bennett's," he whispered.

"Is he still agitated?"

Cobb sensed something different in her voice and took another look through his field glasses. Bennett had popped open the trunk and was removing the carpet.

"You could call it that," he said. "His wife took off with the kids. They had suitcases."

"And what's he doing about it?"

"Washing his fucking car."

She didn't say anything after that. Just a long stretch of silence.

"You need to get out of there," she said finally. "You need to make sure he doesn't see you."

Cobb raised the field glasses again, but couldn't locate Bennett. The door between the house and garage was open now.

"What is it?" he said.

"It's Bennett, Cobb. He's the killer. He's the one."

"What happened?"

"You need to get out of there. I'm with detectives from the Sheriff's Department. Bennett murdered Debi Watson last night."

She gave him Watson's address in West Hollywood and told him that Vaughan was on his way as well. He could hear the worry in her voice.

"You need to hurry, Cobb. It's not safe. You'll see what I mean when you get here."

He slipped the phone into his pocket, his mind skipping through those beats again. He tried to shake himself clear, but it didn't work. He could see Debi Watson's face the way he had seen it when they prepped for the trial. But as he tried to focus on the image, it began to shift and change until he found himself staring at Lily Hight laid out on the floor of her bedroom.

The place where his nightmare began.

He could remember how his chest locked up when he first walked into the room and saw her there. He could remember the feelings he felt. The sounds of her mother and father weeping that carried through the house from downstairs. He remembered sitting with Lily while he waited for the coroner to arrive. He remembered that he didn't want her to be alone. That he had stroked her soft blond hair.

Cobb raised the field glasses for one last look. The door between the house and garage remained open. Bennett was still inside. Pushing himself off the ground, he grabbed hold of the tree and climbed to his feet.

And then he heard the shots. There were three of them. They seemed loud.

He looked at Bennett's house, reaching around to scratch the itch below his shoulder blades. Bennett hadn't been drawn outside by the sound, and Cobb wasn't sure what was happening. He could feel his knees giving out, his body collapsing onto the ground. After a moment, he began to notice the blood leaking out of his chest and flowing into the dusty earth. He lifted his head out of the dirt, struggling to get his bearings. The sky was spinning, the stars leaving trails as they flew through the heavens. He sensed movement behind him and to his right. As he turned his head, a shoe came out of nowhere and crushed his face.

And then it was over. No more movies playing in his head. No more channels. No more money worries. No more bills.

He'd made it. He could see Betty Kim reaching out for him and pulling him into her arms. He was living the life he'd always dreamed about, the one that always seemed so far away. He was living on Easy Street now.

52

His eyes fucking opened and his body jerked its way up and out of the nosedive. He could feel himself pulling out of the death stall. He batted his eyes and looked around, grunting like an animal. He tried to think, tried to figure out what had just happened and what if anything came next.

He was alone.

Bennett's house was dark.

He'd been left for dead.

Cobb reached for his gun in panic. It was still there, holstered to his belt. He looked for his cell phone, but it was gone. He looked again, but it was still gone. Turning his body into the streetlight, he gazed at his chest. He had heard three shots, but saw only two exit wounds. He needed help. The closest emergency room was at UCLA in Westwood. But he didn't want Bennett to find him. He'd have to make sure the doctors talked to Gamble.

His Lincoln was parked around the corner on Highwood Street. Pulling himself to his feet, he concentrated on his balance and started down the hill. He moved slowly, crashing into bushes that seemed to jump out at him from the darkness. Something had happened to his vision. Everything seemed to be glowing. When he reached the street and a car passed, the headlights were so bright that they burned his eyes.

He pulled himself together. He was close now, just passing Bennett's house on the right. It occurred to him that he needed to leave some kind of trail behind. Something for Gamble to follow—no matter how small—just in case. Drawing his gun, he put two 9-mm rounds in the garage door, then emptied the Sig's mag into the living room windows until he'd shattered enough glass to light up the house and kick in the silent alarm. He glanced at his shell casings in the street, kicking them toward the curb so that they wouldn't get run over and could be found easily.

He felt a small burst of energy after that. Reaching the corner, he saw his Lincoln in the shadows and almost tripped as he dug his keys out of his pocket. He got the door open and managed to climb in. But that burst of energy was gone now.

Cobb took a moment to catch his breath.

He thought about Bennett's trick with the door between the house and garage, and wondered how he could have been beaten by an idiot like that. He wished that Bennett had still been washing his asshole car when he walked by with his gun. He wished that he could have greased the little prick, kicked every tooth out of his head, and hit a home run.

He switched on the interior light, eyeing the wounds in his chest and wrestling with his disbelief and terror. He needed to slow down the bleeding. Opening the glove box, he grabbed the extra napkins he'd collected after ordering fast food and twisted the paper into two tight rolls. Then he pushed them into the exit wounds hoping to plug the holes.

There was no pain. Just weakness.

And Cobb had no idea how long he'd been out. The entrance wounds he couldn't see and couldn't reach behind his back were probably far worse. He knew enough about blood loss and shock to see this as the last problem he would probably ever face.

He got the car moving, coasted down to Sunset and made a right. He tried to find the lane. Tried to center the car between the lines.

There was a horseshoe curve ahead and it felt like a roller coaster tumbling down and around on a shaky track. Somehow he got through it by just holding onto the wheel. But he couldn't get past the headlights shooting his way. They seemed to stick to the windshield even as the cars passed. The lights got brighter and brighter and he closed his eyes. Seconds ticked by before he forced himself to open up and look at the twisting road ahead of him.

He was losing it. He wasn't going to make it.

And when he finally rolled down the last hill and saw the Pacific Coast Highway on the other side of his windshield, he realized that he'd made a wrong turn on Sunset. The emergency room at UCLA had probably been less than five miles east of Bennett's house.

He started to panic. He saw storefronts. A neon sign.

L.A. DOG AND CAT.

He pulled over and groaned when he noticed that the lights were on and someone was inside. He jacked open the door and got out. His gun was in his hand—his Sig Sauer—and he didn't know why. And his balance was off—the air was still—yet it felt like he'd walked into a stiff wind.

He reached the door. He was surprised about that. Through the glass he could see the vet doing paperwork behind the front desk.

Cobb knocked on the glass. It was a weak knock—more of a tap, really—but the vet looked up, pointing at the sign in the door and mouthing the words, "We're closed."

Cobb groaned like an animal again.

We're closed.

The vet had said it louder this time. Loud enough for Cobb to hear his voice through the glass.

We're closed.

He thought that he might vomit, but fought it off. He tried to get his head straight, but knew with certainty that he had no chance. He looked at the door—the wood frame and the wood panels below the glass. Then he took two steps back and charged forward, driving his shoulder into the lock.

The door burst open and the vet jumped to his feet.

Cobb raised his gun. "If you say 'We're closed' one more time, I'm gonna blow your fuckin' head off."

The vet's mouth dropped open. Cobb could see him staring at the napkins pushed into his chest. The blood wicking through the paper and dripping onto the floor like a couple of leaky pipes.

"I'm a police officer," he said. "And I need your help."

The vet tried to speak, but stumbled on his words. He looked young. Thirty-five with light features, wearing jeans and a lab coat. The tag over his pocket read DR. FRANK.

"I'll call an ambulance," the vet said.

Cobb shook his head back and forth, almost losing his balance. "I'll bleed to death before it gets here. You gotta do it. You gotta help me."

"But I'm a veterinarian," he said. "I take care of animals."

"I've been an animal most of my life, Doc. And this isn't exactly a request."

Cobb realized that he'd emptied the gun's mag into Bennett's bullshit dream house, but flicked the muzzle in the vet's face just the same. When he saw Frank's eyes widen slightly, he knew that it had worked. The Sig was a good-looking piece. Cobb had always admired it.

"Okay, okay," Dr. Frank said. "Let's go. Let's do it."

He grabbed Cobb's arm and helped him into the back room. There was a stainless steel table here and the tiles on the walls were the same color blue as Gamble's eyes. Cobb took this as a good sign, but had to admit to himself that good signs were selling cheap right now.

Dr. Frank lifted him onto the table, then slipped his hands into a pair of vinyl gloves. He pulled off Cobb's shirt and started working on the wounds. He worked quickly, like a medic in the field, and Cobb wondered if the guy had ever served.

"You've gotta tell me what happened," the vet was saying. "I need to know what I'm dealing with."

Cobb looked up at him. He was the right age, and he didn't look scared anymore.

"Three shots fired behind my back," he said. "I count two exit wounds. I'm hoping one of the three missed. I lost my cell phone, Doc. If something happens to me—"

A wave passed over his body. A big one with a lot of roll to it.

It felt like he was sinking in a sea of exhaustion. He tried to keep talking. Tried to convey the situation as best he could. Tried to give the vet the real deal in broad strokes and tell him that Gamble was in danger. But he wasn't sure he was making much sense anymore. He wasn't even sure if he was really talking.

53

Lena was weaving through heavy traffic on the west end of Sunset Boulevard on a Friday night. She didn't know how fast the car was moving because she hadn't checked the speedometer. All she knew was that the car couldn't go fast enough. She glanced over at Vaughan in the passenger seat.

"It'll be okay," he said.

Over the past hour every time she'd looked at him, Vaughan had said the same thing.

It'll be okay.

She had waited for Vaughan at Debi Watson's house in West Hollywood and walked him through the crime scene with detectives from the Sheriff's Department. Vaughan had spent the day rooting through the district attorney's computer system with Keith Upshaw. They'd found something and he wanted to talk about it. But Lena's mind was on Cobb. She couldn't stop worrying about him. He was supposed to meet them at Watson's house, but he never showed up. When she tried calling him, his message service kept picking up after a single ring as if his phone had been turned off.

Everything about it felt grim. Everything about it, wrong.

She found a clear stretch of road and picked up speed.

"Rockingham's just around the corner," Vaughan said. "It's gonna be on the right and come up fast."

She spotted the street sign as she rolled out of the curve. Once she made the turn, she saw the flashing lights and felt the pull in her gut. The street had been blocked off by a handful of black and white cruisers out of the West L.A. Station. A cop directing traffic was motioning her to make a U-turn and drive away. Lena grit her teeth and shook her head at the guy. When she flashed her badge, she was redirected to a spot on the first side street that hadn't been blocked off.

Vaughan touched her arm. "Are you gonna be okay?"

She looked at him. She couldn't tell. Everything seemed so raw.

She ripped open the door, met Vaughan on the other side, and they hurried up the street. As they checked in, she glanced at Bennett's house and noticed the shattered windows and the bullet holes in the garage door. Vaughan gave her a nudge and pointed across the street to a hill overlooking the house. There were two men up there searching the ground with flashlights. It had to be the spot Cobb had told her about. The one with the view.

"I don't see an ambulance," Vaughan whispered.

"And I don't see the coroner's van. Maybe we got lucky."

Someone called out her name.

She turned and saw a detective standing at the curb in front of Bennett's house. She knew him. His name was Clayton Hu. They had spent a year on patrol together when they both wore uniforms and worked out of Hollywood.

Hu seemed surprised as he approached them and offered his hand. "What are you guys doing here, Lena?"

"Looking for a detective named Dan Cobb. Have you seen him, Clayton?"

The detective shook his head. "We're still trying to figure out what happened. This house belongs to a deputy district attorney."

Vaughan nodded. "We know," he said. "Steven Bennett."

"No one's around," Hu said. "We've been trying to locate Bennett for the last hour. We've got his phone numbers, but he's not responding to the messages we've left. We've got calls into every hospital in the city. Anyone walks in with a gunshot wound and we'll know about it."

Vaughan gave Lena a look, then turned back to Hu. "Maybe you should tell us what you've got."

Hu nodded again, switching on his flashlight and walking them over to the curb. He pointed out the shell casings, then turned the light on the trail of spilled blood that led up and down the street. Lena forced herself to look, but found it painful. Personal.

Hu turned to her. "What was Cobb doing here?"

"Keeping an eye on Bennett."

"And Bennett's a suspect?"

"Yeah," she said. "He's a suspect. It's murder, Clayton. Multiple counts."

"I was afraid you were gonna say that. Let's take a walk up the hill."

They followed the blood trail up the street, then cut into the brush once they'd passed the crime scene tape. When they reached the top of the hill, the two men already there lowered their flashlights and pointed out three more shell casings. After a few moments, the beams of light panned back toward the edge of the hill and Lena's eyes came to rest on the blood that had soaked into the dry ground. There was a lot of it.

"I'm sorry," Hu said in a quiet voice. "I'm guessing this is where your detective was keeping an eye on things when he got shot. Is he a friend?"

Lena nodded without saying anything.

"He lost a lot of blood, Lena. But he's gotta be pretty tough because he walked out and drove away. The blood trail goes all the way down to the next street and then stops where we think he parked his car. We didn't know he was a cop."

Vaughan cleared his throat. "He would have driven into Westwood."

Hu nodded. "We thought so, too, but no one's shown up yet. Not with a gunshot wound."

Lena looked over the hill at Bennett's house, then turned back to Hu. "You've got people looking for him between here and there?"

"Not yet," he said. "But I'll make it happen."

She gave him as much information as she had, a description of Cobb's car, the name of his supervisor at the Pacific Station, the number to his cell phone. Then they started down the hill, avoiding the yellow tape that charted the path that Cobb had taken through the brush. As Lena and Vaughan left Hu behind, she remained silent until they reached the car, climbed in and were alone. The sadness seemed overwhelming.

"What do you think?" she whispered. "Why didn't Cobb show up at the hospital?"

"I don't know," Vaughan said gently.

"Do you think—"

Her voice broke, and she couldn't manage to keep her game face on any longer. She didn't understand her emotions. She could feel the tears beginning to drip down her cheeks. When she tried to turn away, Vaughan pulled her into his arms and held her. Moments passed and she sighed as her body met his and began to relax. She smoothed her hands over his shoulders and buried her face in his neck. She could feel his face—rough as sandpaper—and then his lips, kissing her cheek. She turned and gazed at him. Their eyes met in the darkness. And then their lips. Lena's body flushed with warmth. She could taste the salt on his skin.

54

She was sitting out by the pool in the early morning light with a tall glass of ice tea. She felt weary—her muscles, her bones, her mind. In spite of Vaughan and the comfort he had given her, she hadn't been able to sleep. Clayton Hu had called three times, each update more alarming than the next. West L.A. patrol units had covered every conceivable route between Bennett's house and the emergency room at UCLA in Westwood. Additional units had been brought in to search every possible route between the house and St. John's Medical Center in Santa Monica.

Cobb was nowhere to be found.

She heard her cell phone begin ringing from its charging base inside the house. She was assuming that Hu's next call would be the one where she learned that Cobb's body had finally been located and her new friend was dead. She wasn't exactly rushing inside to hear the news.

By the time she reached the phone, the call had been picked up by her service. She read the caller ID. It looked like a wrong number. Someone from a place called *L.A. DOG AND CAT* had dialed her number on a Saturday morning before 7:00 a.m. When the phone started ringing again and she saw the same ID, her instincts kicked in and she realized that it couldn't be a wrong number.

"Is this Lena Gamble?"

It was a man's voice and he sounded extremely tentative.

"This is Lena Gamble," she said carefully. "Whom am I speaking with?"

"You're a homicide detective? You work for the Los Angeles Police Department?"

She tried to keep cool. "Yes," she said. "Now whom am I speaking with?"

"It's a long story," the man said. "And I'm not sure there's enough time left to tell it."

"Does this have anything to do with someone named Dan Cobb?"

He paused a moment. "Yes," he said. "It has everything to do with someone named Dan Cobb."

Lena pushed the stool aside and grabbed a pad and pen off the counter. The man called himself Dr. Frank and claimed to be a veterinarian in Santa Monica. He gave her his address and told her to hurry.

The drive west seemed to last a lifetime. She spent most of it wrestling with an internal dialogue that had begun when Cobb handed her Lily Hight's boot and she realized that he had seen something no one else had. That the murder of a teenage girl and a trial that had captivated a city and worked its way across the digital universe, had been completely staged by a killer no one was even looking for. A killer who had been standing right beside them. A killer who hadn't stopped killing and was still loose.

She spotted L.A. Dog and Cat on the right, saw Cobb's Lincoln up on the curb, and struggled to maintain her composure. As she parked she noticed a dent in the Lincoln's front fender and a mailbox that had been knocked over on the sidewalk. When she climbed the steps and pushed open the front door, a man in a white lab coat looked up at her from behind the desk.

"Lena Gamble?" he said.

She nodded. "Where is he?"

"Back here."

He led her into an operating room. Cobb was lying on a stainless steel table, wrapped in sheets and blankets and pointing his gun at the ceiling. Rushing over to him, she got a look at his face, his blank stare, and thought that he was dead.

"I'm too late."

Dr. Frank checked Cobb's neck for a pulse. "He's close, but he's still here."

"Why didn't you call an ambulance?"

"He wouldn't let me. He had the gun. He said he'd blow my head off."

Lena's eyes danced over Cobb's body as she took in the incredulous shock and tried to understand. She smoothed her hand over his scalp. Dr. Frank seemed just as distressed, his voice shaky and worn out from the ordeal.

"He told me he'd lost his phone, but I found it in his pocket this morning. I saw your number and called. He talked about you a lot. He'd drift in and out. Most of the time I couldn't understand what he was saying. But he trusts you . . . I got that much. And he's worried about you. Who's Steven Bennett?"

"Why?"

"He said that Bennett tricked him."

"Did he say how?"

"No, but I'm guessing that it has something to do with the fact that he was shot in the back."

The words hung there. The gristle on the bone. Bennett had shot Cobb in the back.

She watched Dr. Frank move to the other side of the table. He was pulling the sheets away from Cobb's chest. He was showing her the exit wounds.

"Two slugs passed through and out," he said. "But there's one left in his shoulder. I stopped the bleeding, but we really need to get him to a hospital."

"Help me get him into my car."

Lena wrapped one hand around Cobb's pistol and pulled with the other. His fierce resistance to let go of his weapon surprised her. Still, she managed to pry the gun away and slip it into her jacket. Dr. Frank rolled a small steel table on wheels over and gave Lena a look like that's all he had. Once they made the transfer, they pushed Cobb out the back door and into the parking lot. Lena swung her car around, and with considerable effort they managed to get Cobb strapped into the passenger seat. Cobb groaned several times. And as Lena climbed in behind the wheel, he reached out for her hand and held it as tight as he had held his gun.

St. John's Medical Center was twenty-two blocks east on Santa Monica Boulevard. It would be a grind, stop-and-go traffic with signal lights on every corner. But Lena would never get past the first mile on the Pacific Coast Highway. That's when Cobb let go of her hand. That's when she looked over at her new friend, saw him take his last breath, and knew.

She slowed the car down, tried to get a grip on herself.

She saw Temescal Canyon Road ahead and made a left turn. There was a park on top of the hill. Pulling into the lot, she found the only spot with a view of the ocean that included palm trees. It was a beautiful view—maybe not quite the one Cobb had photographed in Hawaii . . . but close enough. She opened the windows to let in the smell of the ocean. When she noticed the pack of Camel Lights on the dash, she lit one and drew the nicotine into her lungs. She couldn't help it. She wasn't really thinking anymore.

She wished Cobb could have lasted long enough to see the palm trees.

She felt his Sig Sauer in her jacket and pulled it out. Ejecting the mag, she realized that Cobb had held the vet at bay with an empty gun. She smiled—not where it shows, but underneath where it counts. As she smoothed her hand over his forehead, she noticed that the radio was playing softly in the background. The music seemed familiar and she turned up the volume. It was Miles Davis, and she hadn't heard the cut for a long time.

"My Funny Valentine."

55

Lena had called Vaughan and given him the news. She had called Clayton Hu as well. In spite of the fact that Bennett was wanted for the murders of six people—a killing spree that until last night began with Lily Hight and ended with Debi Watson—it was his seventh victim that would burn through the system like rocket fuel.

Bennett was a cop killer now. Even worse, he'd put three rounds into Cobb's back. No one carrying a badge would show the piece of shit any mercy.

Lena wanted a look at the spot where Cobb had been shot in daylight. Both Vaughan and Hu agreed to meet her there. She was driving from St. John's where she'd left Cobb behind. And she was carrying his Sig Sauer, the gun locked up in her glove box for safekeeping.

The radio had been switched off ever since she left Temescal Canyon Park. All she wanted to listen to was the sound of the engine under the hood. The sound of the machine grinding forward.

She was heading north on Twenty-sixth Street with the Riviera Country Club on her left. She could see people driving golf carts and hitting little white balls on manicured lawns as if this Saturday was like every other Saturday in sunny L.A. She turned back to the road and lit another cigarette. She wasn't sure why, but something about seeing those people playing golf fed the rage and only made the day darker than it already was.

She wanted to hit something. Kick something. Kill it.

When she reached Sunset, she made a right, rolled through the horseshoe curve and up the hill, then made the left onto Rockingham. The patrol units were gone, a woman in a Land Rover packed with kids drove by—the events of last night seemingly forgotten, or even more likely, entirely missed by all. Although it didn't look like Vaughan or Hu had arrived yet, she saw a van parked in front of Bennett's house and imagined that the workers were busy replacing the living room windows. But as she cleared the van, she glanced back at the house and skidded to a stop.

Bennett was home—his BMW backed into the garage with the trunk open. The door between the house and garage was open as well.

Lena pulled into the driveway, blocking the BMW and jacking back the slide on her .45. She stepped out of her car, took a last hit on her smoke, and ground the butt into the driveway with her toe. And then she started moving forward. One round in the chamber—the rest, ready to go.

Entering the garage, it crossed her mind that it would have been more poetic to use Cobb's Sig Sauer. That if she had ammunition for the gun it would have had more meaning somehow. But Cobb carried a 9 mm, and Lena preferred a .45—particularly when coming face to face with a monster. An alien.

She had killed people before.

She had shot them dead in the line of duty. But no matter what the circumstances, no matter what the victim may have deserved, taking a human life carried with it a certain toll that she thought about every day. A price that haunted her and would follow her for the rest of her days.

But she wondered about Bennett. She didn't think it would be the same.

She took a quick peek inside the trunk and spotted his suitcase.

Reaching the door between the garage and house, she looked down a long hallway to a set of French doors that opened into the backyard. The house was dead quiet . . . so quiet that she began to sense something might be wrong. She turned and gazed at the van parked in the street. It took a moment to register, but she realized that it was the same make, model, and color as the van Dick Harvey drove.

Something was going on.

Stepping into the house, she moved down the hall without making any sound. She passed a laundry room, a large pantry filled with cooking supplies, a powder room, and finally the entrance to a kitchen. The room was enormous and looked as if it had been remodeled over the past year. She thought about what Cobb had said. No one could afford to live here on Bennett's salary. Either he married rich or his crimes involved more than—

She froze.

There was a man sitting at the breakfast table with a cup of coffee. His face was turned as he looked out the bay window at the pool. She took a deep breath and did a gut check. Her hands were steady. Then she raised the .45 and entered the room.

The man didn't seem to notice her and didn't move. Lena inched closer for a look at his face. As she cleared the counter, she caught the blood splattered against the wall behind his head. Even more blood was pooling on the floor.

It was Dick Harvey from *Blanket Hollywood,* and his days ruining other people's lives for fun and profit seemed to be over. His eyes were crossed, his mouth was open, and he had a bullet hole in the center of his forehead. Remarkably, he still appeared to be sweating through his wrinkled suit.

Lena steadied herself against the table, her eyes skipping about the room until they landed on the window and spotted Bennett in the backyard. He had a shovel in his hands and was digging a hole in the lawn by the rear fence.

She hustled out the door and across the yard. As she ran toward him, he looked up and yelped in panic—then started shrieking.

"Oh my God," he kept repeating. "Oh my God. I didn't do it, Gamble. I didn't do it."

Lena's eyes zeroed in on the gun laying in the grass. The one he was trying to bury. The 9-mm Smith.

"Jesus Christ—you've gotta believe me. This isn't what it looks like."

He threw the shovel down, lunged for the Smith, and dug it out of the grass just as Lena reached him.

"Drop the gun, Bennett. Then we'll talk about what it looks like."

He pointed the muzzle at her, his hands jittery. "Screw it," he said. "You'd never fuckin' believe me."

"I'm a better shot than you are. You'll miss and I won't. Now, drop the gun and we'll talk."

He was chewing it over. She could see the wild look in his eyes. Every muscle in his face twitching back and forth and out of control. Beads of sweat were percolating all over his forehead. After a long moment, he turned the muzzle away from her and made a slow arc up and around until he found the side of his own head. Lena grimaced. If the prick blew his own brains out, she was okay with that.

"This isn't what it fucking looks like," he said.

"Tell me what it looks like, Bennett."

"I didn't shoot anybody. I didn't kill anybody. I'm innocent."

"But that's what everybody says."

He took it in, his body shivering in terror. His gaze shifted to the house. Lena could hear footsteps on the lawn behind her and took a quick peek. Hu was rushing toward them with his gun drawn. Vaughan was behind him with a handful of cops carrying shotguns.

Lena turned back to Bennett. "It's over," she said. "And we already have everything we need. The suit you wore when you met Lily Hight at Club 3 AM. Security video that shows you walking out with her."

Bennett's eyes flicked from face to face. When they slid back to Lena, he pressed the muzzle into his head even harder and began weeping.

"But I'm innocent."

"Yeah," she said. "Innocent. I had my share of hunches, Bennett. But I never really understood why you prosecuted Jacob Gant when you knew that he'd passed a polygraph. Now everything makes sense. You needed someone to take the fall for what you did to the girl. That's what this is about, right? That's what this has always been about. When you lost the trial, when you saw your career tanking, you needed a new way out. You needed to keep your eye on things. When Gant got too close and took what he knew to Bosco, you shot them and tried to frame Lily's father. It made sense, right? Everybody in the city thought it made sense. Tim Hight out for revenge."

"I know how it looks, but—"

"But what?" she said. "On a scale of one to ten, how low can a guy go? You're off the charts, Bennett. And what about Escabar and the guard? What about Debi Watson? What about your woman, Bennett? Look what you did to her on the very same day she tried to come forward and talk."

He shook his head back and forth like he could see Watson's dead body in the trunk. When he spoke, he spewed the words out with spit.

"I didn't," he said. "I didn't kill her."

"And what about the gun you used? The gun you're holding to your head? The gun from the drive-by case you worked with Cobb? The gun you knew we'd trace because you needed insurance? You're a genius, Bennett. A real genius. If all the fall guys you came up with hit the skids and fell down, you had the ultimate backup. You had your old mentor. You had Cobb. By the way, he died this morning. You're everything you ever were, Bennett. And today you're even more. You're a cop killer now."

"Stop," he said. "Stop it."

She took a step forward. "Drop the gun, and let's go."

"Don't come any closer. I'm gonna blow my fucking head off."

"You don't have what it takes, Bennett. You're a coward."

"Fuck you, you stupid bitch."

He jerked the gun around and fired a shot into the lawn by Lena's feet, then bolted into the gardens. There was a gate that opened to a narrow lane and a pair of trash Dumpsters. Lena didn't see him running down the lane. When she turned back, she caught a glimpse of him hiding against the wall behind the far Dumpster. She traded looks with Vaughan, then Hu, who motioned his men closer. Bennett was surrounded.

Lena inched forward until she had a clean view. He was sitting on the ground holding the 9-mm Smith on his lap. He was weeping. Mumbling. Out of his fucking mind.

"Come on, Bennett. Let's get this over with. Let's go in before anyone else gets hurt."

"I don't want to."

Lena traded looks with Vaughan, then turned back to Bennett. "Sometimes you have to do things you don't want to do."

"Not me, Gamble. I only do what I wanna do."

"But there's no place to run," she said. "No place to hide. You own this."

She could see his wheels turning. She could see the machine crashing—his soul tapped out at zero with no fuel and no backup. His eyes inched along the ground, then rose slowly until they found her kneeling before him just ten feet away. He met her gaze and held it. When he noticed her gun pointed at the center of his chest, he smiled at her.

"Fuck it," he said.

Bennett raised the gun, wrapped his mouth around the muzzle, and pulled the trigger. Lena watched as his head snapped back against the wall and the blood gushed out. But the gun didn't stop firing.

Hu and Vaughan rushed over. The guys with the shotguns moved in as well.

It looked like Bennett's finger had become stuck in the trigger guard. As his body greeted death and began twitching, the 9-mm Smith fired one round after the next, blasting his head away in chunks. The gun didn't stop firing until the mag finally emptied out.

And then the sound dissipated. The smoke cleared. And Lena watched with Vaughan as one of the guys walked over to Bennett's corpse, pulled the pistol away, and tossed it on the ground. When he gave the body a stiff kick with his boot, no one said anything. It seemed like the right thing to do.

56

Cobb needed a fresh set of clothes to be buried in.

Lena remembered that gray suit she'd seen him wearing on video during Jacob Gant's trial. The one that had looked new and perfectly tailored. Vaughan said he'd ride over with her to pick it up.

Over the last three days, they had spent a lot of time together. A lot of time not being alone with themselves or their thoughts. A lot of time in bed.

Lena pulled out of the garage at Parker Center, saw the cameras turning their way from the media camped out around the building, and drove through the red light. Instead of dealing with midday traffic on the 110 Freeway, she decided to take surface streets around Dodger Stadium and pick up the Golden State Freeway on the other side of the hill.

The press was swarming again. The story of Lily Hight's murder bigger than ever with a fresh set of storylines and a cast of seven new victims capped off by the killer of all killers—Bad Boy Bennett—a deputy DA who committed suicide rather than face his arrest and prosecution and the humiliation and shame that would have come with it.

On Saturday night they had confronted the district attorney for his

own odd behavior—a no-nonsense meeting ordered by Deputy Chief
Ramsey. Ramsey wanted to know what Higgins and Spadell had been
looking for that could have been picked up by Club 3 AM security
cameras. Ramsey wanted to know what was so important to Higgins
that it required breaking into Johnny Bosco's house and running away
when Lena identified herself as a police officer. Spadell never showed
up for the meeting and was believed to have fled the city. Higgins refused to talk until he'd had a chance to confer with his political consultants. Ramsey pointed out to the district attorney that burglary was
still considered a crime in Los Angeles County and suggested that he
confer with his attorney instead of his asshole consultants.

But if Jimmy J. Higgins had been searching out video that showed
him using cocaine, it hardly made any difference now.

Bennett had been his protégé and everybody knew it. Higgins had
overseen Bennett and Watson's work on Jacob Gant's trial, hoping to
grab as many headlines as he could. He had received a copy of Gant's
polygraph from Buddy Paladino, just as Bennett and Watson had. Yet
Jimmy J. Higgins had remained quiet about it, essentially paving the
way for the actual killer—an officer of the court—to try an innocent
man for a murder he himself had committed. The mayor, a majority of
the city council and county supervisors—but not all—were calling for
Higgins's resignation. But even more, the sense of outrage was so pervasive that people were taking it to the streets. The story was just three
days old. Higgins had already been attacked twice in restaurants by the
kind of people who aren't prone to acts of violence. He had been chased
down the street by a group of college students who saw him exiting a
parking garage.

Higgins was getting what his office had given Jacob Gant, but with
one essential difference. Every blow Higgins took, he'd earned.

Lena exited the Golden State Freeway, winding her way around the
airport until she reached Vineland Avenue. After passing Fiesta Liquors
and the Rancho Coin Laundry on her left, she spotted a parking space
right in front of Cobb's apartment building and made a hard U-turn
into the curb.

Vaughan seemed confused. "Why are you stopping?"

"We're here," she said. "This is it."

He eyed the run-down building—the lost neighborhood. "I had no idea."

Lena tried not to think about it and got out of the car. She noticed a Hispanic woman draping her sheets over the fence to dry in the sun. Across the street a middle-aged Asian woman was watching them from the sidewalk.

Lena led Vaughan through the broken gate and up the steps to the second floor. Just as before, most of the tenants kept their windows open and they were greeted by the smells of corn tortillas and chicken frying in hot oil. Lena pointed to Cobb's apartment at the end of the walkway and they turned the corner. She could see that old Mexican woman sitting before her window again, her ancient face still expressionless. Still blank and wrinkled. But this time when Lena met her gaze, something different happened. She sensed a certain recognition in the old woman's eyes. A certain sadness. And when she looked ahead to Cobb's door, Lena saw all the flowers and candles that his neighbors had placed around the mat. A snapshot of Cobb taken in the courtyard with an old Polaroid camera had been taped to his door as well.

"They loved him," Vaughan whispered.

Lena nodded, taking in the display as she unlocked the door with Cobb's keys. She didn't want to spend a lot of time here. She didn't want any more memories than she already had. She didn't want to let in anything new.

The heat inside the apartment was stifling. Vaughan left the door standing open, gazing at the shabby furniture and gray walls in disbelief. Lena left him there and walked into the bedroom to search through Cobb's suits. After a few moments, Vaughan stopped in the doorway to watch.

"You know I keep thinking about the day you came to my office," he said. "The day you wanted to talk, but wouldn't do it on the phone. You'd just left Gant's brother, Harry. He'd told you that Jacob was investigating Lily's murder on his own. That he'd found something and had gone to tell Johnny Bosco about it."

Lena spotted the gray suit and laid it out on the bed. "Our first break."

"But I didn't know you then. I didn't know what to think. I thought you might even be crazy."

"Now you know for sure," she said.

"I'm serious, Lena. Gant may have walked out of that courtroom with a NOT GUILTY verdict, but everybody thought he killed Lily. Everybody thought his DNA made it a lock. Do you remember how far out on a limb we were?"

She gave him a look and nodded without saying anything.

Vaughan shook his head as he tried to remember the details. "We started out in the conference room," he said. "The caterer had left food. Watson saw you with me and ran out to tell Bennett. Then Bennett shows up trying to listen to what we were saying."

"We see it now for what it was," she said. "We didn't then."

Vaughan shrugged, still mulling it over as Lena found a tie and pulled a clean white shirt out of the closet. Laying them over the gray suit, she gave them a look and returned to the closet for a pair of black dress shoes.

"Do you remember what we thought of Cobb, Lena? Do you remember your first impression of the man?"

She took a deep breath and tried to push the thought away but couldn't quite make it. She opened Cobb's dresser drawers and found his underwear and socks. The truth was that it felt a lot like the time so many years ago when she buried her dad. She may have only been a teenager at the time, but that's the way it seemed right now. She still didn't understand why she felt this way about Cobb, or how it could come on so fast. His mistakes in life had been horrendous—the size of mountains. Yet it was his mistakes that seemed to make the man. He kept moving forward without looking for someone else to blame. He kept the investigation open, working in secret and helping Paladino out with the gift of all gifts.

The blood samples that pointed to Jacob Gant could no longer be found.

She wished that they could have worked together. Just one more case as true partners.

She glanced back at Vaughan. He'd said something and she'd missed it. Something about Lily's father. She found a plastic garment bag and packed up Cobb's clothing.

"What about him?" Vaughan said. "Lily's dad."

"I owe him an apology," she said. "And his friend."

"The guy who tried to vouch for him?"

"I owe them something," she said, taking a last look at the room. "Let's get out of here, Greg."

Vaughan reached for the garment bag and they walked out of the apartment, locking the door behind them. As they started down the steps into the courtyard, Lena noticed that Asian woman again. She was still standing on the sidewalk across the street. But she wasn't keeping an eye on the woman guarding her laundry. Instead, she was staring at Lena. And it was a long look—the kind of look that wouldn't let go.

Vaughan hung the garment bag behind the driver's seat. Lena climbed in, glancing back at the woman. She wondered if they'd met somewhere before. She looked to be about fifty. She had a gentle face and easy eyes and was dressed in a way that didn't fit the run-down neighborhood. As Lena turned the key in the ignition, the woman waved at her shyly and something clicked.

She turned to Vaughan and told him that she'd be right back. Then she got out of the car and crossed the street. She needed to talk to a friend of a friend. She needed to talk to the woman who described herself on the Internet as *totally hot*. She needed to meet Cobb's woman; Betty Kim.

57

Lena spotted Hight's house in the middle of the block and pulled over. It was late afternoon and she could see the sun nesting over the ocean below the hill. She turned back to the house, then ducked quickly when she noticed Tim Hight walking out the front door.

His Mercedes had been returned to him, and she watched as he backed out onto the street and drove by.

Lena paused a moment, lost in indecision, then made a U-turn and followed him around the bend. Hight made a left on Ocean Park. When he reached Lincoln at the bottom of the hill, he pulled into the parking lot and walked into the grocery store. Lily's father still appeared thin and frail, his gait a beat short of steady.

Lena backed into a space a safe distance away and gazed through the windshield.

She owed this man an apology. She knew that. But she wasn't sure she could find the words. She didn't think she could look him in the eye and meet his gaze. In spite of the guilt she felt, she wasn't sure she was ready.

A truck turned into the shopping center, pulling to a stop in the middle of the aisle and blocking her view of the grocery store. After several minutes it finally drove off, and Lena checked the lot and found Hight's car still parked three rows over.

She was thinking about the burden Hight was carrying. The pain and loss he'd been forced to endure, and now, the new reality he would have to face. But even more, she was thinking about the harsh way she had treated him when she suspected he might have had a hand in his own daughter's death. Hight had been informed that Bennett was the actual killer by Deputy Chief Ramsey and the mayor of Los Angeles, but apparently it hadn't gone well. Hight had refused to let them into his house. From what Barrera had told her in confidence, Hight had refused to even open his front door.

Lena lowered her window. As she checked the store's entrance again, she saw him walking out with two bags. Even from across the lot she could tell that the bag he held close to his chest contained several half-gallon bottles of booze.

She watched Hight open his trunk and place his groceries inside. Rooting through one of the bags, he fished out a pack of cigarettes and lit one. Then he circled around the car and opened the door. Curiously, he didn't climb in. Instead, he leaned his elbows on the roof and gazed at the traffic moving up and down Lincoln Boulevard. For the next five minutes, nothing changed. Hight just stood there, smoking his cigarette and staring at the street.

After a while Lena began to wonder if he wasn't fixated on something and turned around for a look through the rear window. She saw a young man on Rollerblades, pushing a baby stroller across the street. As they glided up the ramp onto the sidewalk, she turned back and watched Hight following their progress down the block. When they vanished, Hight kept his eyes on the empty sidewalk for several moments, then dropped his cigarette on the pavement and finally got into his car.

He drove off slowly. He pulled onto Ocean Park and lumbered up the long hill. It took him a while to reach the top, but Lena kept her eyes on the car until it finally disappeared. Then she pulled onto Lincoln, heading for the freeway. She didn't want to follow Hight home. She wasn't ready yet. She couldn't find the words. And Hight hadn't looked ready, either.

58

She could smell it in the pillow as she pulled it closer. On the sheets as she rolled over in the darkness and searched out cool spots that were not there.

Murder season.

She was floating. Drifting. Cruising through an open seam between sleep and consciousness.

She glanced at the clock radio but didn't really see it, then fell back into the stream and let go. It was somewhere after midnight. Sometime before dawn. Early spring and the air inside the house had been deadened from the oppressive heat.

Murder season had come early this year. It had rolled in with the heat like they were best friends, like they were lovers.

Lena reached across the bed, probing gently for a warm body but finding only emptiness. As she rolled onto her back, she noticed something going on in the house. She could hear it in the background, a noise pulsing in the distance. She tried to ignore it and pretend that it wasn't real. After a while she began to wonder if it wasn't part of a dream.

Until she finally realized that it was her cell.

She opened her eyes. The phone wasn't on the table. When she noticed the light glowing behind the bed, she reached down to the floor and reeled it in. It was 1:30 a.m., and she hoped that it wasn't another callout. She needed more time before working another case. She needed more rest.

She slid the lock open on the touch screen. As she pressed the phone to her ear, she heard a man's voice—an extremely timid voice that she recognized, but couldn't place.

"Who is this?" the man asked.

"Lena Gamble," she said. "Who's this?"

There was a long pause. A long stretch of nothing. Lena looked around the bedroom and realized that she was at Vaughan's house. The bathroom light was on, the door closed. Her memory of the night came back to her. It had been a good one.

Then the caller cleared his throat, his voice even quieter than before.

"What are you doing with this phone?" he said.

Lena sighed in frustration. "You called me," she said. "Now how did you get my number? Who are you?"

He cleared his throat again. He seemed jumpy.

"But that's the problem," he said finally. "I don't have your phone number, Detective, and I didn't call you. I was calling my daughter's phone. I wanted to hear her voice. I wanted to hear her message, but you picked up."

The words hung there. Deep and dark and dead as night.

Lena bolted up to a sitting position. It was Tim Hight. She was holding Lily Hight's cell phone. The one nobody could find. She looked at her naked body under the sheets and remembered that her clothes were in the living room. Worse, much worse, she was officially off-duty. She'd left her gun at home.

Hight broke the silence. "Are you in trouble, Detective Gamble?"

She didn't answer. She couldn't catch her breath. Her eyes rocked back to the bathroom door—everything radioactive now. Everything white-hot and burning down.

"You must be in trouble," Hight said. "If you have Lily's phone, then you're with the man who killed her. You need to tell me where you are. If you can't speak, there's a program on the start page. Just press the icon and the phone will show me where you are."

Vaughan. She'd just slept with the man.

She pulled the phone away from her ear, found the program, and opened it. As she watched the device send out her location, Hight ended the call and she got out of Vaughan's bed. She tried to keep cool. Tried to keep in mind that she wasn't dreaming anymore. As she crept past the bathroom door and rushed into the living room for her clothes, she glanced back at the phone. The icon marked PHOTOS just seemed to jump out at her. When she opened it, a number of files containing still photographs popped up, but she chose to look at the last video instead.

Her hands started quivering. She could feel the fear and terror in her bones.

She was watching Lily make love with her killer in candlelight. They were passing the camera back and forth. They were giggling and laughing. She was watching Vaughan pull Lily into his arms. Watching Vaughan kiss her. Watching them do it in Vaughan's bed.

The light in the bathroom went out and the door opened ever so slowly.

Vaughan looked directly at her. He was dressed in a pair of jeans and a polo shirt, and he was holding a gun. He walked toward her and stopped in the middle of the room. Most of his face was cloaked in darkness, but she could see his eyes, those light brown eyes, glowing from the moonlight that was leaking through the windows at the end of the foyer by the front door.

Somehow Lena steadied herself. Somehow she found her voice.

"Why did you keep this?"

Vaughan reached out for the phone and grabbed it, his voice seething but just above a whisper. "Because I can't stop looking at it," he said. "I can't stop thinking about it. The whole thing was an accident. A mistake."

Lena found her bra and panties and started to dress as Vaughan watched.

"You call what happened a mistake?"

His face moved into the light and hardened. "You saw the video, Lena. You saw what she looked like sitting at that bar. I was in the middle of a divorce. It's funny, but I went to the club with Bennett and Higgins that night. They went upstairs to talk to Bosco, and I walked into the bar and found Lily. She was beautiful. She was gorgeous. I knew that she was younger than me, but that's all I knew. I saw her as a blessing. A gift given to me after my divorce. I was feeding on it. I needed it, and we clicked. We came back here. We drank a bottle of wine. We talked and made love. And then she asked me to drive her home."

Vaughan paused, but only briefly to wipe his mouth.

"She said she lived with her parents. She told me that she was still in high school. Jesus fucking Christ. She was still in school."

Lena tucked in her blouse and pulled her boots over jeans. She glanced at the gun in Vaughan's hand. It looked like a small Glock.

"Your life flashed before your eyes," she said. "You decided murder was your only way out."

"Not at all, Lena. I called her. I bought one of those phones that can't be traced. You saw the number appear on the bill . . . the number Bennett removed for the trial because it didn't point to Gant."

"You tried to explain the situation you were in. You told her that she couldn't talk about it."

"She laughed at me. She said she'd had a great time. She said she wanted to do it again. She said that if we didn't do it again, she'd make sure the whole world knew my name and where I worked."

"You agreed to see her?"

"I did. I agreed to meet her on Friday night. Her parents had gone out to dinner. I picked her up, but I didn't take her anywhere. We drove around in circles while I tried to make her understand what was at stake. I told her that what had happened between us was beautiful and could have happened to anybody. But if anyone else found out about it, they wouldn't understand the circumstances. No one would believe our story and I'd be ruined for life."

"It sounds like you're blaming her for being sixteen, Vaughan. What were you doing even trying to reason with her?"

He laughed, but it was a bitter laugh. "You're right about that, Lena. She didn't want to listen. She didn't give a shit. She said that she didn't even care anymore. She'd made up with her boyfriend and they'd had sex just before I picked her up. She said she was going to tell her father what happened because she felt guilty now. I'm not really sure what happened after that. I know I lost it. I'm pretty sure I scared the shit out of her. And both of us know the rest. She tried to jump out of the car. I had some tools on the floor behind my seat. I reached around, saw the screwdriver in my hand, and drove it into her fucking back."

Both of us know the rest.

Lena could see it so clearly that it might have been happening before her eyes. Lily had given Vaughan everything he needed to push the murder onto someone else. He knew that she'd had sex with Gant and that the odds were in his favor that traces of their lovemaking had been left behind. He knew that they got back together after a breakup.

"How did you make it look like a rape?" she said. "What did you use, Vaughan?"

His face stiffened and he looked at her for a long time with those glowing eyes of his. "You don't want to know what I did to her. But I'll tell you this. Everybody has their breaking point. When you reach it, you realize that you can do just about *anything*."

A moment passed. Another stretch of silence. Lena tried to focus. She needed time. She needed to keep the monster talking.

"How did you keep such close tabs on Jacob Gant?"

Vaughan shrugged. "I didn't. I thought I was free and clear. When the evidence went missing in the lab, I knew someone was out there. But it's like I said over at Cobb's place. No matter what the verdict, everyone still thought Gant did the murder. After the trial ended, after it became a public relations disaster, everyone involved at your end and mine needed Gant to stay guilty because the alternative would have been so much worse."

"You didn't think anyone would be looking for you."

"I didn't, but that afternoon Johnny Bosco called me. He was worried about his business. Gant had told him that Lily had been to his club a week before her murder. That she had come with her friend and probably left with a guy. That's why Bosco agreed to help Gant. And that's why Lily's friend, Julia Hackford, never spoke up. You were right, Lena. It was all about self-preservation and self-interest. Gant had searched Lily's house and found her cell phone. He'd seen the video you just watched and was bringing it over so that Bosco could help identify the man he thought killed her. Bosco was worried that it might be a VIP and didn't know how to handle it. He didn't trust Higgins because he was up for reelection and needed a fresh set of headlines. He didn't go to Bennett because he and Higgins were tied at the hip and he thought the guy was a loser. He told me that he didn't even let his partner in on it because he wanted to protect him."

Lena shook her head. "Bosco handed it to you," she said. "He told you everything you needed to know."

"He even gave me the time."

"And you knew that it needed to end at the club."

"Actually, no. I didn't think it would. Everyone would think Hight shot them in an act of revenge, but I never counted on it ending there. I never counted on it sticking. That's why I pulled the gun out of Property. The one that went back to the drive-by shootings eight years ago. I knew that Higgins and Bennett were cowards. That in a crisis like the prosecution of Tim Hight, they'd run for cover and make me the new face of the DA's office. I knew that I'd be working with you. That you wouldn't buy it unless the case seemed challenging. Because we were working together, I thought I could provide that challenge. That's why it had to end with Bennett. He had the right background. Everything that you discovered about him happens to be true . . . except for the murders. He fingered his witness and had Wes Brown killed. He had a bad history with women and openly cheated on his wife. He prosecuted Jacob Gant for Lily's murder when he knew six weeks out that he had the wrong man. It had to end with Bennett because he fit like a glove. Because he was perfect. Because he was vicious. Because everything he did to corrupt the evidence and build a case against Jacob Gant could be turned upside down until it looked like he was covering his own tracks. Why do you think he killed himself? Don't you think he knew?"

Lena's cell phone began ringing. It was on the couch where her clothes had been tossed. Something in Vaughan's eyes changed. He crossed the room stiff as a machine, then tilted his head and peered down at the phone.

"Take the call," he shouted. "Take it."

"Who is it?"

"Martin Orth, calling you at almost two in the morning."

He pushed the Glock into her side just below her ribs.

"Take the fuckin' call, Lena."

Vaughan was losing it. And she could see that he still had a way out. If he killed her and managed to get rid of her body, he was free. Hight knew where she was and knew that she had recovered his daughter's phone, but that's all he knew. When he assumed she was with the man who murdered his daughter, it could easily be taken as nothing more than a wrong guess.

She picked up the phone. "Marty," she said.

"Lena, I know it's late—the middle of the night—but it's important."

Orth was upset and rushing. From the noise in the background, she thought he might be calling from the crime lab.

"What is it?" she said.

"The touch DNA. Lily Hight's jeans."

"What about them?"

Vaughan gave the gun a harder push and nicked one of her ribs. Lena flinched at the pain, but remained quiet. When Orth came back on, he sounded frantic.

"We made a run," he said. "Nothing came up in the system, but the samples included all county employees. Lena, I don't know how to say this any other way. We got the wrong guy. The killer wasn't Bennett. It's Vaughan."

She could have laughed at the irony. The timing.

"Are you doing anything about it?" she said.

"I called Deputy Chief Ramsey before I called you. What's wrong with your voice? You sound funny."

"Thanks for the tip, Marty. I've gotta go now."

Vaughan grabbed the phone and threw it on the floor. "What did he fucking want? What did he fucking say?"

"They made a run on the DNA they picked up on Lily's jeans. It covered all county employees. They know it's you. They're on their way."

He struck her—a hard blow to the face that knocked her down to her knees—but she didn't stop.

"You fucked up, Vaughan. You covered everything except for the one piece of evidence that had your fucking name on it."

He hit her again. He kicked her and jabbed the gun to her head. Something in the room changed. She looked at the windows by the front door and thought maybe someone had run through the moonlight.

Vaughan moved back to the center of the room, looked up at the ceiling, arched his back, and screamed like a madman. His arms shook and his entire body shuddered. He was panicking now, falling apart, shaky. He stared back at her and hissed. Then he grabbed his wallet and keys and ran down the foyer to the front door.

"You should wait for the police, Vaughan. You should stay inside."

He turned back to her and shrieked. "Why?"

"Because I think someone's out there."

"Is that the best you can do?"

"I think someone's outside," she said quietly.

He laughed at her. Then he threw the locks, yanked open the door, and fled into the night.

The shots came quickly. There were five of them. One loud and made from close to the house. The next four from a slight distance. She ran to the open door and gazed outside. Tim Hight was standing over Vaughan's dead body, pointing a gun at his head. She could hear Hight weeping as she rushed across the lawn. She could see him wiping his eyes as he stared at the corpse.

Lena pulled the gun out of his hand and tossed it onto the grass. Hight turned to her and buried his head in her chest. His body was trembling, the tears splashing off his cheeks like rain. She could hear sirens approaching in the distance. She could feel herself supporting Hight and shouldering his weight.

"Did I get him?" he whispered to her. "Did I get the guy who murdered Lily?"